The Tainted Wars
Heretic

W. J. Grupe Jr

Twin Pines Publishing

ISBN (Hardback) 978-1-952662-08-9
ISBN (Paperback) 978-1-952662-07-2
ISBN (Ebook) : 978-1-952662-06-5

For Luca.
Through your eyes I can see a great big beautiful tomorrow.

The Tainted Wars

Heretic

Chapter One

"The cliffs of insanity!"

THE PRINCESS BRIDE - 1987

"*CHRIS, ARE YOU SURE this is a good idea?*" Marie asked.

"Of course," I replied. "What could go wrong?"

"*With you? Anything.*"

The wind picked up straight into my face and I had to turn. "You risk your life all the time."

"*To prevent drugs from getting on the street so people don't do things like this.*"

"Yes, but they don't have superpowers to heal them."

"Is she trying to talk you out of it?" Adam walked up behind me.

I tilted the phone away from my mouth and turned to my fellow Bishop. The title identified us not as a Roman Catholic priest of rank, but as a member of a secret supernatural sect dating back to the dawn of humankind. So we've got that going for us. "Yeah, she said it was a stupid idea."

"She's not wrong." A hawk cried out not too far away as if accenting his point.

I stuck my tongue out at him. "You're no help."

"Not trying to be."

I talked back into the phone. "Alright, I'm going now."

"Okay, have fun storming the castle."

I hung up smiling and put my phone away. My new girlfriend had a tendency to try to dissuade me from doing things she saw as unnecessarily risky endeavors. As a DEA agent, I would have expected her to be more adventurous.

"You ready?" I asked him.

"Not really."

"Then why did you agree?"

"You wouldn't shut up about it."

I zipped up my sleeves, stepping up to the edge. Adam did the same, shaking his head.

"Three."

"Two."

"One!"

We jumped off the cliff. The wingsuits caught the air as we started soaring down the mountain. The ground streaked by, becoming a familiar blur. After about fifteen seconds, trees started dotting the landscape. A few at first, which increased quickly, turning into a forest. We were skimming the top branches consistently by the height of a tall house, as the slope of the ground matched our descent angle. You can't fly with a wingsuit, nor are you gliding. Your plunge to the earth is simply elongated. For every fifty feet you drop, you move two-hundred feet laterally. The whole process gives you *a feeling* of flying.

After a few glorious seconds like this, the ground dropped and we were out in open air. I looked behind me at Adam and saw him grinning. How could he not? If I wanted to turn, I tilted my body. To slow myself I arched my back. There were no handles to pull, no motor driving me, nothing to sit on. It was just me riding the wind. Off to the left, I saw my objective. A large outcropping jetted out. The center of it had fallen away a millennium ago, leaving a gap about thirty feet wide and a few hundred long. I aimed towards the fissure.

"Chris, what are you doing?" Adam's voice buzzed in my ear through the com, just audible over the rushing of the air.

"I've got to do it."

"No, you really don't."

"You only live once."

"Yeah, and you only die once as well. I'm not sure even we can survive face planting into a mountain going eighty miles an hour."

I kept on my heading, more determined. "Relax, I've got my helmet on."

"It won't stop you from becoming a human pancake." Adam sounded like a parent trying to explain to a child that the stove was hot.

"Then why did I wear it again?"

"You're not funny."

"You can't really believe that."

"Chris veer off." An edge of panic was creeping into his voice. I appreciated the concern for my safety, but no one was talking me out of this.

The mountain side rapidly approached. The gap somehow looked narrower than it did in pictures.

"Chris, shit!"

"Tower, this is Ghost Rider requesting a flyby."

"Chris!"

I rocketed at the cliff face at inhuman speed, even from my heightened perspective. One second I had elbow room to spare, the next I was surrounded by rock, then out in the open again. The flush of adrenaline had me buzzing, and it was all I could do to not attempt a barrel roll. I arced towards Adam as we came within sight of our landing area, a large clearing where Marie and Jelena waited for us. We both leaned back, slowing our forward momentum, then pulled our chutes. There was an intense quiet that permeated the seconds before the silk caught the air, then a loud pop almost like a gunshot. My whole body jerked with the dramatic deceleration.

Drifting slowly down, I tugged hard on the maneuvering cords and landed lightly, then turned and pulled in my chute.

Marie stepped up; giving me a hug and a kiss. "That was pretty impressive. Crazy but impressive."

I smiled at her. "If that impressed you, just wait for tonight."

"Another attempt to beat the wing record at the Buffalo Lodge?"

"I can do it this time. I only missed by four."

She kissed me again, leaned back, and looked into my eyes. "You're an idiot."

I was going to pull her in for another embrace, but Jelena stepped up. As soon as Marie had stood clear, she punched me in the stomach.

"Estúpido estás loco?"

"Glad to see you, too." I grunted. She knew I couldn't prepare myself for fear of activating my powers. If that happened, my skin would turn to iron and she would break her hand. Both she and Marie were human, with no additives. Unless you considered Jelena's other worldly ability to shoot a wart off a frog's ass at six hundred yards. I'd hired the former marine sniper as the first major violation of my career as a Bishop. Up till then we didn't solicit help from those they considered *unblessed.*

"What was the point of that stunt?" she asked.

"It was fun." My voice was still laced with pain.

"And do you think it would be fun for us scraping you off the mountainside?"

"Why are you yelling at me? Marie wasn't upset. Why are you?"

"Are you that thick? Just because she doesn't yell about it doesn't mean she's not feeling it. You are not immortal and you have a job to do. Remember the Tainted? The—" She wiggled her fingers in the air like she was playing the piano, then turned to Adam. "What's the word?"

"Puppet masters."

"Si. Puppet masters. You killed one, starting a shit storm all over the world."

"Which is why we came here," I countered, getting defensive. "To get away from all that for a few moments. To forget for a time that my actions have made everything worse." I stalked a few paces away.

"We are barely hanging on *with* you. What would we do without you?"

I faced all of them. "I don't know what I'm doing, okay? I said it. I'm clueless back there." Stepping forward again, I stood toe to toe with her. She didn't retreat, staring up at me with a look that made me think sparks were going to shoot from her eyes. I pointed at the mountain without breaking eye contact. "But that! That I know. That I can do."

"They taught you to have a death wish in the Rangers?"

"Three jumps a day for a month. I am more in control hurtling down the earth than I am battling the Tainted and their minions."

I looked over at Marie. "I just needed to feel in command again."

She smiled at me. "I know, but we've been here a week." Looking closer, I could see the concern etched in her face.

Jelena yanked my head back to her. "Now that we have settled that, can we get out of this friggin jungle?"

"Forest," I corrected.

"What the fuck is the difference? There are a shitload of trees and nowhere to get good tacos."

Marie stepped up and wrapped her arms around me. "Maybe going back is a good idea."

Adam added. "It's the right thing to do."

I took a deep breath of clean mountain air and realized they weren't wrong. I nodded. "Let's go home."

Chapter Two

"You aint so bad."

Rocky III - 1982

"THIS WAS NOT MY fault." I stared down the hulk of a man in front of me. I wondered if he had been accidentally shrink-wrapped into a sack of potatoes. I had to look up at him and for me, that is saying something.

"How is it not your fault?" Marie stood next to me, holding her DEA issued Glock pointed at the monster. "He was dozing. I warned you not to wake him up. Don't wake the sleeping giant. Isn't that one of the Bishop rules?"

"Yes, but only after climbing a beanstalk. Did you see a beanstalk?" I looked around to further make my point. "Nope. Also, let me remind you that had we still been in the woods, the likelihood of running into a supernaturally drug enhanced pro wrestler would be dramatically reduced."

"You're an ass."

"You would think you could come up with something new."

"Fine, you're a giant ass."

I shrugged. "Not original, but topically relevant."

"Can you focus on the task at hand?"

The big man shifted his gaze between us, not sure who he wanted to pummel first. "Hey, Hodor!" I pulled his attention to me. "Where are the drugs? Once we get them, we will be on our way and you can return to your nap."

He roared and ran at me.

As he got in close, I side stepped with my left foot, ducked under his grab, then stood up quickly. I let the momentum launch him over my back. With the added force from my boon, the giant sailed across the gym and into the boxing ring.

"You did that on purpose just so you could get in the ring with him," Marie accused.

"Yeah, I made sure I was in the perfect position and goaded him so I could put him in that exact spot." Not for nothing, but if I could have, I definitely would have. I climbed into the ring as the big man got to his feet and faced me. We started circling each other; knees bent, hunched over, hands in claws like a scene out of the World Wrestling Federation. He must have felt more comfortable than I was because a smile crept onto his face. I went into a blur—when Bishops move faster than humanly possible—and tried to get behind him. He backhanded me when I moved in close and the blow tossed me into one corner in a heap.

This man's powers, unlike mine, were derived from a drug laced with the blood of a fallen Bishop. Another tale that you can research on your own.

In my upside-down position, I watched as the hulk-moron looked out at nonexistent fans and raised his hands in triumph. He pounded both fists in the air, then started flexing his muscles.

Marie stepped up next to the elevated ring, playing the role of my manager. "You good?"

I righted myself to sit on the correct part of my anatomy. "Oh yeah."

"Let me guess, you've got him right where you want him."

I gave her a side eye. "Of course."

"Getting bitch slapped was the plan?"

"Of course, I'm lulling him into a false sense of security."

Marie repeated the last four words in stereo with me, nodding with a corner of her mouth clenched. "How about you get up off your ass and finish this?"

"See, I knew you were always in my corner."

"Geek."

I was about to get back up when rock-brain grabbed my foot and dragged me into the center of the ring.

"Not cool, man!" I yelled. "I didn't hear no bell."

He ignored me. I planted my other foot and launched myself over his head. He turned to see what I was doing, and I ended up landing behind him. I was in a playful mood, shocking I know, so I tapped him on the shoulder. When he turned around, I landed a powered up punch to the chest with an accompanying dramatic foot stomp. It staggered him for a moment and when he came back in to grab me, I hooked one arm between his legs. Draping the other over his shoulder, I body slammed him.

The force of the supernaturally enhanced move sent out a concussive wave so that the heavy bags swung and rattled the metal weights, sounding like a cacophony of gongs. Not wanting to take any chances, I followed it up with a flying elbow to the chest. I didn't put everything I had into it, but it was a lot. The give in the floor of the ring caused his whole body to lift a few inches before slamming down again. Without hesitation, I hooked my arm around the back of his knee and hauled his bulk up so there was nothing touching the mat except his shoulders. With my free hand, I slapped the mat three times then released him, leaping up and performing my own celebratory dance where I struck a few poses and growled for effect.

Marie must have climbed in at some point because she was in the corner with her arms crossed. "Are you done?"

I stood up straight, looked around, then down at the now unconscious man, and nodded. "Yup, I'm good."

She threw me a small pen injector. I caught it and removed the cap with my teeth. Stepping over the giant, shoved it into the muscle between his neck and shoulder. It was our version of Naloxone that Dorothy, the Covenant's cranky ninety-year-old lab tech, had created to counteract the tainted drugs.

Recapping it, I tossed the pen across the room into the small garbage.

"You are a showoff. You know that, right?"

I mimed shock. "How could you say that? I am simply doing my part in this epic battle against the evil immortal Tainted who..." The rest of what I was saying was lost in Marie's kiss.

When she finally pulled back, she narrowed her eyes. "You also talk too much as well."

"Now *that* I've heard."

I leaned in for more.

There was a groan from behind me. "What happened? How did I get here?"

I turned. "Dude, timing."

Marie smacked me in the arm then extended her hand towards the man, now sitting up in the middle of the ring.

"Fine." I climbed up while hanging onto the top rope. "The drugs you have been taking were laced with a deadly chemical. We saved your life. Now, where are they?"

"I don't take drugs."

"The fugue state you were in would disagree," Marie said.

"What?"

I shook my head. "Let me guess, steroids?"

"Uhhhh."

Marie flashed her badge. "I don't want you to struggle too hard, so I'll read it for you. It says DEA, which stands for—"

"I know."

"Good, then you know the only thing that can get you unscrewed is for you to tell me where the drugs are, and where you got them from."

"Hey, that reminds me of a joke."

Marie ignored me. "What's your name?"

The big guy rubbed his neck. "André."

"Are you serious? Marie, he's André the…"

"Yes, I get it."

I asked, "Fezzik, are there rocks ahead?"

"What?"

Apparently, Andre hadn't seen one of my favorite movies of all time. I was very disappointed.

"Where are the drugs?" Marie continued prodding like I wasn't there.

He hesitated and I just couldn't resist. "Did I make it clear that your job is at stake?"

Marie pulled her Glock and pointed it at me. "Speak again, and I'll shoot you."

I pantomimed zipping my lips.

"André," Marie said. "The drugs."

Whether it was Marie's badge, her gun, or not being able to stand any more Princess Bride quotes, he gave us the drugs and his dealer's info. I followed Marie out the door, but not before peaking back in for a last dig. "I'm going to have to find myself a new giant, that's all."

Chapter Three

"If you've got the time, we've got the beer."

MILLER HIGH LIFE - 1979

WE RETURNED TO THE Covenant house in Miami, Florida. It was a five-acre complex containing three buildings: a large garage, a dilapidated building in the back, and a church. The latter stood in the frontmost area and was charming, but minimalistic. Mass was still held in the front section, but the larger add-on was where we plotted all of our secret defensive operations against the Tainted.

I had been in this little slice of supernatural-addict-infested paradise just shy of six months. We had weeded out most of them since we reclaimed Kristina. She was the Bishop who we had believed to be dead. Instead, she was captured, tortured, and converted. It was her blood that had been laced into illegal narcotics to give normal people inhuman abilities and urges. Well, I guess the impulses were theirs, just magnified about a thousand times.

"I long for the days it was only Ecstasy we were worried about," Marie said.

"Ah ignorance. Thou art a fickle bitch."

We stopped in the kitchen and I grabbed a beer. "You want anything?"

"No, I'm good. It's a little early to get my drink on."

"What are you talking about?" I put on my best announcer voice. "Your morning started when most of the city was just turning over. Navigating a powder keg of otherworldly forces that any other person would call Hell, but you just call Tuesday. The sun is setting, the demon is caged, and the drugs are seized. Now comes Miller time. So, head for the best tasting beer you can find. America's quality beer, Miller Highlife. If you've—"

"If you sing, your chances of sex tonight are almost nil."

I considered. It was really hard not to finish the theme song, and she did say almost. I decided it was not worth the risk. Instead, I popped the top and took a long pull, ending in the global vocalization for being refreshed. "Ahhhhhhhhhhhh."

I looked over at her smiling and shaking her head. "I'm going to check in with the office." She left me, saying over her shoulder, "See you in a little bit."

That was code for a few hours. According to official channels, she was still recovering from her injuries sustained in the raid on Uji Enterprises. It was the legal business entity for Uji no Hashame: the Tainted leader we had defeated in Miami a few months ago. The company was used for many things—most of them not so legal. No one but a select few knew Marie had been fully recovered for a while now. Her doctor, Tira Gupta, was also a Bishop. I had healed her, something other Bishops could do for themselves but not others. Except me.

My thoughts of healing pulled me in another direction.

"Mari, where is Krissy?" Mari was Marianismo, the Covenant AI. She was a combination of Alexa and Jarvis but without the snark or the creepy feeling that a corporation is listening over your shoulder.

"She is in the gym."

"Thanks."

"You are quite welcome."

I've been trying to be more polite to everyone. That included Artificial Intelligence. Or maybe she preferred artificial person? Whatever. I resealed the beer and placed it back in the fridge, hoping it would survive until later. I then made my way to the basement. I entered a secret hallway via a cabinet that held all the paint thinners and other chemicals you would expect to find to maintain an old church, striding down the long corridor to the high-tech gymnasium cleverly disguised as the dilapidated building I mentioned before. This was the only way in. Doors welded shut and bulletproof windows would frustrate any urban explorers. The gym could change its structure based on the user's requirements, kind of like a Transformer. The layout Krissy was using was very simple. She was working a heavy bag, which was twice as big as normal weighing about four hundred pounds, in the middle of the spacious room. She was still beating the literal stuffing out of it. I quietly made my way over to the padded bench against one wall where her towel and water bottle waited and took a seat.

She threw a last couple of punches, then leaned against the bag, head on her arm, panting. She turned, saw me, snarled, and fell into a defensive stance.

"Hey! Krissy, it's Chris!"

She looked confused, then embarrassed. Standing up straighter, she hastened to pick up her towel and wiped sweat off her face. "What the fuck are you doing sneaking up on me like that?"

"Sorry, I didn't mean to startle you. I assumed you felt when I came in."

"Yeah, well, you know what assuming gets you."

"I'm sorry."

"Forget it." She took a swig of water. "What are you doing here, anyway?"

"I came to see how you're doing."

She sat down next to me. "I didn't throw up my breakfast, so that's a plus."

Krissy was in her thirties, and extremely lean due to her year in captivity. She had just recently put on weight again, all of it muscle thanks to the heavy workout regimen. She had been nourished on little more than the blood of betrayers, the Wheaties for any spawn of the Tainted. Her stomach was not used to actual food. She was still mostly vegetarian, not having the tolerance for meat. If I had vomited as much blood as she did on our first meeting, I would probably go that way as well.

"How are you sleeping? Still having nightmares?"

"Can you really call them that when they are memories of what I've actually done?"

"But not as many, right?"

"Why do people have to keep searching for a positive? Let's cut to the chase. Yes, my life doesn't suck as badly as it did. But let me clue you in to reality, it still sucks. I sleep two or three hours a night. We already said what happens when I do. While awake, I can't stop the visions of what I've done or had done to me. I see the faces of my victims. Hear them pleading for their lives." She put her hands to her head. "Tasting their blood as they screamed and remembering how much I enjoyed it."

I heard her stomach gurgle. She put a hand to it, taking a few deep breaths. The wave of nausea must have passed, as I saw color return to her face. She met my eyes. "Yeah, everything is peachy." Shaking her head, she took another sip of water. "I can't even get a decent workout in. Everyone's afraid they're gonna hurt me, or that I will lose it."

I thought about that for a second, tried to restrain a smirk, then reached over and pushed her shoulder. It was a small nudge. She elbowed me back halfheartedly. I shoved her again, hard. She wasn't ready for it and fell sideways.

"What the hell Chris?"

"You don't seem so tough."

Krissy squinted at me until she realized. Then they opened up wide. "Yeah, you want to test me, newbie?"

I stood up. "Let's see what you got."

She hopped to her feet. "Mari, sparring mats." Turning her back to me, she fired over her shoulder, "You're gonna regret this."

I took the opportunity to push her again, then blurred onto the fighting square. She spun around to face me only to realize I was behind her.

"I'm waiting."

The look on her face could have been confused with malice, but I saw the joy behind it. She blurred at me and we exchanged punches and kicks, each blocking the other, then countering. I could feel that she was holding back so relaxed my guard and she tagged me with a left cross. Here's the funny thing about getting punched for real:

there isn't a blooming pain on contact. Your first reaction is shock, even when you know it's coming. Like your body is trying to protect you. Then a heartbeat later, the pain hits.

We had a rule when sparring, no powers. The idea was to sharpen natural reaction time, which would increase overall performance. We had other exercises to focus abilities. Plus, we could heal ourselves, so what was the point? When she hit me, it was for real. No protection, no added strength.

As soon as she connected, Krissy stepped back. "Oh, shit, sorry."

"You should be." I said.

Her eyes got big again.

"That was a pitiful punch." I wiped a spot of blood from the corner of my mouth. "I would say you hit like a girl, but I don't want to insult girls around the world."

She hid a happy smile behind a predatory grin, then attacked. Her blows were coming hard and fast now, nothing held back. She was formidable—got a few good shots in. But I had been training with Soon-Li, one of the most feared and respected fighters on the planet. When I threw Krissy to the mat for the third time, the frustration got to her. Something snapped. She screamed and launched herself, taking me to the ground with a combination of unharnessed rage and enhanced power. It felt like a bull had just taken a run at me. She straddled my stomach, hammering blows down on me. I didn't protect myself, thinking that would just enrage her more.

I just kept yelling her name, trying to get through to her. She came back to herself like a light switching on, staring down at me in horror. Tears welled in her eyes. She tried to run, but I grabbed her. Just moving hurt. I could feel my face swelling up and could barely see out of one eye. Blood itched as it trailed down my face from several cuts.

I pulled her into an embrace so she couldn't dash off. She didn't return it, her body stiff against mine. "Using me as your personal punching bag is one thing. Punching and running—that's just rude."

A half-laugh, half-sob escaped from her and she relaxed into my arms. She hugged me back, wrapping her legs around my abdomen as she cried quietly. After a moment, she pulled away. "I'm sorry."

"For what? You needed to work through some shit. You're not much of a talker, so I figured I could punch it out of you." Krissy laughed, sniffled, and gave me a play shot. "But you could do me a favor, though."

"What's that?"

"Get off me before Marie shows up."

She looked down, realizing the position we were in.

"If she walks in, this beating will feel like a deep tissue massage in comparison."

"She is kind of scary."

I smiled. "You have no idea."

Chapter Four

"You'd need three promotions to get to be an asshole"

Biloxi Blues - 1988

A FEW HOURS LATER, after Krissy and I had a long talk, I had healed myself and showered. Marie met me in the kitchen. I pulled out my beer and re-popped it.

"I'm glad you two are back. We have a problem."

I turned and found Adam standing in the doorway to the kitchen.

"What's going on?" Marie asked.

Adam didn't respond, but beckoned for us to follow him. Marie did so immediately while I just stood there, beer in hand, leaning against the counter.

"Come on Chris," Marie said.

I looked at the beer and sighed. "Alas mon chéri. This was not to be."

"Come on, Chris!" they both said in unison from further down the hall.

I huffed, took another sip, put it on the table, and followed the party poopers.

Adam led us to the conference room. We walked in to see Imaculada, the head of the Miami Covenant, Jelena, and Krissy, who gave me a smile. They were all talking with John McCaw, a member of the New York Covenant where I was originally recruited.

"Hey John!" I said. He looked up, dreadlocks swinging around his face against his thick rimmed black glasses as he smiled. I walked up and greeted him with a bro hug. "Had I known you were here, I would have included you."

"In what?"

"It's Miller time!"

"Not yet, it's not."

The seriousness of his expression caused me to stop and switch gears. "What's going on?"

"There has been another attack."

"In New York?" I asked.

"No." John's face was grim. "New Orleans."

"Your hometown? Sorry. What can I do?" I asked.

He nodded. "We are getting reports of outright supernatural attacks on Bishops in broad daylight."

"That's crazy," I said. "In this age of video? The blowback will be massive."

"What blowback?" Marie asked.

"The last time the tainted showed their hand was the late seventeenth century." Adam said.

"Okay?" Marie drew out the word.

"You heard of the Salem witch trials?" I added.

"Oh."

"Yeah." John took up the conversation. "Our records are much better than most historical documents. We know that over two hundred stood accused. Thirty were found guilty."

"That's terrible."

"That was only Salem. The surrounding areas were even worse. Nearly a thousand were implicated. Most of them were Converted. A few were Bishops."

"Sorry, what is a Converted again?"

"A normal human that one of the Tainted has turned into a minion." I answered. "Minus the yellow bodies and banana obsession. They have powers, but to a lesser degree."

Ima eyed me. "Done?"

I gave her a thumbs up. John continued. "It was a terrible time. Afterwards, we established a silent agreement not to show our powers out in public. Since then, we all keep to the shadows. Neither side wanted this issue to reoccur."

"Until now," Ima added.

Marie put a hand on her hip. "Yeah, but they can't think the witch trials will start up again."

"Why not?" Adam said. "People have proven time and again that, given the chance, they will lay their blame at the feet of any convenient scapegoat. They may not call them witches, but they just have to look, talk or act differently, or just believe in something against the grain. In World War II it was the Japanese and Germans. The Gulf War? It was anyone Muslim. Pandemic? It was the Chinese. People need a place to aim their frustration and misery."

Ima took up the thread. "The real concern is the military. If the wrong person at the right level of government gets wind of this, we will have a big problem. We could easily be looked at as a threat or a weapon to be used."

I crossed my arms. "So, let's take steps to make sure that doesn't happen."

"That's why I'm here," John adjusted his glasses. "The council has convened and put together a task force to address the issue. I was asked to be a part of it based on my history with the area."

"Cool, good choice."

Ima, Adam, Jelena, and John all stared at me.

"What? You want me to join? Forget it. I have too much going on here. The tainted drugs are still all over the city from the missing stash. We have been picking at the edges, but we are getting close to the source."

"Chris." John interrupted my tirade.

"What?"

"They don't want you to join the team."

"Good."

"They want you to lead it."

"Why me?" I took another pull at my beer, which I had returned to after retreating out of the conference room.

"Just off the top of my head, I would say that it might be because you are the only person in history to kill one of the Tainted."

"Great. Let's put the guy in charge with the least amount of experience simply because he got lucky."

"I think you're not giving yourself enough credit. You were the one who felt the poem held some deeper meaning. You figured out how to kill Uji."

"That was more dumb luck than anything else. Plus if it wasn't for Jelena using her for target practice, I would probably be dead."

"And you hired her."

"So?"

"The only person who could have helped you at that moment. A Marine sniper. The first non Bishop ever to be enlisted by a Covenant. You can call it what you want, you pulled the pieces together."

Marie was at her most annoying when she presented logical arguments. Every time I started to regain a little control, life threw something else at me. I felt off balance, like walking a tightrope in a hurricane.

"I don't want to leave you."

"How do you know I'm not coming with you?"

"Your sense of duty. Special Agent in Charge."

Marie didn't respond, but came up behind me and wrapped me in her arms. She felt good. Better than good. She felt like home. That was a feeling I hadn't had in decades. I didn't want to lose it. To lose her. I had a hunch that if I left, I would.

Jelena popped her head in. "We've got New Orleans on the monitor," then disappeared again.

I put my now empty bottle in the recycle bin and followed her.

The large screen was on when we got there: black with streaks of light hopping in, then out again. Muted, garbled voices emanated from the speakers in the ceiling.

"What's going on?" I asked John.

"We're not sure. Tiffany called with an update, but she told us to hang on and…" John gestured at the back screen.

"Who is Tiffany?" Marie asked.

"A Bishop from the NOC," John said, still staring at the screen, presumably trying to make out the occasional flash of light or mumbled word.

Marie looked at me as I leaned over. "New Orleans Covenant, I presume."

She mouthed, 'Ah.'

There was a scraping noise and the screen came to life. The scene whipped by like the view from a carnival ride, then centered on a woman. She had dark skin and an afro that was large enough to go out of camera range. Her lips were a bright red and her eye shadow a pale blue. *"John, thank God."*

"Tiffany, what is going on?"

She looked around before answering. *"They attacked the Covenant House."*

"Who did?"

"Who do you think?"

Ima leaned in. "Did they find the pool?"

"Hang on." The video went blank, then came back less than ten seconds later. *"No, it hasn't been compromised yet."*

"Well, at least there's that."

"Where are you?" John asked.

"At the emergency rendezvous."

"Wait, the house fell?" John's voice went up an octave.

"We had no one to defend it. When it was clear we weren't going to be able to hold, Terrance ordered the evacuation."

"He was there?" John's tone reached a level of stress that I had never heard before.

"Of course."

"Where is he now?"

"He stayed behind to scuttle the hard drives."

"What about the kill switch I installed?"

"He disconnected it after you left. He didn't like the idea of everything being lost with the push of a button."

John slammed the table and the sound made me jump. This was not the man I had come to know. When the shit hit the fan, he was the one you wanted by your side. Nothing fazed him. Except this, whatever this was.

"Where is he, Tiffany?"

"I don't know. He didn't make it here."

"I will be there tonight. I'll send you my flight info. Pick us up at the airport."

She nodded and ended the call.

John faced me. "I need your help with this one."

"You've got it," I said without hesitation.

He walked past me and out of the room.

"Who is Terrance?" I asked.

Ima crossed her arms. "John's father."

Chapter Five

"I love you. - I know"

STAR WARS EPISODE V:
THE EMPIRE STRIKES BACK - 1980

ARIE DROVE JOHN AND me to the airport in my Range Rover. While she would have preferred to take her Chevy Camaro IROC-Z, I didn't think John or I would have cherished the ride from the backseat. She drove as she always did, fast. I appreciated it this time, since it was an uncomfortably quiet ride. John was still brooding, which meant his normally subdued personality had descended to functionally mute. No one thought music was appropriate. Or should I say music that would have been appropriate would not have been tolerable.

We entered Miami-Opa Locka Executive Airport and Marie pulled up to the Atlantic building. This was a new level of travel that I had never experienced. Take every image you have of commercial flying and throw it out the window. There were no traffic jams lined up at the departures gate with taxis trying to mow people down as they exited. In fact, there were no cabs at all. We did pass a line of Escalades, Denalis, Navigators, and other high end executive transportation options. Off to one side, there was what looked to be reserved parking spaces for cars able to break two hundred miles an hour: McLaren, Ferrari, Audi, Lamborghini. Mine, while not inexpensive, would have stood out like a Sesame Street lesson.

Marie screeched to a stop and John practically vaulted from the car with a backward, "Thanks." He slammed the door closed and we were alone. It took only a few seconds for the silence to become uncomfortable. We had only been together for a few months, but they had been the best of my life. I wanted to tell her that, but the words carried with them a transition; an expectation that those early days were coming to an end. I didn't want that to be true.

There was also the genuine possibility that I might not survive the next few days. The Tainted generally worked from the shadows, acting like puppet masters. Whenever they became bold, the body count went up. Including for Bishops. Until today, they had never outwardly attacked a Covenant house.

My palms started sweating, and my mouth dried up. Marie just kept staring out the windshield at an undetermined point of interest. I had confessed multiple times throughout my life that I was no good at small talk. A friend had pointed out once that my actual issue was real talk. This was as real as it got and I felt like I had lockjaw.

I took a deep breath, frustrated at my incompetence. "Fuck this. Look Marie, I don't know what this is for you, but I'm in love with you. This is not the way I wanted to express it, and definitely not the circumstances. I don't know what's coming next, not even sure how long I will be gone or if I'll make it back in one piece. But I can tell you I want to come back. To Miami, to this Covenant, but mostly to you."

Marie stared at me, eyes filling more of her face than I thought possible. I knew it. It was too soon. I'd freaked her out. Well, chalk up another relationship to my bumbling ineptitude.

I opened my mouth to say something else but Marie grabbed the back of my neck and pulled me into a kiss with enough force to lift me out of my seat. We stayed there for a few seconds, letting the emotions take us. Falling into the well of passion.

I moved to speak when we finally pulled apart but she placed a finger over my lips. The scent of her perfume drifted up into my nostrils. She only sprayed it in one spot, in the middle of her cleavage. Whenever I breathed it in, it would bring me back to our most intimate moments and threaten to drag down into that floaty headspace.

"Do us both a favor and don't say another word. But understand this; if you don't come back to me after this is all over, or if you get yourself killed, you will have me to answer to."

I nodded and smiled at her. "As you wish."

I got out of the car, watched Marie drive off, then went inside. I found John at the check-in desk. On any other day, he would have busted my chops about what went down in the car after he left. His silence, though understandable, freaked me out a little. We were escorted to a lounge with a bar and a mini restaurant. The chairs we selected were plush and I sank into mine, feeling that a cloud could not be more comfortable. I wanted a drink, but I didn't want to give John the impression I was enjoying this. I was dancing on that middle ground between joy and misery, similar to what I had experienced soon after my mother's death. Anything that made me happy would quickly turn to guilt and sorrow.

I thought back to my parting words with Marie, a smile on my face. I had finally told her I loved her. Then a thought occurred to me. She didn't say it back.

Chapter Six

"Roger Roger. What's our vector Victor?"

Airplane! - 1980

I HAD BARELY TIME to flip through the issue of Soar Magazine, reading about the five most flown jets in the fleet, when a man approached dressed in a light gray tailored suit. "Mr. McCaw, Mr. Bateleur? My name is David. Your plane is ready."

I didn't know what to make of that statement, but John stood and grabbed his bag.

"May I take that for you, Mr. McCaw?"

"Naw, I got it," John mumbled.

As I stood, the man looked at me silently asking me the same question.

"I'm good as well," I said, holding up a hand.

He nodded. "Very good. If you gentlemen will follow me."

There was no enclosed gangway like I was used to in New York. David led us outside into the warm Florida air and onto the tarmac, where a sleek jet sat waiting. Another man in a twin suit to David's stood to the side of the plane's folding stairway.

"Good afternoon, gentlemen. My name is Anthony. I will be taking care of you today."

John nodded and stepped up onto the plane.

I stopped. "Do you know how long until we will take off? My friend is anxious to leave."

"No worries, Mr. Bateleur, we have priority status. As soon as you are settled, we'll start our flight."

I looked around. "What about everyone else?"

"You and Mr. McCaw are our only two passengers for this flight."

I didn't know how to respond to that. After a second I said, "Excellent." Blinking, I stepped onto the plane.

I was not ready for the luxury. Ten minutes ago, I would not have been able tell you what type of plane it was. Thanks to my recent magazine perusal, I identified it as the Hawker 400XP with a range of fifteen hundred miles. I had to duck to get to my seat, as did John though not nearly as low. The interior consisted of two sets of plush looking tan leather chairs facing each other with a mounted table separating them. Yes, I said chairs. While they were bolted in place, they did not qualify under the name seat. A couch sat along one bulkhead closer to the front. I had seen these types of planes in the movies, of course, but experiencing it was a completely different matter.

John picked one of the back seats, and I dropped into the adjacent one. Anthony closed the cabin door, signaled to the cockpit that they were ready, and approached.

"Can I get you gentlemen anything to drink?"

I started to answer, "I think we are all—"

"Vodka on the rocks," John didn't look up.

"Alrighty then. I guess I'll have a Bombay Sapphire and tonic with a lime wedge."

"Very good," Anthony moved off to fetch our aperitifs.

"I've never seen you drink anything but beer."

John shrugged. "Needed something a little stronger."

"Worried about your father?"

He looked at me and raised his eyebrows over the rim of his glasses.

"Yeah, okay, stupid question. He's a Bishop right?"

He nodded.

"So he can take care of himself?"

"It doesn't stop the dark thoughts."

I understood the feeling. I tried to think of something else to say that didn't sound stupid when Anthony returned handing us our drinks. My normal reaction would be to clink glasses with whomever I was drinking with. Even if it was appropriate, I didn't have a chance to propose it. John drained his glass before I had mine completely in my hand. He handed it back and asked for another.

I thought I was going to have to carry John off the plane, but he sipped his second drink. We disembarked into the somewhat cooler air of New Orleans two hours later. We landed at the small Lakefront Airport, in the middle of downtown instead of the more popular Louis Armstrong International Airport. The terminal was a large Art Déco building the color of sand, featuring one main wing in the center and two slightly smaller on either side. Its frieze was sculpted with depictions of what looked to be the myth of Icarus done in an artistic blocky flair that reminded me of Disney's Hercules. In my mind, I questioned an airport's use of a figure who perished by plummeting to earth after his wings had fallen off.

Despite the symbolic representation of death in the architecture, the personalized service we received was, once again, stellar. A representative who also called us by name was waiting just outside our plane with a fancy golf cart that whisked us the short distance to the terminal. In the parking lot was an older model white Chevy Colorado. John snorted.

"What?"

He pointed. "That is the last vehicle to be produced in the Shreveport Louisiana General Motors facility before it closed. That was two-thousand-twelve. My Father insisted on having it. Swore he would never get rid of the thing."

I recognized Tiffany, sitting grim-faced in the passenger seat, from our video call this morning. It felt weird that it had been such a short time ago. She waved us over. John hopped in the back and I followed.

Tiffany leaned around the seat. "Thank God you're here."

"Any word?"

"No."

"Has anyone been to the house?" I asked.

"No. That would go against procedure," said the man in the driver's seat.

Tiffany nodded towards the driver. "This is David Ritter. He's from the Philly Covenant."

I knew little about the branch, but what I did know made me nervous. It was the equivalent of being from D.C. for a government agency or, if you were a Roman Catholic, the Vatican. David was here for oversight. I nodded towards the front. "Hey Dave. Good to meet you."

Tiffany cringed.

"It's David," he said without humor.

"David, sorry. As I was saying, nice to meet you. I'm Chris, this is John."

He nodded at the rearview mirror.

I smiled back. "We would like to check out the house."

"As I said, that is against regulations."

"Understood, and thanks for letting me know. I'm kind of still new at this, so I'm not as versed with all the rules." I was tying to be as diplomatic as I possibly could. In the army, I would have simply informed him that when I wanted his input, I would beat it out of him. However, we were not in the military and I needed to proceed cautiously.

David nodded again.

"Be that as it may, I still would like to go to the house."

"Emergency protocols clearly state—"

"I'm sorry to interrupt, but I was under the impression that I was put in charge of this operation. Was I misinformed?"

I presumed David came up with several replies during the ensuing silence that he discarded. He finally just replied, "No."

It was my turn to nod. "Then if you would be so kind." I left the rest unsaid because if I had to repeat myself again I was going to lose my sunny disposition. To David's credit, he didn't argue or quote regulations any further and pulled away from the curb.

I had never been to New Orleans. My image of it comes from movies like Live and Let Die, Undercover Blues, Interview with a Vampire, as well as NCIS spin offs. The Covenant house for the local chapter of superheroes divinely tasked with a hidden war did not disappoint. Similar to the house in which I started this journey, a whopping six months ago, it was on a packed urban street. In fact, it was at the corner of two. A building between Bourbon Street and Dumaine. It had two balconies, the lower of which started on one street and wrapped around to the other. While the upper was smaller and spanned three of the four shuttered doors on Dumaine. The last looked like a forgotten portal hanging out there by itself. It had slate gray shutters on the windows, real ones not the plastic decorative type, and the stucco was a light greenish gray. We parked a few blocks away and walked to a spot where we could watch the building from across the street from a bar by the name of Cafe Lefitte in Exile.

"I don't see any movement," I was trying to peer into the windows from our vantage point.

Tiffany stepped up next to me. "You wouldn't. The windows don't allow you to see in, and anything visible would be simulated. The internal sensors are offline so there is no way to determine if there is anyone inside."

"Okay. Anybody have thermal vision as a power?"

I felt John turn and stare at me. "That's not a thing."

"Seems like it should be."

John narrowed his eyes at me. "I'm going in."

"That is against protocol," David argued.

"So, stay here and cover our backs," I said. "Let us know if anyone follows us in." I looked at Tiffany. "How about you?"

"I'm going too."

I nodded. "John, take point. I'll follow when you get to the door."

He gave no sign that he heard me, but started walking. When he was nearly at the door I said, "Let's go. You watch westward."

"Got it."

"David, watch our six."

David huffed but said, "Acknowledged."

We crossed over Dumaine, trying to be nonchalant, just a couple out for a walk. Then we ducked through the door John had left partly open. I wasn't sure what I was expecting, but a pub was not it.

It wasn't large. The room held a few tables on either side, some now overturned or broken. The bar was three sides of an octagon, the middle section facing the front door. We performed a quick search of the area but uncovered nothing. Behind the bar, double doors led to a kitchen. A large pot of gumbo simmered on the stove. The smell of the holy trinity of vegetables—celery, onions and green peppers—paired with the andouille sausage, chicken and shrimp had my mouth watering. It quickly changed as I caught sight of the three bodies and caught a whiff of the clawing odor of death. Flies feasted readily on both. A door on the perpendicular wall from the bar opened to a hallway that provided access to several storage areas.

At the end of the hall a stairway doubled back on itself, leading to the upper floors. It was a similar layout to the Manhattan house, where one floor was dedicated to offices, one to living areas, and one to prayer. I noted the inside appeared bigger than the outside and pointed it out to John.

"We own the buildings on either side as well."

The one difference I saw in this setup was all the worship areas were facing inward and ringed by a common hallway. Well, that and all the bodies. I hadn't seen a massacre like this since Poseidon's Grove. But these weren't innocent scientists, they were military for hire. Groups of one or two could be found in several places along the route. Death came in many forms but none from gun fire as though the victims were picked off little by little. Whatever this was had ended in the foyer opening into the worship floor.

A large open area at the top of the steps was filled with art and artifacts from many religions. There were paintings by Giotto and van Eyck, a tignon under glass identifying its owner as Marie Laveau, and an old trombone belonging to Mother Catherine Seals. Benches were staggered around for viewing or quiet reflection. In the middle of the sizeable floor, a wide pool of congealed blood. Drag marks stretched out from it emanating from the middle. The source of the blood was no longer here. It was surrounded, however, by seven bodies.

John kneeled down next to the bloody puddle, looking into it for something. I wanted to comfort him, but didn't know how. We were friends, brothers in battle, and drinking partners. But were we close enough for this? Would my words be a balm or an irritant? With every passing heartbeat, speaking up became more awkward. I shook off my doubt and was about to reassure him when our ear pieces cut through the silence.

"Local LEOs incoming." David's voice held an 'I told you so' air. Had he been under military command, I would have cured it with enough pushups to make him throw up. I couldn't utilize that tried-and-true discipline method now. I couldn't, right?

"NOPD!" voices called from below.

Chapter Seven

"There are rules for policemen."

Die Hard - 1988

J OHN'S HEAD SHOT UP, then he stood and got moving. "Follow me."

John entered the Christian worship area, which served any of the faiths that followed Jesus, dipped his fingers into the holy water hanging on the wall and made the sign of the cross. I followed suit, but Tiffany did not. He led us past the small altar and up to the tabernacle. Behind it, mosaic tiles depicted the Christmas scene. John pushed the Christmas star, opening a panel in the floor revealing a set of stairs. He descended, expecting everyone would follow. I looked at Tiffany. She motioned for me to go ahead, and I did so. I don't know if it was her age, that she was an Acolyte, or that I still adhered to the ladies first edict that caused me to hesitate. The fact this was her Covenant house finally moved my feet. She followed, flipping a switch at the bottom that closed the hole in the ceiling. The corridor below was narrow, the width of two average sized people, and dimly lit by strips of LEDs below the floor on either side. After about ten yards, we came to a solid metal wall.

"Welcome back, John," said a female voice.

"Thank you, Trinity."

"Hello, Tiffany. Nice to meet you, Christian."

Tiffany returned the greeting.

I said, "I prefer Chris."

"Noted. John, I can't allow you access to the chamber. We are in lockdown."

"Override code: malt, hops, yeast and water."

"Verified. Welcome home."

I caught John's eye and by way of explanation, said, "My father is a big believer in the German rule for beer purity."

"I can't argue with that."

The door slid up. It was thick as a bank vault. When closed, it sank into the floor and walls by six inches. If someone didn't have access, they were not getting past this. Beyond was a circular room about fifteen feet across made completely of steel. When the wall through which we entered slid shut, I saw that the space was barren of any features. The chamber resembled what I pictured the inside of a large water tank would look like. I was waiting for the disembodied voice from the Haunted Mansion to inform me that the only way out was his way. Before I could say anything, a muted thud echoed through the chamber—something I felt more than heard. A railing extended up through the floor and we started moving downward.

The platform picked up speed. Lights embedded in the open sides flashed by. After a few seconds, my stomach sank as we slowed again. At the bottom was a single closed door which opened with a whoosh very reminiscent of the Original Series of Star Trek. We stepped out into a corridor that curved away in both directions. I got the impression if you were to head off down one direction, you would eventually end up where you started.

"Trinity, is there anyone down here besides us?" Tiffany asked.

"No, you three are the only residents."

John led us to the right about thirty yards and entered the next door on the same wall as the huge turbo lift we had just exited. It was the main security room. A grid of monitors mounted on the wall all showed different views of NOPD officers swarming through the main building.

I pointed at the screen. "Do you think Anton had someone watching the house who called the police?"

"Seems plausible. Many areas of the building are damn near sound-proof. It's likely no one would have had a clue what happened here.

Trinity, show me thirty minutes before the lockdown."

"Sure, John."

The bank of screens all went momentarily black before coming back to the same rooms without the contingent of New Orleans' finest. John's father stood in the kitchen, putting spices in a large pot of simmering seafood, and singing along with the jazz that was playing. Every once in a while, he would pause to focus on a few dance steps, or sing into the wooden spoon in his hand. All of us had smiles on our faces. How could we not when watching the sheer joy he displayed during the simple act of preparing a meal?

On another display, a squadron of paramilitary fighters flooded into the bar. They split up. Most flowing in the doorway that led to the rest of the house, while four entered the kitchen. Terrance moved like lightning and hit like a thunderclap. He kicked the first one through the door so hard I could see his chest cave in on the camera. The next two, he dispatched with the wooden spoon which had been a cooking instrument and microphone. He struck hard with it in the soft parts of the intruders. Neck, groin, solar plexus. The small team never even got a shot off. The last attacker had his neck snapped. They died as quickly as they'd entered.

When the one-sided skirmish ended, he contacted Tiffany.

"The house is under attack. Get out now."

"We can take them."

"No, there are too many. Just go. I am going to lock things down and retreat as well."

"But—"

"Don't argue, just move."

"Yes, sir."

"Trinity, go into lockdown."

"Lockdown confirmed."

John's father looked at the bloody spoon and tossed it aside. He covered the pot and turned it down to a simmer, then walked through the door into the bar area. He looked really pissed. We watched him meticulously stalk the rest of the team through the house as they broke off to check rooms or transitioned to the next floor. The deployment was lightning fast, as though they expected no resistance.

As the unit moved onto the top floor, Terrance seemed to lose his patience. He blurred up through their ranks, knocking them back. He stood in the middle of the room, face contorted in rage. Before they could regain their upper hand, he struck. I had never seen anyone flow from a blur to strength, to solidity, and back into a blur as quickly or as laser focused as he did. Terrance would zip to one opponent, hit them with a volley of attacks, breaking bones or flinging them across the room before appearing in front of the next. He appeared to have a sixth sense about when an enemy was about to take a shot and would harden his skin just in time. Then he'd blur away before they could try another. He took advantage of the enclosed space where the fear of cross fire was very real for the intruders. Anxiety overwhelmed one of the team and he panic-fired, taking out one of his comrades.

Of the fifteen men that had stepped onto the fifth floor, only five remained. That was when another figure blurred in. He was a huge, nearly seven feet tall and pushing four hundred pounds. His great bulk looked to be a fifty fifty combination of muscle and fat. He grabbed John's father and hurled him across the room. Regaining his footing, Terrance launched back into the attack. The monster of a man simply snagged him out of the air and held him in place. He nodded at another intruder who immediately stepped up. The goon raised his automatic rifle and started shooting at Terrance until one bullet finally penetrated into his shoulder. He grabbed the wound crumpling.

The big man let him fall to the ground and walked away, ordering, "Take him." His voice was deep, though melodious. He stopped to look up at the camera and grin.

John froze the image, one hand white knuckled on the desk. I heard him mumble, "Still alive."

I watched him for a second, then pulling my attention back to the monitor. "Who the hell is that?"

"Anton Mueller." John replied in more of a growl than usual. "Better known as The Giant."

"No shit," I said.

Tiffany crossed her arms. "I'm sorry John. This is my fault. I should have stayed."

John shook his head. "There was nothing you could have done. You would have just been killed."

I cocked my head. "Not captured?"

"I don't think so," he said. "They are making an example of him for what we did to Uji."

"You mean what I did."

"You were only the tip of the spear. Either way, you only need one example, and the Creole Knight is a much more poignant one."

"Who?" I asked.

"John's father," Tiffany said. "It's what the locals nicknamed him fifty years ago after he rescued a bunch of kids trapped in a burning building. People never got a good look at him, but from then on, any unclaimed act of kindness was attributed to the Knight."

John tapped the keyboard and switched to an outside view of our location, where an ambulance sat waiting. After loading Terrance inside, they sped away in several cars. Anton climbed into the back of a silver Lincoln Navigator. Tiffany noted the make, model, license plate and other markings of all the vehicles.

"I don't suppose there is another way out of here?" I asked.

Nodding, he motioned to us to follow.

"Maybe we should get some supplies before we go?" I suggested.

"Agreed."

We stopped off at the armory and selected several automatic rifles, various attachments, and a few sidearms, knives, etc. They all went into a duffle bag pulled from a drawer. The next room over was the gadget room. We packed another bag with night vision goggles, laser listening devices, com units, tactical binoculars, and wireless bugs.

Tiffany picked up a bag. "We're traveling rather heavy."

I slung one onto my shoulder. "We don't want to chance coming back."

I estimated we walked about halfway around the circular hallway, passing several doors on either side before we came to the one John wanted.

As he was opening it, I said, "Do you think we will be a little too conspicuous with all these bags?"

We stepped into what was obviously a garage and he selected big black Chevy Suburban.

"Beulah?" I asked. It was the name he had given to the twin vehicle in New York, after his aunt because, as he put it, *she's big black and mean, but will always take care of you.*

John smiled for the first time. "Deloris."

We drove up behind the bar where we'd left David. I hopped out and went through the back door. He was still perched near the main entrance, staring out at the house, but now he was on the phone. "No, they are definitely caught. There is no sign of them. You should have put me in charge."

I pulled the phone out of his hand and held it up to my ear. "Fortunately, we were not captured. All is well. Thanks for checking on us." It was one of those new foldable ones that reminded me of the flip phones from the past. It gave a satisfying snap as I closed it before tossing it back to him. He snapped it out of the air with ease, robbing me of the bumbling move I was hoping for. Damned powers.

"David, how about we make a deal? You've been at this longer than I have—Let's face it, so has Tiffany. Your experience and familiarity with the regulations is invaluable. I need you to tell me when I am breaking protocol."

"I can do that." David looked smug.

"But only once."

He frowned.

I continued. "I want your insights, but the decision I make may go against regulations. You need to be okay with that."

David considered that. "And if I'm not?"

"Then you can catch the next plane back to Pennsylvania."

His eyebrows pulled together and his mouth quirked in a look that said, *yeah right.*

"Based on what we saw, I am going to need as much help as I can get. But I would rather be down a man than be constantly battling you along the way."

He gave me a side eye.

"I'm not asking you to trust me. Just give me the benefit of the doubt until I prove to be incompetent."

"And when that incompetence gets someone killed?"

"How about we work together to make sure that doesn't happen?" I stuck my hand out.

David looked at it for a heartbeat too long before finally grasping it in a firm, confident handshake.

"I'll follow until you screw up, then I'm taking you down."

"Just do me one favor."

"What's that?"

"Don't spend more time focused on me than you do on the reason we are here."

His grin told me it would be about fifty-fifty.

David hopped in the back and I took shotgun.

John pulled away and glanced in my direction. "Where to?"

"We need a base of operations. Do you have a safe house?"

"I know one."

"Let's start there." I pulled out my phone and selected a contact. "Hi Chris, how's it going? How is John?"

"Hey Soon-Li. As good as can be expected in both cases."

"He's right next to you?"

"Yup."

"Give him a hug for me."

I took the phone away from my mouth. "Soon-Li says, hey."

"That's not what I said."

"Close enough. He's driving. If I hug him, he will crash."

"Have you gotten anywhere?"

"A little." I filled her in on what we found while being conscious of John's feelings. Look at me being sensitive. "I need everything we have on Anton."

"Know thy enemy?"

"Something like that."

"I will get it together and send it over."

"Thanks."

"Be careful."

"Come on. You know what a cautious fellow I am."

"M-hm." Soon-Li hung up, unconvinced.

About fifteen minutes later, we pulled up to the gates of a large gorgeous house on the water. John rolled down the window next to an intercom. He punched in a code, waited for a second, and they opened silently. He proceeded up the driveway and parked between a Mercedes and an old Ford Pickup truck.

I looked around, feeling like my mouth was hanging open. "This is quite a safe house."

"It has the best food, too." John opened the door and hopped out.

We all piled out of the SUV and I walked to the back to grab our gear. That was when I noticed the woman standing in the drive watching us. She was a little shorter than John, but with the same dark skin. Her curly hair was worn high on her head and was dressed in a green skirt suit.

"What happened to your father?" she asked with a hint of a Nigerian accent.

"Why did something have to happen?"

"Because I taught you better than to arrive unannounced with a truckload of people and he would have called even if you forgot."

"He's been taken."

"Again?"

John nodded.

"What do you need?"

"A place to stay and work out of."

"The bayou is compromised?"

He nodded again.

"Let's get you settled. Who are your friends?"

John half turned and introduced us. "This is Blessing McCaw, my mother."

Chapter Eight

"I suggest you put on a tie."

YOUNG FRANKENSTEIN - 1974

BLESSING WAS TRUE TO her name. She whipped up one of the best meals I've had on a moment's notice. This after being told that her husband had been abducted and was possibly near death. I didn't think we should spend our time sitting around a table and hinted as much to John.

"Not sitting and enjoying her hospitality would be insulting, no matter the circumstances. She has already allowed us to not come to dinner dressed."

I looked down at myself, miming a sarcastic response about the clothes I had on.

John said with a smirk, "Jackets at minimum, ties suggested."

"You're kidding, right?"

He raised his eyebrows. "There is only one thing that scares me more than the tainted; earning my mother's ire."

I settled into my chair and accepted a glass of wine when it was offered. How long could this take, anyway? Two hours later Blessing stood up and showed us to the guest rooms.

My room, complete with an attached bathroom, overlooked the water. The bed with head and foot boards, dresser, nightstand and desk were all made of poplar, off white with matching styles.

I put my duffle bag on the small seat in front of the bed, pulled out my laptop, and set it up at the desk. I logged in and realized I needed the Wi-Fi password. That's when I noticed the small note.

Guest Wi-Fi password: De$tinyJob18:15

Shaking my head, I plugged it in. The email from Soon-Li had arrived about an hour ago.

> Chris,
>
> The attached file has everything we know about Anton, but here are the highlights. He is well known for being the strongest of all the Tainted. While he has other supernatural abilities, he favors his brute strength. He is also ruthless even compared to the rest, which is saying something. If he took Terrance rather than just kill him, there is a reason for it. That scares me more than anything.
>
> You have a tendency to rush in where angels fear to tread. Try to take this one a little more cautiously. Let me know how I can help.
>
> Soon-Li.

Great, I was going from the original dragon lady to a giant the size of Hagrid with a demeanor that made Genghis Khan look like Barney the Dinosaur. Just ducky.

I opened the attachments and started reading about the centuries of destruction Anton had wrought. According to the reports, he "mentored" Alexander the Great, Julius Caesar, and Napoleon. Some of the bloodiest wars were secretly influenced by Anton. Whereas Uji avoided cameras or the limelight, Anton appeared to revel in it. He was prominently depicted in paintings, on pottery, and later in photographs. I looked through the photos she'd included. In one ancient painting, Anton stood behind Julius Caesar, arms akimbo, a heavy cloak draped over his massive shoulders clasped by a gold star. He didn't seem to care that he was showing off his immortality, and either no one pieced it together, or those that did passed it off as a tremendous coincidence.

A knock came at the partially open door and I turned to find Blessing peeking in. I closed the laptop and stood. "Please, come." It felt an awkward thing to say about a room in her house.

"I thought we might talk." She glided in, her hands folded at her waist and sat on the bed.

"Sure." I turned the desk chair around and sat again. "I really appreciate you letting us stay here. You have a beautiful house."

She waved away my statement as unimportant and looked around. "This was my daughter's room."

I wasn't sure how I was supposed to respond to that. I settled on "It's very nice. She had good taste."

"None of this is hers. When she moved out I turned it into proper guest quarters."

I blinked at her and swallowed hard.

"I understand you saved my son's life." It was not a question.

It took me a second to realize she meant the battle with the two demons back in New York. I shrugged. "I don't see it that way."

"No?"

"We were a team, each doing our part to complete the mission."

She nodded like she approved of my view. "I have heard about you, Mr. Bateleur."

"Don't believe everything you hear."

Blessing raised her eyebrows. "Even the good things?"

"Especially them."

She smiled. "You are special."

"That's just a nice way to say I'm different."

"You have a problem with niceness?"

"I prefer candor."

"Then I will give it to you. You are him. The rebirth. The…"

I held up a hand. "Not that much candor."

"Do you deny it?" Blessing looked down her nose at me.

"Let's say I believe I am me, and no one else."

"That doesn't change anything."

"It changes perspective, which is everything."

"Whose perspective?"

"Mine. It means that my decisions and my actions are my own. Not predetermined, not controlled, not guided. I do what I feel is best, what I believe to be right. Not because someone told me to. Not because it said so in a book written centuries ago by people that might as well have come from another world for all the resemblance they have to modern day humanity. I don't need someone, man or deity, to tell me what is honorable. I can feel it." I tapped my sternum. "Right here. It doesn't make me special. Nearly every person on earth has it. Many just decide to stop listening to it because it's easier."

I wasn't sure how we'd gotten here. I felt like we missed the left turn at Albuquerque and ended up too far south. Blessing, however, smiled.

My brow furrowed. "What?"

"You are indeed the man my son has described."

"That's a good thing. Right?"

She pushed off on her knees and stood. "Indeed, it is. My husband believed we would witness the end of this war in our lifetime. I can see that you are the key to that."

I stood as well. "No pressure."

Blessing stepped up to me and patted my arm with enough force to shift my equilibrium. "Luckily, you have broad shoulders. Please let me know how I may be of service." This last as she glided from the room.

"Thanks?" I shook my head, wondering what had just happened.

Leaning back from my studies, I scrubbed at my face and rubbed my neck. I checked the clock, which said just after eleven. I considered going to bed, but the way my head was buzzing I would be tossing and turning for hours. A workout might tire me out enough to quiet the storm. My naturally lazy tendencies fought against the idea of strenuous activities so near the witching hour. After an internal battle, my productive side won. I changed and headed for the gym John had pointed out during the tour.

It wasn't overly large, but contained everything you could need to get into shape. One corner was dedicated to free weights, with setups for bench work, squats, and leg presses. Another looked like it belonged in a boxing gym with a heavy bag, speed bag, and jump ropes. Along the opposite side was the martial arts wall holding weapons mostly from Japan, as well as sparing dummies, targets, and so forth. The center of the area was a large mat for sparring, or practicing, forms.

Apparently, I wasn't the only one who'd had the same idea. David was just finishing up a kata, wearing a very formal-looking karategi. The uniform lines were perfectly ironed, even the rolled-up sleeves looked like they were sewn in place. In contrast, I wore gray sweat-pants with a tight fitting soft t-shirt with 'Game over man. Game Over' printed on the front. He moved deliberately. Every motion was perfect, powerful, but from my perspective, stiff. He finished, stood and made a formal salute.

"Nicely executed." I was going to say performed, but there wasn't much in the way of performance in it.

David nodded. I don't think he was happy to see me. He walked over to a bench, picked up a towel, and blotted his forehead and neck.

"May I?" I asked, indicating the mat he had just vacated.

He gave a tilt of his head. Apparently, he was not in a talking mood.

I started my own form. There is a vast difference between Japanese and Chinese martial arts. I was trained in Shaolin Hung Ga Kung Fu. My moves were very fluid, with sudden bursts of power. A mix of quiet dance interlaced with ferocious attacks that tend to startle onlookers. I could have exercised with any of the methods, but none silenced my mind like running through a form. They were second nature and became a method of meditation for me. I put all of myself into each move. Picturing invisible opponents that I blocked and took down, driving my foot into others, and plowing through a crowd with long arm movements.

I finished, sweat dripping down my back. A *thunk* drew my atten-tion. It had been there in the background during my workout, but I was too detached to acknowledge it. Now, as I reconnected with my environment, it was more pronounced.

Thunk, thunk.

I looked over to where David was standing at one end of the room, facing the wall like he was being punished. He spun like lightning and his hands flicked out. *Thunk, thunk, thunk.* I traced the sound to the other end, where one target was peppered with spikes. It took my brain to register what they were. Throwing stars. They were in a tight grouping around the center.

I think my mouth was hanging open as he walked up and casually pulled them free of the target. "David."

He looked back at me as he continued to extract the stars from the target. His expression told me he was expecting to be mocked.

"That was awesome!" I said, in honest awe.

He tried to hide the smile that forced its way out. "Thanks."

I walked up next to him. "How long have you been training with these?"

"Since I was a kid. I always thought they were cool when I was young. I guess I never grew out of them."

"Cool is an understatement. May I?"

He met my gaze, realized what I was asking, and handed one over. It had four points to it and the sides were beveled to be razor sharp. The points themselves were menacing. I touched one as a person does to something pointy and it drew blood.

"Damn." I dragged out the word, wiping my thumb with my forefinger as it healed. I met David's gaze. He looked unsure, like waiting for the punchline. "Can you show me?"

He watched me for a second, then nodded. I helped him remove the rest of the stars from the target, trying not to skewer myself, and we returned to his spot against the wall.

"Why don't you face it?" I asked.

"Surikens are not for hand to hand combat. Their blade length is too short to kill in most situations. Depending on the size of the adversary, sometimes the only path is through the eye. They are more for disarming or incapacitating. If I'm facing them, I have other options. I carry these for quick action in my periphery. Someone to the side about to shoot. Giving aid to a teammate that might be struggling. Things like that. I want to be able to lock onto a mark and release with little thought. So I face away, or at an angle. At least for the first throw."

I nodded and stepped back. He spun like the crack of a whip and sent the star flying.

"Bullseye! Damn, David. That is friggin' outstanding."

He actually blushed, trying desperately to control his smile. "Thanks."

"Do you use your boon?"

David made a face. "My what?"

"You know, your powers."

"No. I don't want to rely on it."

"Do you mind if I try?"

This smile while he handed me the star would have been appropriate on a carnival worker as they stacked up the milk bottles for a third time. I didn't bother facing the wall. I had used throwing knives before and I was okay with them, but I knew my limitations and I didn't want Terrance to come home to holes in the walls. Plus, I was more than a little scared of Blessing.

I took the star, switched places with David, and held the weapon by one point. Taking aim, I held it over my ear, simulating the motion a few times, then threw it. It bounced off the target and stuck in the floor.

I sucked air in through my teeth. "Shit."

David chuckled, almost under his breath. "It's not like a throwing knife. Using a Suriken is more like flipping a frisbee. While not all in the wrist, that is the critical part." He offered up another.

I held up my hand. "No. I feel like Blessing is going to kick my ass already."

David made a face.

I felt he and I had bridged a gap and I didn't want to lose that. "What?"

"Nothing."

"Don't give me that," I said. "You made a face."

"It's nothing."

"If it was nothing, you wouldn't have made a face. Just tell me."

"It's not a big deal."

"Great, then it should be no problem telling me."

David sighed. "It's the cursing."

"You have a problem with cursing?"

He started to pack up his things. "Not a problem. I just don't understand it."

"What's to understand? They are words used to express emotions."

"I find people use them when they are unable to express themselves properly."

"They can be used that way. They can also articulate a point clearly and more efficiently."

He seemed skeptical. "How so?"

"How would you get someone to stop talking and pay attention to you?"

"Please be quiet."

"Are you a librarian? Because no one's hearing that if they're talking."

David raised his voice a tad. "I order you to be silent!"

"Order, eh? Who do you think you are, the king?"

"Well, I…" He searched for the right words.

"The only ones who know you are Bishops and the Tainted who are trying to kill you. Try again."

He took a deep breath and spoke authoritatively, "Now see here, I will have—"

"Shut the FUCK up!" I bellowed.

David stopped and blinked at me.

"See, I got my point across in four words and clearly imparted my severe dislike for what was going on."

His mouth was still hanging open and he continued to try to find his voice.

I walked over and removed the throwing star from the floor and wiped at the new gouge, shaking my head. "You're correct, though. Cursing has its time and place. But if not overused, and delivered at the right time, the impact is immeasurable." I placed the weapon in his hand. "Have a good night." I left the gym.

Chapter Nine

"You're nothing but a sister!"

ARISTOCATS - 1970

THE NEXT MORNING, I woke early and went for a run. This was a habit I had gotten into over the last couple of months, mostly because Marie jogged, and I would do anything to spend time with her. Even cardio. I found it to be a great time to organize my thoughts and connect the dots where my theories had gaps. It also made me less pruny than extra long showers, my other area for deep thinking. So far, it wasn't doing much.

I tried to lose myself in putting one foot in front of the other. I focused on keeping an even stride, controlling my breathing, and the soft slapping of my running sneakers as they struck the sidewalks. There weren't many people up and moving at this hour except those still partying from last night. They stumbled from the last bar in what was likely the final stop of a bar crawl. Some got sick on the street, a waste of good alcohol. I barely saw them as I sped by. But my brain kept drifting back to the issues at hand.

How was it I was dealing with another abduction so close to Kristina's return? Despite the key similarities, these were vastly different circumstances. Terrance was taken publicly. Anton all but challenged us to stop him. I didn't think he had any plans for him other than leverage and a display of his prowess. Or was I underestimating him? Was I falling victim to the big, dumb stereotype? Soon-Li said he didn't take prisoners, but he had. A superhuman possessing that much destructive power as well as a gift for strategy was a very scary prospect. I stumbled and had to refocus momentarily on staying upright.

What's more, Terrance being snatched from within the safety of the Covenant house put everything in question. We were more vulnerable than we believed. Had Anton always known of the location or was it recently discovered information? The only saving grace was they didn't get to the sanctuary or the pool. I couldn't tell if the Tainted were aware of its existence.

If they ever knew how easy it would be to wipe us out. Deny us access to the holy waters that give us our powers and we would become no more dangerous than a normal human. Did they not know? Or did they know and not care? I was not sure which was worse.

I needed to figure out how to find John's father. When I was searching for Krissi, I discovered a portal pointing the way. Though finding and opening it was a puzzle in itself. One no one had solved before me. Now I had bupkis. We traced the escape vehicles through street cams, but it had come up empty. They were driven into a parking garage where they must have been switched out.

How was I going to track them now? I wasn't even sure how much time I had. Terrance had been shot and lost a lot of blood. He had run out of his boon. I stopped short, my breathing faster despite my efforts to control it. Anton had held him while his goon had pumped bullets into him, then dropped him as though he knew he was out of juice. He had to know. That was a dangerous realization. If the tainted knew that our powers had limitations—I didn't want to finish that thought. They didn't have the same disadvantage, at least not that we were yet aware of

I looked around at where I was, surrounded by bars and nightclubs on both sides, along with the other miscellaneous stores. Small grocery vendors, convenience stores, Chinese restaurants. Apparently, even in the bayou, people got a hanker'n for moo goo gai pan. Only one place was open that I could see, a pub with a sign in the window that said *breakfast served here*. My growling stomach won over.

I entered the establishment. An old-fashioned bell at the top of the door rang out, announcing my arrival. There were six square wooden tables that could seat four people each. The high back red metal chairs each had a thin cushion. Red bricks formed the outside wall and the rest were painted a bright yellow. The bar was to the right. A dark-skinned woman with long, very curly hair came out from what I assumed was the kitchen.

"Good morning," she said.

"Good morning. I'm not really dressed for breakfast, but maybe I could pick something up to go?"

"Don't be silly. Have a seat. Start off with some coffee?"

I nodded with gusto. "Please, and maybe a glass of water as well."

"Take whatever seat you would like." She nodded towards the tables.

I sat down, feeling a little uncomfortable in my current attire, like that naked dream everyone has. I watched the woman as she worked. She wore a short-sleeved blouse under her slate gray apron, her bare arms rippled with muscles. Not large, but well toned. As she came around the bar with the coffee and water, one in each hand, I could see she didn't skip leg day. Her full hair bounced as she walked to the table.

"Cream and sugar, mister?" she asked while placing down the glass, mug, and a menu that she pulled from the pocket of her apron.

"Chris, and black is fine."

"Yes, I am, and thanks for noticing."

I barked out a laugh, completely caught off guard. "That's great. I would steal it, but I don't think it would translate."

"Not even if they cooked you over a spit."

I laughed again. She was good.

"When you figure out what you want, my name is Charity." She twisted her hip a little when she said it.

"Huh. That's the second beautifully uncommon name I've heard in two days."

"Oh yeah, what was the first?" I could tell she was just being polite with the question as she moved to return to the kitchen.

"Blessing."

Charity stopped dead in her tracks and spun around. Her eyes may as well have been looking at me through a microscope. Her expression went from polite and happy to deadly serious. She backed away slowly, as one would from an agitated cobra. "When did you see Blessing last?"

"Last night," I said, my confusion coloring my voice. "I'm sorry. Did I say something wrong?"

"Why were you with her last night?" She took another step away and her left hand had disappeared behind her back.

"She said we could stay there for a bit."

"Who is we?"

"Me, David, Tiffany, and John."

Her eyebrows shot up at John's name and she took a few quick steps back to the table. "Wait, you said your name was Chris. You're *that* Chris? The Bishop?"

It was my turn to be suspicious. It was clear she had prior knowledge of the secret world, but how much, and what side was she on? I took a chance and followed my gut. "Yes, that Chris."

She plopped down into the opposite chair, dropped a huge knife on the table and put her forehead on her hands, elbows resting on her knees. "You scared the shit out of me."

"I'm sorry. I didn't mean to. What did I say?"

"You mentioned my mother's name."

"That's it?"

Charity picked her head up. "No, you are also here stupid early, not dressed like a typical tourist, and no one just happens to bump into Blessing."

"Blessing's your mother?" I said in unison with her, "Did you say John's here?"

The bell on the door chimed as she grabbed my forearm resting on the table in a firm grip. "Why are you and John here? What's happened? Is it my father?"

I opened my mouth, but nothing came out. I barely knew this woman. This was not my news to deliver.

"Yes."

Charity and I both looked towards the door. John stood framed in the opening. She released my arm and ran over to her brother, giving him a big hug. His thick arms folded around her. Pulling back, her voice quivered. "Is he dead?"

John said, "We don't think so."

They both returned to the table and John slapped my shoulder. "How did you end up here? Is that how you come dressed to breakfast? My mother would hang you from the clothesline."

I told him.

"Then he scared me half to death," Charity added and repeated what I had told her.

"I don't think I made it sound quite so creepy."

"You definitely did."

"You make me sound like a Scooby Doo villain."

John watched tennis between us. "Are you two finished?"

We both shrugged and laughed though hers still carried an edge of worry. John sighed and caught her up with why they were there. She showed much more shock and concern than her mother had.

"What's the next move?" she asked.

It took him a few moments to answer. "We don't know."

"What do you mean you don't know? You have to do something."

"Obviously Charity, but what? The van they left in was a dead end. Wiped clean. We haven't located where they are working out of. Hell, we didn't even know he was in Louisiana before he hit the house."

"I had a thought on that," I said and they both looked toward me. "Do you have a contact in NOPD?"

"Maybe. I'm not sure after this raid. Why?"

"Well, they brought a bunch of men with them. Chances are they didn't all just get a call, put on their mercenary uniforms and converge on the house at the designated time. If we can get some names and cross reference them with DMV records to get vehicles…"

"We can see if there were any GPS locations they had in common," John finished my sentence.

"You probably don't need the car info." Charity held up her phone and waggled it in the air.

John snapped his finger and pointed at it. "That would be even easier if I didn't reengage lockdown protocols." We both looked at him. "Trinity identifies and collects every unknown wireless device that enters the building. She would have all that information stored and ready for analysis."

"Okay," I said, "so what's the problem?"

"The only way to break a lockdown is in person by one of two people coded to do so. One current resident of the house or one from outside."

"Not sure where you're going with this," I said. "I saw you disable the lockdown yesterday."

"You didn't let me finish. They need to be inside the house."

"The passage we used to get out?"

John nodded. "Not available during a lockdown." He got up and walked toward the kitchen. "You want coffee?"

"When don't I?" I said.

"Char?"

"Yeah, thanks," his sister said.

I looked at her. "Char?" I mumbled.

She quirked her mouth. "Ever since the Pokémon cartoon, that's what he calls me. He used to run around the house yelling, Char, Char!"

I smiled. "That is hard to believe."

"I will have to show you our family photo album."

"Please don't," John yelled from the kitchen.

Charity displayed a maniacal grin that lit her face. She was stunning. I thought of Marie, and a pang of guilt ran through me. I was simply enjoying the witty repartee with John's sister, who just happened to be gorgeous. Yeah, that's it. I looked around to distract myself and noticed an old, very cheap-looking trophy up on a shelf.

"What is that?" I pointed, and Charity followed my line of sight.

She smiled again. "That's the Patrick."

"The trophy has a name?"

She nodded. "Named after Patrick Ewing. John and I had our own private basketball tournament. As you can see, I won."

"You cheated." John yelled.

"I was eleven, playing against my older brother with supernatural powers. How did I cheat?"

"I don't know, but you must have."

"Is there another way in?" I called towards the kitchen.

"What about the roof access?" Charity said.

John exited the kitchen carrying a tray with three coffees and assorted pastries on it. They were filled to the top, unlike many restaurants that love to pour you little more than a half a cup. He expertly served without causing an imbalance, then placed the tray on a nearby table. "That's a possibility."

"Any additional lockdown protocols on the roof?" I asked.

"No, we keep up the appearance that we are just another religious clubhouse. Steel emergency shutters contradict that."

We all selected a pastry and sampled our cup of Joe. "Good coffee," I said to Charity.

"Thanks. I get it flown in from Jamaica." She smiled.

John looked from her to me, then back. "Did he tell you about his girlfriend yet?"

Charity shot him a dark look.

"What? I'm just saying."

"No, we didn't get the chance. Why?" I asked.

"Because my brother's an ass, and can't keep his nose out of other people's business."

He raised his hands, palms out. "Just looking out for you."

"I appreciate it, but I can take care of myself."

I took another bite of the cranberry scone I had chosen and did my best to ignore the staring contest.

"Back to the roof." John finally said. Charity nodded as if they had come to an agreement via telepathy.

"Do you think they will be watching it?" I asked.

John paused briefly with his cherry danish an inch from his mouth. "Somebody will. Either the cops or the tainted." He took a bite.

"We need to find who and distract them long enough to get in."

John swallowed. "Yeah, we don't want a repeat of yesterday."

I took another sip of coffee and considered John's shift in attitude. It seemed like being with family had pulled him out of his deep melancholy.

"Maybe we should do it now?" I offered.

John considered that. "David?"

I nodded. "David."

"Who's he?"

"They sent him from Philly," John said.

"Oh." Charity's eyes widened and did a slow nod.

"If we get over there now, we can be in and out before he realizes."

"I'll drive." Charity said.

John looked at her and frowned. "You're not going."

"You can't tell me…"

"Don't you have customers?" I asked.

"The first regulars don't get here for over an hour, and I finished all the prep work."

"Why so early?"

"Charity doesn't sleep."

"I sleep. I just don't need as much."

"Like how much?" I asked.

"Usually three or four."

I shuddered. "That's nuts."

She smiled. "It's helpful when you own a bar that serves breakfast."

"You're still not going."

"John, you have to go in to get the info. I have to distract whomever is watching and I could use someone who knows the city to identify anything out of place. It's not like we are taking her into battle."

He stared at her for a long moment. Charity smiled and fluttered her eyelashes at him. He gave a deep sigh. "Fine. But you're not driving."

Chapter Ten

"Can I borrow your towel for a sec? My car just hit a water buffalo."

Fletch - 1985

I F YOU HAVEN'T BEEN to New Orleans before—or have seen none of the plethora of movies based there—let me paint a picture. Like many urban areas, the buildings were all attached. What sets this city apart from, say, New York, is that a good number of these were only a few stories high, and overrun with balconies. A fairly athletic person can hop from roof to roof without too much of an issue. For a Bishop, with the ability to leap small buildings in a single bound, they could make their way from Canal Street to Esplanade Avenue without ever touching the pavement.

We parked on Burgundy Street a few blocks away. John scaled the nearest set of balconies like a parkour legend and disappeared onto the roof. Charity and I kept pace on the ground while the Cajun acrobat danced along the rooftops. Every once in a while, we glimpsed him sailing overhead.

I broke the silence of our stroll. "How does it feel to have a Bishop as an older brother?"

"It sucks."

"No gray area there."

She laughed and put her hand on my bicep. "I love John. He's a great guy, but talk about overprotective. Take your typical big brother, add in the knowledge of actual monsters and superpowers, and what do you think is the result?"

"Billy from hell."

"What's that now?"

I side stepped to avoid a pedestrian. "The brother of a girl I was interested in. We started hanging around together, and he and his goons tried to scare me away."

"Did it work?"

"I guess it did. I decided she was not worth the trouble."

"See what I mean."

I nodded. "How often does he come home?"

She kicked a beer can onto the road. "This is the first time in three years."

"Then, he can't be that much of a deterrence."

"No, I guess it's just triggering."

"Wouldn't that have been better on the sidewalk?" I said, pointing at the can she kicked.

She shook her head, and her afro shimmied. "Street sweepers come through daily."

"Really?"

She nodded. "Another little known fact: we have brick water ducts under the streets. Actual red bricks."

"They must be old."

"Very."

I looked up and saw John staring down at us and I gave him the international sign for *What?* He continued the long distance staring contest for a few more seconds, then moved on.

"Girlfriend, huh?" Charity said.

"Yeah."

"Is it serious?"

"I think so."

"Think?"

"It's complicated."

"Always is."

We rounded the corner onto Bourbon Street. There were still a few blocks to go so we focused more on looking for things out of place. What they might be, I had no idea. I looked down alleys, up at windows, even eyed a few suspicious cats. It all appeared the same to me. Then it didn't.

"Got him," I said.

"Where?"

I nodded. "Homeless guy up ahead."

"How do you know?"

"He's got a cell phone."

"Homeless people can have cell phones," she pointed out.

"How about a shoulder holster? I recognize the shape and position of the bulge."

Charity eyed me. "Alright, I'll give you that."

"How do we distract him?" I asked.

"You're supposed to be the expert. I was just here to find the guy."

We were getting close to him and I wasn't coming up with anything. "Since I did your job, how 'bout you help a little?"

Charity rounded on me and yelled, "What the hell is that supposed to mean?"

I could feel the shocked look on my face and the flush of embarrassment. "I'm sorry…"

"You should be! I have been holding up my end of this relationship. What have you done for me lately?"

It took me a second, but once she said relationship, I understood my part. "I guess the dinner I made you the other night was nothing."

"Spaghetti, yeah real tough. I want to go out! Go to a club and dance."

"This again? All you want to do is dance." Several song lyrics popped into my head and I had to restrain myself. In my peripheral vision, I saw the homeless man watching us. We had gotten his attention, but we were not in the best position. I grabbed her wrist and started dragging her into a better one. "Come on, we are going to be late."

She caught on faster than me, ripping her hand back when the watcher's view was aimed away from the other building. "Don't you be pulling me anywhere. And what do I care if we are late to see your friends?"

"I thought you liked them!"

"Sure, if you think I like Neanderthals that swill beer and belch the alphabet."

I saw John sail overhead onto the Covenant house roof. Time for the big finish.

"For your information, we weren't going to see my friends. That was just a ruse to get you to your surprise party."

Charity gave a sharp intake of breath and actually touched a hand to her chest. "I thought you forgot."

Behind her I saw John making his way to the door and out of the corner of my eye I noticed we were losing the man's interest. She must have thought the same, because she launched herself forward and kissed me.

John met us at the car filled with an awkward silence. We drove to the pub and Charity got out of the backseat and stopped at the passenger window.

"It was nice meeting you, Chris."

"You too."

"Sorry about the…"

"Don't worry about it."

She put a hand on my shoulder. Then looked over at her brother. "Tell Mom I'll be over later."

He nodded and she walked away, her hand sliding slowly off my shoulder.

John pulled away from the curb. "What was that about?"

"What?"

"What was she sorry for?"

"Nothing. Just a misunderstanding."

"Uh-huh."

"What did you find out?" I asked, trying to change the subject.

"That you're a player."

"I'm not a player."

"Then why didn't you mention Marie?"

"Because it is not the first thing that pops out of my mouth when

I meet a woman."

"Uh-huh."

"Seriously, I got there, sat down. She told me her name and I told her it was the second interesting name I had heard, then mentioned your mother's. She looked like she wanted to kill me."

John shook his head. "Wow."

"What?"

"You're right, you are not a player."

"Exactly. Wait, why not?"

"You have no game."

"What do you mean, I have no game?"

"That's the second interesting name I have heard?"

"I wasn't trying to pick her up," I said defensively. "I was just making conversation."

"Yeah, okay." John rolled his eyes.

"Why don't you believe me?"

"Cause everyone tries to pick up Charity."

"Okay, she's gorgeous, but that doesn't matter."

His eyebrows bunched up. "What, is she not good enough for you?"

"No, I didn't say that."

"What's wrong with her?"

"Nothing."

"Then why aren't you interested?"

"Because I'm in love with Marie, okay?"

John smiled. "Damn, it took you long enough."

"What? Are you serious? This whole big brother thing was bullshit?"

"No, if you go near my sister, I will kick your ass. But I knew you were too into Marie. I just wanted you to admit it."

"You're an asshole."

"Yup."

Chapter Eleven

"Why don't you gentlemen have a Pepsi?"

Spies Like Us - 1985

W E GOT BACK TO the house with pastries and information. We decided to say the info came from John's contact in the NOPD. The analysis showed all the cell phones had one location in common. We had to deal with David accusing us of running an investigation without him. Which was true, but my jogging outfit and the delicacies mollified him.

"What's the plan?" Tiffany asked.

"Step one, eat pastries and drink coffee. Then we need to check out this building."

I took one for the team and ate a second breakfast like Frodo. John did the same, but I don't think it was much of a stretch for him. He was infamous for eating massive amounts of sugar filled treats and still sporting an eight pack. It must have been his special power. Cosmic ability to turn carbohydrates into lean muscle.

The location was off the beaten path, and more modern than the Covenant house. It was an office building with as much glass as concrete on the outside, like the builders couldn't decide if they wanted all one or the other, so they opted for splitting it down the middle. The name of the bank it had once been was still engraved in the marble facade. It had eight floors and was now leased out to various different businesses. All of them seemed to be legit on the surface. There were several law firms, a small insurance corporation, an actual bank though not the one whose name was carved on the front, a modeling agency which I felt needed additional scrutiny but was outvoted, and a private security company which had a separate entrance and a fleet of black SUVs.

We geared up and moved out. Blessing walked us to the driveway. John climbed in and started the car.

"You bring him back to me, you hear?"

He nodded. "Yes, ma'am."

I studied the blueprints John had downloaded, working through the scenarios. Eight floors meant a roof attack was not feasible. There were possibilities, but none worked for four people, except maybe creating a portal. I had created a rift through the realm of the divine on three separate occasions. The first time, I'd followed the path someone had left behind. The only way I knew how to map it out myself was to study the harmonic resonance of the dimensional fabric at each location which gets into the whole chicken/egg argument. I couldn't go there until I'd been there. You get the idea.

So we were performing a direct assault in the middle of New Orleans in broad daylight. The first thing we had to do was ensure no one saw us coming. "John, did you pack anything to take out the cameras?"

"Yeah." He thumbed backwards. "Tiffany."

I looked back like a typical teenager, she had her nose in her phone. She gave me a thumbs up. I moved my gaze to John, who was looking in the rearview mirror and smirking. To me he said, "She's good with electronics."

"Okay." I drew the word out. "The separate entrance has a single guard sitting behind a small desk next to an elevator. The problem is the door is glass, so unless he's sleeping, or very distracted, he is going to notice four people in tactical gear. Can anyone blur from far enough away to not be seen?"

Daniel made an annoyed sound.

"Something to add?" I asked, trying to keep the aggravation out of my voice.

I caught his eye roll in the windshield's reflection. "We may not obey the laws of physics, but the door still will. Contrary to the Flash comics, doors don't open and close faster than a human can see. That's if it's not locked. Again, we can't unlock while blurring."

A comment about the attitude was fighting to get out, but I was trying to build a rapport, not widen the gap. "Great point, thanks."

"Standard procedure would be to eliminate the sentry with a silenced subsonic round from a discrete distance," David continued.

John sighed, knowing what was coming.

"We are not killing him," I said.

"I'm not following the logic."

I turned in my seat. "Because there is no logic in killing. It is not a calculation. There is no equation that, when all the factors are aligned, concludes that the best course of action is to rip a fellow soul from the earth. You all might be fighting against the Tainted and their legions of converted, but I'm not."

"What are you fighting against?" David asked.

"Nothing. I am fighting *for* humanity. All of it, even those that may, by circumstance, have found themselves on the other side."

David crossed his arms. "Okay, fine. So how do we get in?"

"The old-fashioned way."

"This is stupid and embarrassing. I'm not four," Tiffany said.

"It doesn't matter how old you are, it matters how old he believes you to be. Now keep dancing." I replied out of the side of my mouth.

I rapped on the glass door while Tiffany danced around with her knees touching. We had stripped down to the shorts and tee-shirts we had under our gear. She actually had no shorts, but her t-shirt was extra long and was barely covering her.

The guard tried to wave us away. I wrapped harder and yelled, "Bathroom! My daughter just needs to use the bathroom."

I saw him give an exaggerated sigh and get up from the chair behind the small desk he was sitting at. He had been diligently working at the computer when we had walked up, presumably trying to figure out what went wrong with the outside and lobby cameras. Tiffany had disabled the first when we entered the parking lot and the other as we approached the door. The guard lumbered slowly toward us like he wanted to do anything else but have this conversation, which was probably the case.

"We don't have a bathroom," he said through the glass.

"Yes you do," I yelled back.

"You need to go somewhere else." He pointed.

"She won't make it anywhere else. Come on, do me a solid. You look like a parent."

"I'm sorry I can't let you in. Try the coffee shop around the corner."

"What?"

"Daddy, I gotta go real bad."

The guard opened the door to tell me where to go, probably both literally and figuratively. He was watching me like we were in the middle of The Purge. Big mistake.

Tiffany leaped onto his shoulders from the front, wrapping her thighs around his neck. It was, shall we say, a very intimate position, especially with her current level of dress. He reached up to grab her and she snatched both hands out of the air, then threw her weight to one side, toppling them to the floor. She squeezed her thighs together, cutting off the circulation flowing through the carotid artery. It took eleven seconds for him to lose consciousness. Tiffany tossed his limp arms to the side.

I reached down to offer a hand getting up, which she took. "Nicely done."

She smiled and even blushed a little.

"We're clear," I said into the coms plugged into my ear.

"And make sure you bring my clothes," Tiffany said.

The team scrambled in and we gave Tiffany thirty seconds to get decent again. John acted as a privacy screen like a big brother, his eyes daring anyone to peek. I put mine on with considerably less concern had by all. Meanwhile, David zip tied the guard, pulled him behind the desk out of sight, and called the elevator. It was fairly plain as they went. Not many decorative adornments. Each of the three walls had a wood panel to break up the metal box. The antiqued mirrored tiles didn't do too much to hide the hatch in the ceiling of the elevator, which he pushed open.

We all piled in and David started things up by leaping up through the opening and landing soundlessly onto the top of the elevator car. *Shit.* This was not my area of expertise. I could blur consistently, as well as using my iron skin and enhanced strength. I'd also gotten very good at telekinetically locking and unlocking doors since it was something I could practice while lying in bed. Enhanced jumping, however, I had not trained enough at. I could do it, but it was more of an on-off switch. Leaping a specific distance was beyond me. I was equally likely to fall short of the hatch as I was to overshoot and land like a boulder, announcing our presence to people on every floor.

"You want to go next?" Tiffany asked.

I extended my arm. "Ladies first."

Her eyebrows knitted together and her mouth quirked on one side like it was the stupidest thing she had ever heard. Then she leaped up with as much effort as it would for me to play hopscotch.

"Issue?" John asked in a whisper.

"I'm not great at Jumping."

"Don't overthink it. Connect with your blessing, then jump like you would normally. You're not going for a world record. Just act as though you're grabbing something off a shelf just out of reach."

I nodded. "Thanks."

"You've got this."

I metaphysically reached out and opened the floodgates, letting the inner light of my boon in. It felt like standing in a ray of sunshine through a window on a winter day. I visualized where I wanted to be, gathered myself and bent my knees ever so slightly, then jumped. I sailed through the door and kept going. My ascent slowed about two floors up. I managed to grab the ladder rungs attached to the wall while I was still in a zero G state.

"Showoff," Tiffany whisper-yelled from below.

"Yeah, right," I mumbled.

I looked down and caught John's expression in the elevator's light, a mix of confusion and awe. Then he followed through the hatch as David closed it. I started climbing, pretending I was just trying to save time instead of being incompetent. The team climbed the ladder behind me and we reached the top floor in minutes. I was a little above the ceiling, Tiffany level with the doors. David's hands were just below the floor line, while John was closer to the floor below.

If you have ever seen the inner workings of an elevator shaft, there is not much to see. The car runs on a set of metal tracks on either side. The car itself is suspended by a massive cable the size of my wrist, which is attached to a pulley system on the roof. At each floor there is a set of doors that keep people too focused on their phones from falling down the shaft.

From the outside they are very plain, but inside there's a long locking mechanism which prevents the door from being forced open despite what they show on TV. Inside, there was a latch that could be disengaged with little effort. The ladder was on the side wall nearest the doors, so the latch was in easy reach. I looked down at the rest of the team.

"Ready?"

They all gave a thumbs up. I unlatched the door, trying not to make any noise, then nodded at David, who counted down from three on his fingers ending with a fist. I yanked the doors open. Tiffany swung in from the side, landing on the right of the opening. David hopped from his spot to the left side. John grabbed the bottom of the doorway and leapfrogged himself to a standing position with one swift move. They cleared the opening and I swung down from above. It probably looked impressive, but there wasn't anyone there to witness it. The hallway was empty.

So were the rest of the rooms. It appeared to be any office on a weekend. Except for the armory, which told us we were in the right place. Behind one door was a slop sink. It was basically a janitorial closet that had a drain in the corner with a water spigot attached to the wall so mops could be rinsed out and the like. This one, however, was being used for other activities. There was a folding chair sitting in the middle. Cut plastic ties lay discarded. Blood pooled on the floor below.

David pulled out a device from a pocket about the size and shape of a scientific calculator. He ripped off a thin plastic applicator dispensed from one side, then dipped it into the blood and stuck it into a small slot in the front. After a few seconds, it dinged, and the display lit up with information.

"It's your father's blood."

"They moved him," I said, stating the obvious.

"Why did they do that? Did they know we were coming?" Tiffany asked.

David placed the applicator into a separate container and put the unit away. "Unlikely. This was probably only a temporary holding location. But I think we just missed them. The cleanup crew hasn't been here yet."

"Tiffany, computers. David, give her a hand. I want everything. John and I will check the hard files if they have any to see what else we can find out. Ten minutes, people. Leave no trace we were here."

David only hesitated for a second, but complied. The teams started at opposite sides to not get in each other's way. John and I took the left, rustling through papers.

He pulled open a drawer and started his search. "Ballsy move, having him help Tiffany."

"Not really," I said as I flipped through some files on the other end of the room. "She's practically a technical prodigy. David's focus was biology, chemistry, and forensics."

"Tiffany's not even a full Bishop."

"David is a rules guy. Standard procedure states that seniority rules, except in the case of field expertise." I closed the drawer I was rooting around in and opened another.

"I thought you told David you didn't know the procedures."

"Eavesdropping? Isn't that an abuse of your powers?"

"Just watching your six."

I closed the last drawer. "I've got nothing here. Next room?"

"Well?"

It was a vague question, but I knew what he meant. "I read them before we left."

"All of them?"

"The global one, the New Orleans Chapter, and the New York Chapter."

"That's it?" John asked in a sarcastic tone. "Not the Philly?"

"I read that last night along with everyone's files."

"Have you always been an overachiever?"

I made a scoffing sound. "I'm just trying to catch up for twenty-plus years of training I missed out on."

We walked to the next room and started the process over again. Then the following room and the one after that. We passed Tiffany and David. They worked quietly except when he ran into an issue for which she had a ready solution. They moved on before we finished.

I looked up from my search. "How you doin'?"

John paused but didn't meet my gaze. "Okay."

"That's not very descriptive."

"How do you think I am?"

"Are you and your father close?"

"We've had our ups and downs." John went to the next drawer.

"About anything in particular?"

"You thinking my relationship with my father may shed light on where Anton is keeping him?"

"No. I was just—"

"Then let it go."

Chapter Twelve

"...I like to think that there always are possibilities."

Star Trek II: The Wrath Of Khan - 1982

W E ARRIVED BACK AT the house empty-handed, apart from the knowledge that we were on the right track. But it was a trail that led to a dead end. Tiffany had locked herself away for several hours, poring through the data she'd collected from all the computers. We all offered to help but she declined politely, saying that she could work faster by herself. After she finally emerged, she provided a few locations the security company leased. We checked them all, but nothing panned out.

We were back to square one. Worse, since we had no leads. We sat around the dinner table, though nobody was eating the oxtail soup that Blessing had prepared.

"Eat," She said. "Even *your* bodies need to be properly fed to work right."

"Yes, ma'am." John pulled some meat off the bone and scooped it up between his fork and a piece of bread. His movements were robotic.

The rest of us followed suit. The stew was delicious. It tasted like it was made with red wine and had carrots, onions and parsnips. It must also have had magical properties, since all our moods lightened after digging in.

Charity sat across from me, having arrived while we were analyzing data. I caught her watching me a few times. She wasn't being overt, but apparently I wasn't the only one to notice. Her mother shifted in her chair and Charity yelped. John thought the whole scenario immensely amusing.

Not wanting to play favorites Blessing asked, "So, how will you rescue your father?"

John started choking on a biscuit while his sister smiled, so I spoke up, "We are not sure."

"Not acceptable. Do better."

"Well, the problem is—"

"I am not interested in problems. Life is full of them. Bring me solutions."

John took up the thread. "We're trying, but we have run out of options."

"There are always possibilities." Blessing popped a carrot slice into her mouth. My head perked up, but I discounted the Spockism as coincidence. When she'd finished chewing, she continued. "Stop focusing on what hasn't worked. You know what your father says."

John nodded. "Work the problem."

"Okay," I said. "Let's do that. What do we have?"

"They broke into the Covenant house and kidnapped Terrance," Tiffany offered.

I looked over at John as a question just occurred to me. "Why?"

He frowned at me. "Why what? When a croc takes down a bird floating on top of the water, it's just in its nature."

"Agreed, but taking a Bishop prisoner is not in their nature. David, how many times in the history of this war has one been taken?"

"Seven, including this one."

"And how many of those were battle line captures?"

"Six."

"But wasn't this a battle line capture?" Tiffany asked.

"No," John sat up a little straighter. "You saw the video. Once they had him, they withdrew."

"But they went all the way through the house," Tiffany argued.

I nodded. "Looking for *him*,"

"They found him in the kitchen first thing."

John put down his fork. "Dad moved too fast for them. He took them down before they could radio in. Maybe he was getting too close to something."

David made a little circle with his fork as he chewed. "The why of it still doesn't make sense."

"Exactly." They all looked at me. "It doesn't make sense. That's the key. John, I think you're right. Terrance was closing in on something, and they needed to stop his investigation."

"So, why not just kill him?" David's expression changed. "Sorry. But what is gained by capturing him? They lost a lot of men trying to take him alive. To what end?"

"Distraction." I looked at each in turn. "We have been spending all of our time trying to figure out what happened to him, and how to get him back, that we are missing the big picture."

"Isn't this just retaliation for killing Uji?" Tiffany asked.

"If it were, then why capture Terrance? Like David said, why *not* just kill him?" No one could think of a reason.

"We need to get back into the Covenant house." John's voice was etched with the realization that we had gotten this all wrong.

"We can't," Tiffany said

At the same time David said, "I agree."

"I know regulations say…" I started, then David's words finally filtered through. "Wait, what did you say?"

"I agree with John. We need to find out what his father was working on. If they will go through this much trouble just as a distraction, it has to be something big."

I nodded. "Okay good. It won't be easy though, it is being watched."

"How do you know that?" David asked.

I explained how we really obtained the information about the security office location.

"Of course, I should have known. And you got your sister involved?"

Charity's back stiffened. "I can take care of myself."

"That's not the point. You are an unblessed."

I jumped in before she threw a fork at him. "You people are way too stuck up about that."

"It is not about being stuck up. We cannot guarantee protection for an—"

"Please stop using that word," I interrupted. "The fact is, many humans put themselves at risk to protect the larger population. Military, federal agencies, police, fire departments, emergency rescue teams. Every day they go up against all kinds of dangers out of a sense of duty. Calling them unblessed is an insult. Like saying they are not complete."

"As you wish." I realized that when David said this, he was really saying fuck you. I took the loss and moved on.

"It won't be a problem this time," John said and we all looked at him. "I opened the tunnel."

"You broke lockdown protocols?" David sounded more shocked than normal.

"Let's say I altered them. We are still in lockdown, but now it has an alternate entrance only available to me. I didn't need my sister performing any more public displays of affection for the sake of the Covenant."

"You saw that, huh?" I said.

"Relax. I know it wasn't your idea. It's why you're still breathing."

"Again," Charity raised her voice. "I can take care of myself. If I want to kiss a guy in the middle of the street it's my business."

"Don't I have a say in this." I asked.

Both John and Charity said "No," in unison.

"Enough." Blessing said with a tone to stop the bickering. "Now that you have extracted your heads from your nether regions, finish your stew and get out. I have guests coming tonight." Blessing led by example, and popped a piece of meat into her mouth that she had just expertly detached from the bone.

"Book club?" John asked.

Blessing swallowed. "We must keep up appearances."

Chapter Thirteen

"Ferris Bueller, you're my hero."

Ferris Bueller's Day Off - 1986

W E PACKED EVERYTHING UP, and the McCaw women followed us out. Charity walked beside me. "So about that kiss."

"It's all good." I said. "I know you were just trying to help John."

She chewed on a thumbnail. "Yeah that was just an excuse."

"Oh." I didn't know what else to say.

"I wanted to tell you I was sorry. It wasn't cool to do."

"Don't sweat it."

"Really? Is that all you have to say? What didn't you like it? Am I not a good enough kisser?"

A few random syllables came out of my mouth but nothing distinguishable.

Charity smiled. "I'm just screwing with you."

I will never understand women. We all said our farewells and climbed into Deloris.

Blessing grabbed my arm before I could walk away.

"I'll be right there," I called to the team.

"John thinks a lot of you," she said.

"The feeling is mutual."

"He is hotheaded and tends to let his emotions take over."

I smiled.

"Did I say something amusing?"

"In my limited experience, John is the least likely to be controlled by his feelings."

She considered this for a second. "Perhaps he has grown. Neverthe-less, look after him." It was not delivered as a plea, more of a decree.

"I will do my best. But it is your son that normally watches my back."

Blessing smiled at that. "I like you Mr. Bateleur."

I nodded. "And I you."

Her smile faded. "See that you don't disappoint me."

We pulled into the underground garage, grabbed our gear, and made our way to the temporary sleeping quarters within the inner sanctum. They were mostly used by residents to catch a few winks while deeply involved in a project. Or in days past they may act as overflow if the group ran out of space for visiting Bishops. If anyone looked closer, however, they would notice that they were locked from the outside. They were actually fancy prison cells.

Conveniently, there were four rooms. We each selected one and dropped our stuff off, then headed to a small briefing room.

John pulled out his laptop and connected to the Wi-Fi. "This will probably take a while," I stepped up behind him. "And I don't want anyone looking over my shoulder while I work."

I raised my hands and backed away. "Next time, just clear your browser history or log onto those sites incognito."

"Will you go take a walk or something?"

"Fine, I guess I will take a recharging dip. Care to join me?" I directed my question to David and Tiffany.

"Might as well," he said.

She shook her head. "No, I'm good. I'll stay here and help." John eyed her and she smiled at him, then pulled out her own laptop. "Don't worry, I'll stay over here. But I might be able to fill in some blanks if you have questions."

He nodded.

The catch to our powers was that they had to be recharged peri-odically. To do so, we had to bathe in waters from the same river in which John the Baptist did his good work. There were many theories as to the reason. In my view, it was another safety valve. Like the inability of a Bishop to combine powers. We could be fast or strong, but not both.

David and I met outside the entrance to the rejuvenation chamber. We entered through a typical door into what looked like a garden containing a central pond. The ground sloped gently into the water from the front. On the opposite side stood the stone sculpture. It was wider than it was high, and it depicted imagery of many of the mainstream religions all woven together. A testament of how the teams all worked as a unit, despite our backgrounds and beliefs. It was one of my biggest sources of pride about being aligned with these otherworldly people. The superpowers were awesome, don't get me wrong. But the fact that the Covenant made room for all belief systems without prejudice or debate gave me hope for the future of humanity. Though, now that I thought about it, I hadn't met an atheist Bishop. How would that even work?

We entered together, moving to either side and genuflected. We had dressed in our immersion robes, all white with a red sash. Standing, we waded into the water. Nothing happened. It never did until we were completely submerged. It was customary for one person at a time to dunk themselves. I motioned for David to proceed first. He lowered himself down until his head disappeared below the surface. Small lightning streaks danced around his form for nearly ten seconds. He reemerged once they subsided, sluicing the water from his hair with his hands.

"I must have been pretty low," he said.

"You good?"

David nodded. "You ready?"

"Yeah." I took a few slow, deep breaths. I could feel my partner's eyes on me, either trying to figure out why I was being overly dramatic or deciding that my lack of experience was showing itself. I tried to ignore him. Like a free diver, I inhaled for four seconds and exhaled for eight, breathing from my diaphragm. The technique was designed to lower heart rate and blood pressure and to purge as much carbon dioxide from the lungs as possible.

Once the top of my head dipped under the water, the fireworks started. I was used to the intensity of the experience, but most other Bishops were not. I felt a shift as David threw himself backwards away from the light show. Electric currents danced across my body, causing my muscles to twitch. My brain acknowledged all this while I tried to disassociate.

The ten second mark came and went with no reduction in electrical stimuli. I consciously slipped into a meditative state. The familiar meadow by a lake appeared. This was the place where I was closest to the source of my power. Gazing out over the visualized horizon, I felt the breeze as it brushed over me, a welcome shift from the effects of the charging.

Twenty seconds went by and my lungs started to remind me they should be doing something. The sparks dancing around my skin were not diminishing.

Then I heard a familiar sound I had not experienced since the first weeks I had taken up the Bishop's mantle. It was a buzzing. Not the high-pitched reverberation of a fly, the annoying whine of a mosquito or even the deeper vibrato of a bumblebee. This was deeper still. A noise that made itself known not just audibly, but also through feeling.

Then I saw it floating across the lake; occasionally touching down to the water, creating tiny rings where it disturbed the surface: the dragonfly. It came right up to me as it had once before. It then appeared to stare at me as though taking stock. Not simply my physical—or rather metaphysical—form, but the essence of who I was.

I was about to issue a greeting to what I considered an old friend when it shot forward the last few feet and basically head-butted me.

I stood in the middle of the street. Realizing where I was, I looked around to make sure I wasn't going to be hit by a car but there was no traffic to be seen. Only garbage. Mounds of it piled high like it had been bulldozed here. This place seemed familiar, but I couldn't connect it to reality. Then I glanced to my left and saw the Freedom Tower. That view was as familiar as the one out of my childhood bedroom. I took a second look at the building in front of me. It was the New York Covenant. The scaffolding, that hid it in plain sight as just another unending construction area, was gone. I don't know that I had ever seen the building's facade, which could be why I hadn't recognized it.

I fought my way over to the door, which was clear compared with everything else. It still opened to my subcutaneous chip but required effort to open. Inside, dust covered every surface and I left a trail of footprints behind me. The double doors to the common hung partially off their hinges. I stepped through.

The disarray extended into here as well. All the furniture was missing, except for Hager's high-backed chair. The big-screen TV looked as though someone had thrown a fastball at it. Books were pulled off shelves and stacked next to the cold fireplace. Stepping up, I grabbed the poker and pushed through the ashes. I uncovered a charred remnant with the name Melville on it. Wondering how bad it had to have been to start burning books for warmth, I replaced the iron. Turning, I nearly jumped out of my skin. The chair was occupied.

The gaunt face didn't look familiar, but the black clothes, long white beard and curly side locs were unmistakable. I approached slowly, afraid he might turn to dust if I disturbed the surrounding air. I reached out to check his pulse. My fingertips barely grazed the loose flesh when he grabbed my wrist. I met his gaze. His eyes were wide open and he pulled in a ragged breath.

"Christian!"

"Hager. What the hell is going on? What happened here?"

"No time." Hager's voice was strained and his words were drawn out as though forming them took a massive effort.

"Where is everyone?"

"Gone."

"Everyone? The other Covenants?"

Hager just shook his head. He licked his dry cracked lips with a tongue that held little moisture itself.

"Let me get you some water."

His grip held firm. "We lost. They destroyed…pools."

"How? What can I do?"

Hager's other hand shot out, grabbing me around the back of the neck and pulling me in close. We were nose to nose. I stared into his ice-blue eyes. "Find…Heretic."

With some final reserve of strength, he shoved me backwards and everything went black.

Chapter Fourteen

"I can see things no one else can see."

BIG TROUBLE IN LITTLE CHINA - 1986

I LAUNCHED MYSELF BACKWARDS breaching the surface with an explosion nearly knocking David over. I gasped air back into my lungs as water poured off of me. My body, making up for lost time, had me panting like a dog in the desert.

"Are you okay?" he asked

I nodded and gave a thumbs up, not yet able to speak.

"My God, Chris. You were recharging for nearly a full minute. I have never seen anything like that. Your reserves must be incredible. And the intensity of it. I thought we were going to be boiled alive. I shook you when it all subsided, but you just sat there."

I waded over to the side and sat on the rocky ledge that ringed the still sloshing pool. David followed, bombarding me with questions.

"How much of your reserves did you replace? Is it always so intense? Is this normal for you?"

"I don't know if that's the word I'd use," I answered his last question, still breathing hard. "But it is typical." Well, at least the timing was. The vision? That was new. I caught my breath enough to extract myself from the freak show I had created and so pulled my legs out of the water and got to my feet. I headed across the grass to where towels were stacked. Yeah, actual grass, grown inside on actual dirt, not substrate. Whether from tradition or necessity, everything surrounding the pool was natural. Other than, you know, there was a natural body of water in the middle of a secret underground lair.

I had found little information about the immersion pools in my research of the collected works of the Bishops. Being the oldest newbie in history, I was not eager to show my ignorance by asking a ton of questions that everyone thought obvious.

Grabbing a folded towel, I attempted to dry myself. If you have ever tried to towel off while wearing soaking wet clothes, you know what I mean. David walked over and selected one for himself. I could feel his eyes on me. It made me uncomfortable despite this being the reason I asked him to join me. There were several methods to get people to follow you that I'd learned fell into two schools; the long game and the short game.

The long game was simple and was for people leading for the right reasons. Show a genuine interest in people and demonstrate time and time again that you had their best interests in mind. People are happy to follow such a person. I didn't have time for all that.

In my experience, the short game also had two options: domination and awe. Domination was basically the drill sergeant method. Control every aspect of a person, keeping them in line by stamping out any resistance with force and punishment. Not my bag. Awe was some-what different, but no less devious. I'd witnessed it while floundering through what to do after I left the military at the real root of all evil, sales. Here, they tricked people by creating a false sense of awe around the head of the company. I was told things like, '*The first time I saw him I could feel his presence before I laid eyes on him,*' or, '*I have never met anyone like him, simply amazing.*' While I'm sure some of these people actually felt this way about this guy, their descriptions were more from habit than any genuine emotion. If enough people raved about how special and amazing someone is, most people would fall under the same spell. It was the trick evangelists used to gather their flock.

I didn't have a stack of people waiting to tell David how special I was. I had to show him. There was a buzz going around about me after what happened in Miami. Most people either fell on the side of belief or hoax. I was a bit embarrassed. Generally, I didn't like to publicize things that set me apart, but I thought it may help win him over.

David said nothing more about it as he toweled off next to me. What he did say was, "What's our next move?"

I smiled inwardly. He wasn't fully on board, but he was on the path. "What do you know about *the Heretic?*"

David hadn't heard of him. We changed and went to find John who was right where we left him.

"The Heretic?" John looked at me like I was insane. I thought Tiffany was going to break her neck with how fast her head snapped up.

"Does it mean something?" I asked her.

"No, but she sounds really cool."

John closed his laptop and motioned us to follow. We stepped into the hallway. "Where did you hear that name?" He had an air of wariness than I had ever seen him

"Why?" I asked.

He glanced from me to David and back. "Because there are only a handful of people on the planet that have ever heard of him, and fewer still that know anything more than a myth."

"It's a person?" David asked.

"Sorta."

David frowned. "What's sort of a person?"

"A Tainted." I guessed.

John nodded.

"Fantastic," I said.

"Now answer *my* question. Why are you asking about the Heretic? Where did you get that name?"

I hesitated to talk about the vision. I had the feeling it was going to be yet another thing that no one else had experienced. These oddities were piling up, highlighting me as different. I considered making something up, but immediately discounted it as stupid. I would not be one of those people in every story that held back key information because it made them look bad, only to find out it was the pivotal key that would have solved the issue from the beginning.

I took a deep breath. "I had a vision during my immersion."

The two men exchanged glances, then John shrugged. "So?"

"That isn't abnormal?"

"No," David said. "Many Bishops have visions during immersions."

"I've never had one till now."

John adjusted his glasses. "You don't get one every time."

"So, what? It's random?"

"We like to think it's God trying to impart wisdom to help us on our journey," David said.

"The problem is by the time a vision gets started, it is little more than a flash of insight that would take far too long to dissect to be of any real help. It is usually only helpful later on, like the last puzzle piece that completes the picture."

"What if I had a longer vision?"

John cocked his head and his dreadlocks danced around his face. "How long?"

"He was under for almost a minute."

John's eyebrows disappeared under his glasses. "That's crazy."

I described my vision in as much detail as I could.

When I was finished, David crossed his arms and placed his bent index finger against his chin. "Useful immersion visions. I've only read about them. There hasn't been one in hundreds of years."

"Forget that shit. What can we do about it?"

"As I said, there are only a handful of people that even know the Heretic is more than just a legend. There is only one that has built up a file on him. There was a reason he was in your vision."

"Seriously?" Is there anything he is not involved in?

"Probably not."

Amram Hager, the man that pulled me into the life of a Bishop, was my first teacher. When I first met him on the street, dressed in his normal Hasidic Jew regalia, long white beard and curled side locks, I thought he was trying to sell me salvation. I guess I wasn't far off after all. It just wasn't my salvation, it was the world's. Our relationship had developed over the past few months. Early on, he was more of an antagonist. Now I called him regularly to catch up.

I sighed as the phone rang for the third time. You didn't rush Hager and he made sure you knew it. I was wondering if I would have to leave a message when he picked up.

"Amram Hager."

"Hey Hager, it's Chris."

"Chris, how lovely to hear from you! Though it is not Sunday, so I presume this is not a social call."

He knew who was calling. I wasn't using a different phone and the display told him clearly who was on the other end. Hager, though, was raised during the age of analog and rotary dials. Despite technological advances, or maybe because of them, he insisted on maintaining proper phone etiquette. Not being big on meaningless pleasantries, I needed to perform deep breathing exercises almost every time we spoke.

"You presume correctly. I need to find the Heretic."

Silence echoed from Hager's side.

"You still there?"

"Indeed. Though I must have a bad connection, since I thought I heard you say something you could not possibly have."

"What? Heret—"

"Please don't repeat it."

"I can't say he-who-must-not-be-named. I'm pretty sure it's copyrighted." Covering the phone I spoke to John. "It's not you know. HP Lovecraft used it back in 1928, but then it was 'him-who-is-not-to-be-named.'"

John's lips drew into a thin line. "Then why did you say it?"

"Cause it was funny."

Hager continued on. "If you insist on having this conversation, please call me on a secured line."

"We have one of those?" I tilted the phone away from my mouth and directed my next question to John as well. "Do we have a secure communication line?"

He made a face that looked to be questioning my intelligence.

I shrugged. "Okay, call you in five?"

"Better make it ten. I'm in the middle of a workout and I would like to shower first."

"How is that possible? You're not even breathing hard."

"Experience."

"Whatever. Talk to you in ten."

"Very good. Farewell."

I punched the end call button without bidding him adieu. It was a minor victory that would probably only make him less cooperative, but I couldn't help it. I was going to talk to him in literally ten minutes. Why did I need to go through the whole salutation bullshit?

John finished his salad and led David and me to the operations room. There was a wedge-shaped control unit and speaker about the size of a half loaf of bread. John scrolled through the options on its small display and selected Manhattan Ops. The view switched to a simple screen giving the same typical setup you would find on Zoom. He checked his watch, waited for the next minute to click by, then pushed the call button.

It only took one ring this time. I guessed prearranged calls had their own etiquette.

"Hello John, David, Christian." Using my full name was probably my punishment for my abrupt hang up.

We each returned the greeting and I could finally get to the meat of the conversation. "We need to find the Heretic."

"First, I will need some additional information."

"Shoot," I said.

"How did you come to know that name and why must you find that person?"

"You told me." I retold the story of my vision. Hager stayed quiet throughout. I watched his face for micro expressions, but he might as well have been cast in stone. When I was finished, he simply responded with, "I see."

"Well?" I asked after a few seconds of silence.

Hager stroked his beard. "I'm thinking."

"Thinking about what? Do you know where he is or not?"

"It is not that simple."

"It actually is."

"His location is not the question, allowing you to rub this particular lamp is."

I narrowed my eyes at him. "I'm not following."

"That is because you are looking with the wrong lens."

"Should I switch to telephoto?"

Hager's eyebrows knitted together, creating one long white cater-pillar. "Thank you for making up my mind." His hand reached out for the wedge in front of him.

"Amram, please." John's deep voice was soft and poignant. It made Hager hesitate. "Anton has my father. If he can help, we need to try."

He drew his hand back, but remained silent, his fists clenched at his sides. After a moment or two, his whole body relaxed. He leaned forward, laying his finger tips on the table in front of him as though he had run out of strength to remain upright. He looked up at the camera and I could feel the intensity of his gaze over the thousands of miles that separated us.

"Chris, please listen."

I put my hands behind me and stood straighter to show that I was.

"The Heretic is unlike any creature you have encountered, vastly powerful and completely insane. Once you are on its radar, you can never escape. We have only theories as to where it ultimately came from and why it does not follow the path of the other Tainted."

"Don't you think that after dealing with Baldemar and Uji that I can handle this guy?"

"No."

I crossed my arms, but said nothing. Restricting himself to a single word spoke volumes. We stared at each other for what felt like an eternity.

"The Heretic is here in Manhattan."

Chapter Fifteen

"I'm in a New York State of Mind."

BILLY JOEL, TURNSTILES - 1976

LYING INTO NEW YORK City at night is like flying into a swarm of multicolored fireflies. The beauty ended once we landed. John F. Kennedy airport is a small city unto itself, you know, like Gotham. The layout was designed by the Mad Hatter and the traffic pattern by Joker. We walked out of Terminal Four and crossed three lanes of traffic to get to the pickup area. I called for our car, waiting in the cell phone lot. Even from there, it took ten minutes to reach us.

"I still don't see why I couldn't have stayed in New Orleans." Tiffany had been sullen since she lost the argument with John. I would have thought a teenager would want a trip to the Big Apple, but she had been dead set against it.

John ignored her, refusing to be dragged into another debate. I got his attention and mouthed, "Boyfriend." He ignored that as well.

Our driver pulled up two lanes over, partially in traffic, as close as she could get. I spotted the Black Denali and wove my way between the waiting cars, John and David following. One SUV I walked behind started backing up. There were three possibilities here. Either the rearview mirror and backup camera of said SUV has somehow failed, the driver had a sudden heart attack just as he put it in reverse, or he was an asshole. I was leaning towards the last one.

I banged on the rear door to alert this mo-mo there were people in his path. Whether his camera started working, his myocardial infarction turned out to be gas, or my pounding got through to him, the car finally stopped. I kept moving to the Denali. Our driver had exited and was waiting to help with the luggage. That's when I heard him.

"Hey, jackass. Why'd you hit my car?"

I half turned and caught sight of an apparent bodybuilder moonlighting as an Uber driver. He stood over six-foot tall and could have been a double for the Rock. Was I going to run into every pumped up gym rat in the friggin country? "Maybe all the steroids affect your eyesight, but you were about to run over my friends."

"How 'bout you come over here and say that?"

Back in New York less than an hour and I was already in an altercation. I channeled my inner Gandhi and turned the other cheek.

"Why don't you and your girlfriends come here and give me a lap dance?"

His lines were less than original and I had more important things to deal with, so I was willing to let it slide.

The guy tried once more. "Idiot is probably a Met fan."

I stopped.

"Chris, we don't have time for this," John prodded.

"Oh, there we go. I have insulted the pretty boy."

I'm not sure why complimenting my looks was supposed to be a dis, but he had already crossed the line when he attacked the blue, white, and orange. I handed my duffle bag to John.

He sighed and took it. "Please make it quick and don't hurt him too badly." The three of them moved off toward our ride.

As I started towards the heckler, behind me I heard our driver ask, "Shouldn't you help him?"

"Naw, he's just getting back in the New York state of mind," John answered.

I stepped up to the big man, toe to toe, as they say.

"What are you going to do?" he asked, clearly amused.

"Can you see a difference between me and you?" I asked.

"You are tiny and I'm huge."

"Yes, very good. You are great roaring fire. Do you think I should be afraid?"

He nodded and smiled. "Very."

I smiled back and leaned in a little more. "Do I look scared?"

The notion must have dawned on him, and his smile disappeared.

"Now let's think about why that is. Maybe I'm drunk? But then I would probably slur my words and smell like a bar, so that's not it."

His eyebrows got closer together.

"Maybe I have a gun."

His eyes got big and he shot a glance towards the car where I assumed he hid his own weapon.

"Nope, I just walked out of the airport and was carrying a bag, so that's probably not the case, either. So what is it I know that you don't that gives me such confidence?" I checked around to see if anyone had their phones out, but this was in the middle of JFK. The only thing people wanted to do was get out.

He moved, but I moved faster.

Five seconds later, he was sitting behind the steering wheel, the seat belt buckled over his arms with the door closed. He stared at me open mouthed through the window. I gave him a friendly wave.

"You have a nice day, okay? And do me a favor and check your fucking backup camera."

The address I gave the car service was on the same block, but not our actual building. It was a massage place, completely legit. No additional services if you catch my meaning. It was also a place where drivers would not ask too many questions. Especially with three men in their thirties, traveling with a teenager. We waited for them to turn the corner before making our way to the six floor building down the street on the opposite side. It was covered with scaffolding as though under reconstruction, though the exterior had not changed signifi-cantly in the last forty years. This was just a facade so that passersby didn't look twice.

John took the lead. This had been his home for several years since he moved here from New Orleans. The door opened to his subcuta-neous chip and we walked into the bland foyer.

"Lucy, I'm home."

John looked at me.

I shrugged. "I couldn't help it."

He shook his head.

Through the next set of doors, I expected everyone to still be sitting there like the first time I found my way here. The common room, however, was empty. We walked through into the industrial kitchen, which was vacant as well. I looked left towards the hidden elevator behind the pantry leading down to the secured level, then right where the stairs led up to the offices.

"Eve, where is Hager?" I asked. Eve was the Manhattan Covenant's AI. She knew the location of all members based on the same subcutaneous chips implanted in our forearms that John used to gain entry.

"Amram Hager is in the upstairs conference room with Soon-Li and Tira. I have alerted him to your presence," Eve said.

We made our way upstairs and I barely got through the doorway before Soon-Li nearly tackled me with a big hug.

"Chris! It's so great to see you! You look great!"

"You too," I said as I returned the hug. Soon-Li, Chinese by heritage, had long straight black hair that reached to her lower back. Her soft curved mouth and chin were at odds with her sharp cheekbones giving her looks a hard edge. She had been friends with my mother growing up as initiates through to adulthood and had known me as a child, though I have only glimpses of the times she'd spoken about. We'd spent a few evenings after our encounter with Baldemar, talking late into the night.

She would regale me with stories of my mother's adventures and I would ask question after question. I had an insatiable thirst to better understand my mother both as a person and as a Bishop. She was also the youngest to hold the position as head of this very Covenant.

Hager stepped in to shake my hand. He was smiling despite our last conversation. Then Tira was in front of me. She was how I would picture an Indian goddess with full lips, dark brown wavy hair, which she wore just below her shoulder. But her mind surpassed her looks as she held several doctorates, including an MD.

I wasn't sure what to do. We had a roller coaster ride of a relationship during my few short months here. There was always something between us. But from my perspective, she could never decide if she wanted to hug me or slap me. After my abilities started aligning with the likes of Moses, our vibe shifted to more of acquaintances. Out of all the team, she had the strangest reaction to my demigod-like powers.

I hadn't spoken with her since I moved to Miami and started my relationship with Marie. I'm sure she heard about that through Soon-Li, who took an unhealthy interest in my love life. Evidently, she was feeling about the same level of uneasiness. She leaned in for what I assumed was a hug, thought better of it and ended up with a half-shake, half-cheek kiss. That torture ended, I introduced David and Tiffany.

"Aren't you from the Philadelphia Covenant?" Soon-Li asked, though it sounded more like an accusation.

"Yes." David preened, as if she was asking if he was the guy from that popular TV show.

"Great, who do I complain to about the ridiculous regulations that are coming out of there? You would think that none of them had actually been on a mission before."

Hager put a hand on her arm. "Maybe we can defer that conversation for another time?"

David nodded like a bobble head, relief plain on his face. "Happy to do so."

Hager motioned to the seats and we all found seats around the conference table. "What I am about to reveal is highly confidential and does not leave this room." Hager looked at each person individually, lingering longer on the two newest guests. "You are not to discuss this with any other members of any Covenant, including senior ones, and it should be excluded from any reports."

David's head moved backwards as though it were trying to drag him from the chair. "That is highly irregular. As per regulations, nothing should be intentionally withheld from after-action reports."

"This comes from the top." Hager was nonplussed.

"What is higher than the Philadelphia Covenant?"

"The High Council."

David blinked twice, but otherwise made no further comment.

"Is there a file we can look through?" I asked.

Hager crossed his arms. "No file. It was deemed sensitive enough to remain verbal only. Again, from the top."

I sighed. "Okay, so what do we know?"

"Little I'm afraid. It is more of a story, one the Council of Israel felt would be too corruptible for general knowledge. The Heretic's existence would be constrained to a few Covenant heads scattered around the globe, with the more details sitting with Israel and the Covenant where he resides."

I nodded. "Okay, so what's the story?"

"The Heretic approached us about a thousand years ago with a proposition. Forsaking the ways of the other Tainted, the Heretic was no longer interested in death, destruction, and suffering. It had lost the stomach for it."

"And they believed him?" David asked.

"No. At least, not at first. But the chance of taking one of the Tainted off the board was too good to pass up. One less devil on everyone's shoulder, as it were. So they made an offer they assumed would not be accepted. We will leave you be, but you need to let us know where you are living, and allow us to check on you periodically to ensure you are not doing anything untoward."

"Untoward?" I asked, not able to restrain myself.

Hager just nodded. "There was one other stipulation. He would provide us information when requested."

"Wait, we had an informant that is being kept from PC?" David sounded insulted.

"For two excellent reasons. The first I have already covered. The second is that the Heretic has restricted our aid to once every ten years."

"Seriously? And we accepted this?" I asked.

"Early on, we tried to negotiate for additional help. At first we were just refused. Then we were penalized ten years for approaching outside the agreed window. One self righteous Bishop showed up on The

Heretic's door and demanded answers to his questions else he would bring down the wrath of God. He returned to us with his eyes burned out unable to heal them despite having all of his reserves available."

My mouth went dry.

"The story he told was that the Heretic never even twitched from the chair in front of the fireplace. One minute he was threatening to call down Heaven upon him, then next he was on his knees, a searing pain in his head like he had never experienced. Since then, we have been extremely cautious in approaching the Heretic. We go only when in dire need, and after all avenues have been exhausted."

A thought occurred to me. "Why didn't we talk to him last year when a dirty bomb was threatening the city?"

"We need permission to approach from the High Council. I asked. It was denied."

I huffed. "Why am I not surprised? So what about now?"

Hager inhaled deeply. "Now, my dear boy, it is up to you."

"What does that mean?"

"It means you will go before the High Council to plead your case."

I looked at all the rest of the Bishops around the table. Each, including the initiate, had decades more experience than I did. "Why me?"

Hager stared at me for several seconds. "Because you are the one who had the vision."

Chapter Sixteen

"The decision of the council will now be heard."
<small>Superman II - 1980</small>

I SAT IN FRONT of the video display, my image shown back to me on the gargantuan screen as I waited for the High Council to connect. Hager sat to my right; John to my left. I was not prepared for this encounter. Not that I had an issue speaking to a set of high-level individuals. That, I couldn't give a crap about. Status doesn't impress me. I had seen too many stuffed shirts in the army, so hopped up on the modicum of power that had been handed to them with their rank that they practically salivated to deliver their next order.

No, these people were not the issue. It was me. Or rather, the argument I was bringing forward. I like to be armed with facts, statistics, intelligence. A logical argument that held merit. Instead, the arrows I had in my quiver were dreams, feelings, and visions.

The screen shifted and the council appeared. There were seven of them, all women. Their ages looked to range from early fifties to triple digits. They all sat around a crescent-shaped table. Hager had briefed me in the hours before the meeting.

"Who comes before the council?" The speaker was Ali Rashid. She looked to be one of the youngest, wearing a purple abaya with sleeves down to the wrists and a black shayla hijab that wrapped around her head and framed her face. Her eye makeup was minimal but dramatic.

I cleared my throat as quietly as I could. "I do. Chris, son of Angela, descendant of Luke."

Hager cocked his head at my response.

"Who has vouched for this man?"

"Are you quite done, Ali?" Hager asked.

It was my turn to stare.

The woman's eyes danced dangerously until she finally cracked a smile. "You're no fun, Amram."

"So I have been told."

Ali looked back at me. "It is very nice to meet you. Angela and I were friends."

I struggled for words. "Thank you."

An older woman more towards the center spoke up. "We do have other pressing matters. Can we continue?" She was tall with pitch black hair pulled back into a bun so tight it appeared to be yanking her head backwards so that she looked down her nose at everyone. She wore all black. Her name was Miriam Levi, the second highest council member. I wanted to ask if she was Hager's sister but, to my amazement, restrained myself.

Ali nodded. "Of course Miriam. Christian—"

"Chris." I almost drew blood, biting my tongue, but it was too late.

Ali seemed to sense a deeper meaning to my correction and stared at me for several seconds, brow furrowed before she continued. "Chris. First, I would like to thank you for taking the lead in the New Orleans investigation. For one so new to the Covenant, your successes have been extraordinary. How can we help?"

"I want to see the Heretic."

The collective gasp was really satisfying. Then they all started speaking at once.

Miriam's face was a combination of anger and shock. "How do you even know that name?"

Ali said, "That is a very complicated request."

"We can't have a Bishop with so little experience meet with that creature," declared Shakini Maharaj. She wore a sari that left one arm bare which gave her a scandalous look. Her nose ring connected to her earring.

"This is outrageous!" Euzebia Laszowski, a portly woman with long, straight brown hair. Although she was third in line and sat on the high seat's left, she kept glancing over at Miriam as if looking for instructions.

From there, they argued with each other. Some were for utilizing this virtually untapped potential, but most thought I was insane, out of my depth, or both.

Then Speranza De Angelis, who was in the middle and had not spoken since the call started, raised her hand no more than four inches off the table from where it had rested. The ancient Italian woman was the current high seat of the council. She had short, curly white hair and piercing brown eyes. Silence fell instantly, like a maestro conducting an orchestra. She stared at me through the camera, commanding attention better than any General I had ever seen. Her eyes held an intensity that, had it not been for my deep disdain for authority, might have had me sweating. Okay, I was a little.

I met her gaze, though, not letting her win this minor battle. The silence became uncomfortable, and I let it hang there. I had read several books on interrogation after the debacle a few months before when I allowed one of the Tainted to use my interview to learn more about me than I did about them. One common thread in all my research was the adage *let silence do the heavy lifting*.

Her lips cracked into a barely perceptible smile, and she nodded. Then she asked, "Why?" Her body may have looked frail, but her voice held a strength in it that was enough to carry the world. Perhaps it had to.

I launched into a description of what was going on with the investigation, what we had encountered so far, and wrapped it up with my vision. They all did me the courtesy of staying quiet during my presentation. Once it was clear, I had finished, the debate began.

"A dream? We are going to waste a council for a fantasy?" asked Miriam

"Not a dream. A vision," Ali corrected.

"Can you prove it was a vision?" This was from Cili Nemeth who had hair buzzed around the sides and longer on top. She had nine earrings and wore a blazer without a shirt.

"No more than you can say that it was only a dream," Althea

Constantinides countered. She looked like a retired model with long, curly black hair and a neckline that nearly reached her navel.

Ali crossed her arms. "How about the fact that he had never heard of the Heretic until it appeared to him?"

Euzebia put a finger to her chin. "Did he appear, or did the word? It's not like it has only one meaning."

Althea shook her head. "Forget whether this was a dream or a vision. A Covenant was breached and a Bishop taken. This needs to be responded to quickly. We cannot allow this to set a precedent."

Ali nodded. "She's right. We cannot be seen as weak."

Shakini slammed a hand down on the table. "We *are* weak. Our numbers dwindle while theirs swell. More and more are too easily corrupted. We have been on the defensive for decades. I feel that a critical time is approaching. If we squander our opportunity with the Heretic, all may be lost."

Althea leaned in. "The same could be said if we don't take counsel now."

Miriam bent forward as well as if meeting the challenge. "I think some of our younger members are still somewhat reactive."

Ali huffed. "And some of our more senior would rather pray than act."

Euzebia put a hand to her chest. "What's wrong with seeking guidance from Allah?"

Althea countered, "Nothing, as long as you listen to the answer you are given, and not wait for the one you want."

"What is that supposed to mean?" Miriam spat out.

Ali took up the thread. "It's right in front of you. We have prayed and God has answered our prayers. But now that he stands before you, you deny him. AGAIN."

Cili flicked a hand. "Don't be so melodramatic."

Althea leaned further in, putting both hands on the table. "Don't be so blind. What would you have him do? Part the Red Sea?"

Ali lifted her chin. "I have one better. He should perform an act that has never been accomplished in the history of humankind. Something we had never even thought possible. The dispatching of one of the

Tainted." She looked at each of them, daring them to dispute that irrefutable fact. Everyone fell silent.

Speranza sat up straighter. "It is time." She met each woman's eyes as well. "Each of you to decide if what you have heard warrants a meeting with the Heretic." All the women settled in, and Ali opened her mouth to speak, but Speranza continued, "This is a serious matter at a dangerous point. Please consider all aspects carefully." At the first words of the last sentence, council heads turned to the high seat. Shock was plain on some faces, while others covered their surprise a bit better.

It took Ali a second to recover before continuing on with what felt like a ritualistic process. "We will return with our decision in one hour."

The connection was severed from their side.

"What was that about?" I asked.

Hager sighed. "The high seat participates very little in council decisions. She is there as a kind of magistrate. To guide, when needed, to decide on rules of order, and to keep the process moving. She weighs in only to break a tie and should not sway the proceedings in any direction."

"I don't get it. She is a leader that is not supposed to lead?"

"She isn't a leader in the strictest sense of the word."

"Why? How do you have a powerful organization like this without a chief?"

"That's the problem," David said.

"You've lost me."

"Come on Chris, you watch Star Trek. What do they always say about power?" John said.

"Power corrupts. And absolute power corrupts absolutely."

Hager nodded. "What do you think that means for the leader of a company of super humans? We've had many in that position who nearly brought us to ruin or had us lose track of the real enemy. All with the best of intentions, of course. As a side note, the quote originally come from Lord Acton back in 1887."

I frowned at Hager's correction. "Why not adopt an Arthurian style of leadership?"

"The round table?" John asked, and I nodded. "Who do you think invented it?"

"They have been around for that long?"

"No, the High Council is relatively new. For us, that is." John nodded back to the dark screen. "The problem is when you have someone leading, even if they only get one vote in seven, most people will defer to that person."

"It is against protocol for the high seat to take sides in a discussion," David said.

John tilted his head towards the now dark screen. "What she did broke hundreds of years of precedent."

I looked around. "That should be good for us, right? Putting a finger on the scales, if you will?"

Hager appeared more solemn than usual. "Or bad that she felt it necessary at all?"

An hour later, we all sat before the large screen again waiting for the council to reconnect. We had stepped away to get a snack, or a drink, or use the facilities. In my case, all three. I'm not good at waiting. During normal circumstances, I need to be doing something, often several things at once. Having to sit around in anticipation of a pivotal moment was damn near torture. I found myself pacing. Not because I was nervous, but because my brain kept trying to get me to take on different tasks.

I should call Marie. No, I'm gonna want to dedicate more time than I have to talk to her. I still need to know why they took Terrance. Has Tiffany made any headway in her analysis? Is she mad I wanted her to stay behind?

The High Council finally blinked to life and I sat down. While they went through a slimmed-down version of the formalities. I analyzed each of their expressions, but these were experts in hiding their inner thoughts. They may as well have been statues for all they gave away. All that is except Speranza. She looked pissed. My heart sank.

Ali spoke in a very clipped monotone way. "It is the decision of the council that the circumstances do not warrant counsel from the Heretic."

"Excuse me?" John's voice was even slower than normal and held a dangerous edge.

Miriam frowned. She was apparently not used to people questioning the official response. "Your request has been denied."

John clenched his fist, knuckles turning white. He took a deep breath and it shook as he exhaled. "I would ask the High Council to reconsider."

I thought David was going to either throw up or fall out of his chair.

Miriam's eyes narrowed. "Mr. McCaw, you are not the one who has come before us. Up to now, your presence was tolerated as a courtesy."

"My father is still missing. The Heretic may be the only way to save him."

Ali took back the conch. "We are aware, and we do sympathize. However, there is nothing that can be done."

"Nothing that can be done?" John's volume increased and I was quite happy to let him lay into this band of women who seemed unaffected by reality. Hager had other ideas.

"We know this was not an easy decision and there must be other circumstances to which we are unaware."

"Amram." The council's collective jaw dropped as Speranza spoke again. "Sometimes decisions are not as we would hope. Like in Africa."

Hager nodded his head. "I understand."

The screen went black just before what looked like another heated discussion was going to start.

"Amram, they can't be serious. They are going to just sit there while my father is killed?"

"Seriously," I added. "There has to be something we can do to change their mind."

"I'm afraid that once they have made a decision, it would take near catastrophic circumstances to alter it." Hager's voice was a little too conversational after what had just transpired.

"Then we need to—" John began.

"Did I ever tell you about Africa?" Hager interrupted and I almost fell out of my chair.

"You know I love your stories, but I don't think this is the time."

"It was during apartheid."

I let out a deep sigh, knowing that nothing was going to dissuade him from regaling us with this tale.

"A group of indigenous people were being held in a manor house on the fringes of a large piece of property. They were being tried in a mockery of a court for imagined crimes. Their only actual crime was their skin did not match their captors, and they refused to allow that to stop them."

Hager stroked his beard while he reminisced. "Speranza requested permission to deviate from our objective to perform a rescue mission from what was going to be a mass murder. We were denied."

"They were all killed?"

"They would have been." Hager gave me a pointed look. "Had we followed the order."

Chapter Seventeen

"What is your quest?"

MONTY PYTON AND THE HOLY GRAIL - 1975

"I REALLY BELIEVE THAT we should not be doing this," David lamented for what felt like the twentieth time. "Going against the High Council's direct instructions is not a good idea."

We were all in Beulah, John driving of course, heading towards the Heretic's apartment. Hager was in the front passenger seat, while David and I were in the second row.

I was looking out the window, soaking in the New York atmosphere. The feeling I experienced being back after several months away surprised me. I felt—home. "Don't worry about it. We have approval from Speranza."

"She didn't give us express permission and even if she did, it doesn't work that way. Decisions aren't made unilaterally."

Hager shifted in his seat so he could engage David. "I understand your concern. I also have my misgivings about ignoring the High Council's wishes. Unfortunately, we are experiencing a time where politics are interfering with the proper course of action."

"In your opinion."

Hager held David's attention. "Mr. Ritter, what is your analysis of Mr. Bateleur?"

David frowned. "I'm not sure what you mean?"

"Yes, you do. There is a debate going on throughout all the Bishops as to his divine prowess. Many of us have witnessed him perform feats that some would call miracles."

I felt my face flush, listening to them discuss me as though I wasn't there.

"Rumors."

"I watched him heal Tira," John said over his shoulder.

"She must have had some of her blessing left."

"She was lying on the street for several minutes after being beaten to within an inch of her life by a demon. I was about to experience the same before he one armed it and slammed it into the street, killing it."

David's mouth hung open.

Hager nodded then added, "that was after he vanquished another demon by simply forgiving her."

David's jaw got closer to the floor.

"Don't forget when he stopped time." John spoke into the rearview mirror.

Hager nodded. "Indeed. Or when he discovered how to open portals into the Divine."

"Guys," I interrupted. "I think you've made your point."

"Quite right. You can look at these in two ways. One; you might perceive them as flukes, isolated events of luck that have no greater meaning. Two; they are harbingers. Signs that this war we have been fighting for thousands of years may be coming to a head. That God, in whatever form you believe him or her or they to take, has given us a path. Already a rift has been created among the Bishops. You could see that clearly in the High Council's debate. They are split, and not in our favor."

David chewed on his lip. "If that's true, why did they unanimously decide to put him in charge of this mission?"

Up to this point, I had been trying to ignore the fact that they were discussing me. David's question awakened something in me, and I sat up straighter. "They want me to fail."

Hager nodded. "I believe so."

David's expression shifted multiple times as he contemplated what that really meant. "It's a sink or swim test."

"If it were, then why deny him the tools he needs to succeed?"

John asked.

"This is a way to denounce someone publicly whom they believe to be fraud."

John pulled into a garage. The attendant waved him through, and we descended several levels before parking next to an elevator. Turning off the engine, he swiveled in his seat so he, too, could face the back. "Decision time."

David's mouth opened and closed like an animatronic figure whose soundtrack had broken. Finally, it melted into a thin line of resolve. "I will not hinder you, but nor will I actively help either."

John and Hager exchanged glances.

I put a hand on David's shoulder. "That will do for now. But eventually you are going to need to pick a side."

I opened my door and Hager said, "No weapons. Leave everything here."

We all complied and made our way to the elevator. I pushed the call button and the doors immediately opened. Filing in, John selected the button for the penthouse and the car started moving.

Hager stood with his arms folded behind his back as he stared at the floor while the numbers climbed. "I will give you one more piece of evidence for you to consider. As the Covenant Head, I have been here multiple times. The Heretic is not guarded."

"How do you see that as proof?" David asked.

"I believe this time will be different. If I am correct, please let me do the talking."

I looked over at Hager. "You say this after you tell me to abandon my weapons?"

He met my gaze and held it for a moment. "Yes."

The elevator doors opened to a short hallway. There was a small table to one side that served absolutely no purpose other than decoration, and a large indoor apple tree. At the far end was a lone door. Two men with automatic rifles stood at attention, along with one woman who was oozing Bishop vibes.

"We could really use Adam right now," I said under my breath. He had the ability to hide himself from people's vision. It was a skill we'd used several times while battling Uji in Florida a few months back. I wasn't sure if he could do it with three people guarding one door, but I would have liked to see him try.

We only progressed a few steps when both men raised their weapons.

"That's far enough," the woman said. She looked to be middle-aged, maybe a little older. Gray flecked her short blonde hair. A pixie cut, I think they call them. She was average height and wore tight fitting black leather pants with matching boots, and a gray tunic like shirt with a thin belt.

"Ms. Hutchinson."

"Mr. Hager."

"I wasn't aware you were in the area."

"Just stopping by."

"From Germany? It is customary to check in with the local Covenant when arriving."

"I got in last night."

"What is your purpose here?"

"I am on council business."

"That does not answer *my question*."

The woman's eyes narrowed. "I was told there was a possible threat to the Heretic."

"Do I look like a threat?"

"You, no."

Hager inclined his head. "Apologies for my rudeness. May I present Chris Bateleur, John McCaw, and David Ritter. Gentlemen, this is Amanda Hutchinson."

Her eyes lingered on me. Sizing me up. "So, you are Christian."

"Chris."

Her eyes narrowed again, but remained silent. She readdressed Hager. "Then, why are *you* here?"

"We have come to see the Heretic."

"I'm presuming you have spoken to the High Council first."

"We have."

Amanda regarded each of us, taking her time. I wondered at what special talent her gifts had given her. Each Bishop had a core set of skills along with one that was not so common. Could she read minds, sense intentions, or weed out the truth? Is that why she was selected for this?

"Okay then. I hope you find the answers you are looking for."

"What?" one guard exclaimed. I had to restrain myself from echoing him.

Amanda turned to him. "You heard him. They have spoken to the council."

"Our orders are not to let anyone enter."

"Your mandate is to follow my direction."

"I think I should verify with Miriam."

Amanda crossed her arms. "Fine, but be quick about it."

She glanced at Hager, then at the other guard as the first man reached for his radio. He never made it to the mic. The two blurred and the guards were on the ground and unconscious within a second and a half. John, David, and I stood there trying to pick up a surprise plot thread.

"It was lucky Miriam asked me to head up this little coup," Amanda said, while securing her guard.

"Luck, or divine intervention?" Hager offered.

"Either way, I'm burned now."

"We have others."

I looked to John, then David, both shrugged.

"Can someone clue me in?" I asked. "And since when do the High Council hire mercenaries?"

"Since someone hired a sniper."

"Oh, yeah, right." I had broken that rule about six months ago when I hired the Marine sniper that tried to kill me. But like the car that drives on the shoulder to avoid traffic, it only takes one, then everyone follows.

"And what about the rest of—" I waved my hand around "—this."

Hager stood up. "Since your encounter with the demons back in November, a rift has been forming among the Bishops."

"What kind of rift?"

Hager hesitated.

Amanda stepped in. "Between those of us who accept your extraordinary abilities as fact and those that do not."

"I'm not following."

"Is he always so dense?" she asked Hager.

"Only about himself."

Amanda shook her head. "Let's just say there are Bishops that support you and others that don't."

"Support me in what?"

John put a hand on my shoulder. "She means we've got your back."

"Uh, okay," was all I could think of to say.

"The High Seat is one of those that supports you," Hager added. "Unfortunately, four out of the six that can vote on the High Council do not."

Amanda finished hogtying her guard and stood to face me. "Amram has been organizing us to make sure if a move is made against you, we are there to shift the balance."

Hager actually dusted off his hands when he was done. "Key people were asked to play as if they were against you so they would be in a position to take action, or at least provide intel on the plans. Amanda is one such person."

"Miriam believed I was on her side and asked me to ensure you did not reach the Heretic under any circumstances. She was quite clear that I was to use physical force if necessary."

I crossed my arms. "Well, that's not very nice."

"She will know you were playing her now," John said.

Amanda nodded.

"Are you in any danger because of this?" I asked.

She laughed. "We haven't quite gotten to where we are bumping each other off."

"Chris."

I glanced at Hager.

"It is time."

I nodded, then looked at the door. There was nothing special about it. It was nice since this was a high end building. But in my mind, it loomed larger than physically possible. A lot of trouble had precipitated this visit. People I didn't even know were taking risks to ensure that I had this opportunity. What if I was wrong? I remembered something my mother used to say. The past is behind you. Keep an eye on it in your rearview mirror but focus on the future. It is the only thing you can affect.

I walked up to the door and moved to knock. Before my knuckles could connect, the door opened.

Chapter Eighteen

"I am the saint of blasphemy."

THE LAST TEMPTATION OF CHRIST - 1988

THERE WASN'T ANYONE WAITING to greet me as I cautiously stepped inside. The decor was…interesting. It looked to be Niles Crane meets PewDiePie. On one side of the living room was an Ours Polaire couch, which I recognized from when I went through an Antiques Roadshow infatuation, one of three hundred made to order from the French designer Jean Royére. Next to it was a bar with liquors including the Eye of The Dragon Vodka, Louis XIII Cognac, and Ley 925 Diamante Tequila. These held a combined price tag in the eight-digit realm. The bookcase that stood next to it held books that made my breath catch. An original three volume set of Moby Dick, a first folio of the works of Shakespeare opened to its iconic portrait of the author, the publications of both Edger Allan Poe and HP Lovecraft. By the look of them they all appeared to be first editions though I dared not flip through them to confirm. One however caught my eye more than the rest. I remembered the deep almost black maroon color with gold highlights on the spine of Milton's Paradise lost. I couldn't resist. Opening the glass door I eased the book out and opened the plush cover. Inside was written, 'With boundless gratitude for your inspiration to my humble endeavor. With warm regards, John.'

"Holy shit." I whispered, then replaced the book.

The other half of the room held a comfortable-looking couch, a TV that had to be over a hundred inches, and every gaming system in existence.

The apartment was open-concept and spacious. The living and dining rooms were delineated only by the arrangement of furniture. It was a dramatic transition from comfort to formality. I could picture sixteenth century aristocrats sitting around that French Renaissance table deciding how they were going to carve up the new world.

There were other pieces that would have made the Antique Road-show people weep with envy. An actual William Clement long-case clock, quite possibly the first grandfather clock ever made. A solid gold candelabra sat atop the dining table, and a Monet hung above a buffet that could have come out of the White House.

The latest Call of Duty franchise game was being played, though there was no sound. Whomever was in control was decimating the other team single-handedly. The game mode was domination, the aim being to secure as many of the three flags for as long as possible.

"People, play the fucking objective. Can somebody jump on 'B' besides me?"

The voice was in a higher register than I expected and came from a large high-backed chair that faced the TV. Its back was to me, obscuring my view of the person speaking. I approached slowly, not wanting to spook the player, as I was pretty sure they were wearing a headset. Snaking around the couch, I tried to get a peek at this fearful, ageless Demigod. I almost tripped when I finally got a clear look. The Heretic was a teenage girl.

"Hey, Chris. Give me a minute to finish these noobs off. Fix your-self a scotch and pour me one while you're at it. Try the Yamazaki."

I know I sat there with my mouth hanging open. I tried to stop but I couldn't make anything move. She had long red hair tied back in a ponytail, fair, freckled skin that looked like it would burn in the shade. She had on jeans that were ripped to the point of barely being wearable with a Rage Against the Machine concert t-shirt that was cut into a deep V-neck. Her eye makeup bold dramatic colors that extended to the side of her head made her look like one of the fae, but wore no lipstick.

Her eyes diverted to me for a split second, then back to the game. "Stop being creepy and get me that scotch."

I finally snapped out of it and walked over to the bar. I recognized the one she'd requested. It was fifty-five years old and sold for about eight hundred thousand dollars a bottle. I was about to ask if she wanted ice, but one didn't mix liquor of this quality with anything. Thick glass tumblers were sitting on a bar towel. I uncorked the bottle and inhaled the robust aroma of sandalwood and well-ripened fruit, involuntarily closing my eyes. The word that came to mind was heavenly, which didn't fit this scenario. Pouring two fingers' worth into each glass I replaced the bottle and walked the two drinks over.

The Heretic was just finishing up capturing the other team's flag while taking out any defenders. "Win" was appeared across the screen. Despite her previous complaining, it was nowhere near an even match.

"Okay boys, it's been fun. Gotta go." I could hear the moaning of her teammates from where I stood. "Nothing I can do. My father is giving me the stink eye. I need to help with dinner." She pulled off the headset and tossed them on the coffee table. It looked like a Louis XIV with a price of a quarter mil.

"Father?" I asked.

"Should I have told them that a Bishop was looking for advice from the immortal they had been playing with who probably killed some of their ancestors?"

"I guess not." I moved to hand over her drink, but hesitated.

"I only look like a kid."

Somehow, I felt like I was being played. But at this point, adding the charge of contributing to the delinquency of a minor wouldn't make much of a difference. I handed over the glass, expecting her to shoot it. Instead, she held it out, we clinked glasses, and she took a delicate sip. I followed suit. I had tasted expensive scotch but nothing came close to this. It didn't have the bite normally present in hard liquor. To say it was smooth would be doing it a disservice. I believe the nectar of the gods would taste like this. I think I may have had a small orgasm.

"Good, right?"

I pulled myself back, trying to remember that I was there to discuss life and death situations. "Not bad."

Rolling her eyes she took another sip and gestured with the glass. "Sit."

Several sarcastic responses came to mind, but I somehow kept them to myself and did as requested.

"So, you're Christian."

"Chris. How did you know?"

She seemed to find my correction amusing. "Let's say I have a view of things that most of my siblings don't."

"Siblings?"

"What would you call them?"

"Evil."

She scoffed.

"You disagree?" I pushed.

"No, I just don't get how you can take that attitude when your race has basically taken what they wanted throughout history."

"What, white guys?"

The Heretic laughed and I felt like someone just walked across my grave. "The human race."

"With you whispering in our ear."

"You can't be that naïve. How many of us do you think there are?"

"Eighteen. Oh wait, sorry seventeen."

Anger flashed across her face and was gone just as quickly. She smiled. "Yes, I heard about that. I figured that chip on her shoulder would get her killed one day."

"I thought you were immortal."

"I believe you proved we aren't." She took another sip, eyeing me from over the glass. Then she got up and went over to an old wooden cabinet. She opened one door. Inside was a row of LPs. She bent over to shuffle through them. Her ass was directed towards me, as she rubbed her right calf with the top of her left bare foot.

I looked back at the painting. Something tickled my memory about it and I went in for a closer look.

"No, it can't be." I must have said it out loud.

"Yes, it's Waterloo Bridge."

"But it was stolen."

"I know. I commissioned the theft."

"You what?"

"Well in all actuality, it was mine. Claude made it for me. It was the view from our window."

"You lived with Claude Monet?"

"Lived? No. It is where we met up occasionally."

She finally stood up holding one of the old style records. I believe she could have found it without the drawn out searching. The picture on the foot square cardboard cover showed a man playing a trumpet. His cheeks were puffed out as he blew into the instrument. She pulled out the paper sleeve, then removed the black disk by holding it perpendicular to the floor, putting her middle finger on the label and securing it with her thumb on the edge.

I returned to my seat. "Have you heard of this invention called digitization?"

She lifted a panel on the cabinet with her free hand, exposing a turntable. "Digital is so cold." Shifting the album to rest between her two palms so that her fingers never touched the surface, she lowered it into place. "That's why it is so easy to manipulate you. You want everything now, instant gratification."

"Digital is clearer, more cost effective, and allows me to take my music wherever I want."

"Making the music less valuable." She placed the player arm on the record and a crunching sound emanated from the speakers almost like a car rolling over gravel or hard rain on the roof. Then the smooth tones of the trumpet drowned out these more tactile sounds.

She picked up the cover as proof. "This was a communication between the artist and his fans. The album was a total experience. The anticipation of the release. Going to the store to get it. Reading the jacket until you could get it home to listen."

"And now we have TikTok."

She replaced the jacket and returned to her seat, folding her legs up under her. She cupped her scotch the way Marie would her coffee.

"So, how does this work?" I asked.

"Usually I get paid up front. I drift off afterwards, so I would rather not trust you to leave it on the dresser."

It took me a second to catch her meaning, and she looked pleased with my confusion. "Funny," I finally said.

"Based on what I keep hearing, I expected you to be more fun."

"Sorry, my game's a bit off when one of the most feared creatures on the planet turns out to be the girl with the dragon tattoo."

"I have a few tattoos. Would you like to see?" She ran her fingers along the inside of her neckline, tracing them down in the curve of her chest.

"Could you stop that, please?"

"Oh, come on. The only sex I get is from pervy men who are more concerned with their own gratification than mine."

"I'm seeing someone."

"And if you weren't?"

"Sorry."

"Let me guess; it's not you, it's me."

"Oh no, it's you."

The Heretic laughed at that. "I have to say, you have balls to come here without the permission of the High Council."

I tried to keep my expression fixed. "Why do you think that?"

"Because they already came to me a few months ago."

I sat bolt upright before I could stop myself. "That's not possible."

"Were you here?"

"I mean, they didn't mention they had approached you. They even debated over the decision."

"Interesting."

Yes, it was. There were only a few reasons they would not mention it. From what I understood of the High Council, everything they did was public. At least among the Bishops. While I could see one or two of them agreeing to keep something like this a secret, I doubted the entire council would agree. It felt like a decision that needed a unanimous vote. Speranza was obviously unaware, since she sent us on this secret mission. That means someone came here without permission. The only people who knew the Heretic's location were the High Council and the head of the local covenant, in this case Hager. I was confident it was not him. Which left—

I met the Heretic's eyes. "Who came to you?"

"Miriam."

I went to the door.

"Where are you going?"

I didn't answer, but opened it. The team all looked in my direction. "Come in."

No one spoke or moved.

"Chris. This is not how this goes," the Heretic said from behind me.

"It does now."

Everyone gaped at me. I motioned for them to hurry and stepped back so they could pass.

"What about them?" John nodded towards the hogtied men.

"Leave them."

They all hesitated for another second, then Hager led them in where they milled around the door. I closed it after David entered.

"Hey Amram." The Heretic smiled. "Someone's getting old."

"Yes, well, not everyone is blessed with immortality." Hager glanced over at the TV. "Or can while the day away battling eleven-year-olds."

"Quite," she mocked.

I held up a hand. "Okay, you two. We have a problem."

"Really?" Hager said, taking in the jazz music and drinks.

The Heretic leaned up against the stereo cabinet, her elbow leaning on her crossed arm, drink hovering around her lips. "Relax, the Boy Scout here wouldn't do anything." Everyone but Hager openly gawked at her. "Yes, it's me. You may all bow."

It looked like David might actually do it.

I pushed ahead to work through their fear and confusion. "It hasn't been over twenty years since the last council."

Hager pulled his gaze away from our host. "Excuse me?"

"Miriam was here a few months ago. I'm presuming you didn't know."

Hager stroked his beard. "No, which tells me it was not sanctioned by the High Council."

"That can't be." David finally found his voice, but was still staring at the Heretic.

"See, you were so worried about us breaking tradition, and the second highest woman on the High Council beat us to it."

"There must be some mistake."

John slumped down on the floor. "How do we find him now?"

"What's his problem?" the Heretic asked.

"Anton took his father," I said. "We were coming to you to find a location on him."

The Heretic frowned and pushed herself to a standing position. "Anton took Terrance?"

I nodded, more concerned with my friend than everything else. I put a hand on his shoulder. "We will figure out another way."

"Hello? All powerful demigod with a question."

We all looked at her.

"He took him? Not killed him?"

"Yes," Hager answered, then described the incident.

The Heretic's eyes started darting around. Finally, she looked up. "We need to go."

"What do you mean, go? You don't leave these rooms."

"I know this is difficult for you short-termers, but I need you to think for a minute. Number one, Anton doesn't abduct people. He doesn't torture, he doesn't trade for leverage, he doesn't demonstrate his superiority like a samurai by winning without death. Anton is a killer. A butcher. He is like a tornado. When he touches down, there is nothing but destruction."

Her words had resonance to them that aligned with my concerns over the past few days. Why was Anton acting contrary to his nature? What was driving him? Or maybe it wasn't a what, but a who?

"He's not doing this by himself." I interjected.

"Bingo. Someone has a brain."

"The Tainted do not work together," Hager said.

"They have before," she said.

"When?" Amanda finally spoke up.

"To dethrone me."

A buzzer sounded. The Heretic went over to a screen on a table and tapped it to life. It showed the elevator, now crowded with people.

Most were carrying automatic rifles. Anton stood among them, towering over everyone. I almost threw up when I recognized the man standing next to him. Baldemar.

Chapter Nineteen

"Run for it Marty!"

Back to the Future - 1985

"TIME TO GO," I said.

"Is there an alternate way out?" Hager asked.

The Heretic stood frozen, staring at the screen. I wasn't sure what I saw behind those green eyes. Then it came to me. Inevitability. Baldemar looked up at the camera and waved.

I yelled, "Heretic!"

She met my eyes, nodded once, then moved towards the far end of the apartment to a china cabinet. When she pulled, it swung open revealing a short hallway that led to stairs. We all quickly filed through. As the Heretic closed the secret door, I thought about the two mercenaries hogtied in the entryway. I was hoping they were still unconscious and would be left alone, but didn't really believe that. Two more men on my conscience.

"Where do these stairs go?" Amanda asked.

I moved past her. "They go up." I started climbing, taking two at a time. The flight doubled back on itself, then ended in another door. I pushed it open. Daylight flooded in along with the crisp air of spring as I stepped out onto the roof. The view was spectacular, one side looking down on Central Park. The Heretic didn't pause, but led us to an alternate ledge. There was a decent jump to the next building over; lower than our position by about five stories. Death for a normal person, not an issue for a bunch of Bishops.

Following the leap of faith the Heretic ushered us through another door and into an apartment. It was sparsely appointed; the bare minimum, like it was just for show.

"Whose is this?" David asked.

"Mine as well, under an alias."

"For emergencies?" Hager guessed.

"No, mostly for slipping out unnoticed. I know you keep tabs on me. Sometimes I prefer you didn't. Now, toss your phones in here." She opened a heavy metal box. Then grabbed a small device off the table next to it and started waving it over each of us.

"Is this really necessary?" John asked.

"They got to me somehow. One of you is compromised or working with them."

"We are Bishops," Amanda said.

"And I am one of the Tainted. Yet here we are."

"Why would they be after you?" Hager asked.

"Best guess? They think I told you how to kill Uji."

"My father being kidnapped was just a ruse?"

"That is my theory. They kidnap Terrance very publicly. With no other way to find him, you guys come to me leading them right to my door." She finished scanning David. "None of you are carrying trackers."

A bad thought occurred to me. "If they followed us here, they may have discovered the location of—"

"I need a phone," Hager said.

The Heretic opened a cabinet and tossed one to him. He dialed and put it to his ear. "Soon-Li, thank goodness. No time to explain. Lockdown protocol *Eisheth*. Get everyone out. Rendezvous at the safe house." He nodded at whatever she said, then clicked off. He moved to hand it back.

"Keep it."

Out into the hall, we followed her to another door that led to a freight elevator. The Heretic pulled the doors open vertically. We all piled in and she heaved them closed again.

"Are we going to discuss what just happened?" I looked around.

The Heretic shook her head. "Not yet.".

Hager nodded. "Quite right, we need to get to a safe location."

We reached the bottom floor and made our way back onto the street. There were two obvious lookouts guarding the entrance to the garage. The Heretic's face darkened and she took a step towards them. I grabbed her shoulder, and almost instantaneously I was in an arm hold that had me on my toes, her hand around my throat.

"I want blood!" she practically growled the words.

I nodded as much as possible, then croaked out. "Maybe later would be better?"

She dropped me. "Fine, let's go." She turned and stalked to a garage next door, gaining entrance through a biometric scan of her thumb print.

We followed her in, John and I lingering behind as he stared in the direction of the Suburban. "You're bad luck. This is the second time that we have had to abandon Beulah."

I put a hand on his shoulder. "We'll come back for her."

"Whatever."

We stepped into the garage before the guards noticed us.

It was spacious, holding all kinds of high-end vehicles. I saw a Ferrari, Lamborghini, Koenigsegg, Porsche, and Corvette Stingray. I could go on, but you get the idea. Alongside these modern technical wonders were classic cars; A Sixty-eight Chevelle, sixty-nine Camaro, seventy-eight Trans-Am, and so on. I felt like I was dreaming. John looked as though he might pass out.

"Which one is yours?" Hager asked.

"All of them."

"You're kidding me," John breathed.

"Most of these are two seaters." Hager pointed out. "Do you have any that could hold all of us?"

"Please say no, please say no." I only heard John's mumbling because I was right next to him.

"How many seats do I need? Anyway, we should split up into teams. Go off in different directions in case we're followed. Keys are in the ignitions," the Heretic said. "Chris, you come with me."

I got an icy chill down my back.

"Very well," Hager said and John did a little celebratory dance. "Though these aren't the subtlest of vehicles. We will meet up at the uptown safe house."

I followed the Heretic over to the midnight black Koenigsegg. The license plate read two-thirty-four. I was going to ask what it meant, but then I noticed the car next to it read two-thirty-five. Shaking my head, I pulled the door handle, and it swung up. I climbed into what felt more like a spaceship than an automobile. I tugged it closed and the Heretic slipped behind the steering wheel. She fired up the engine. I felt the rumble up through my seat into my chest. Pulling out her phone, she launched an app and plugged in a seven-digit code, triggering the large garage door.

"Why do you still have *your* phone?"

"Because I know mine is not compromised. Now, hang on."

I had already buckled myself in, but grabbed the 'oh shit handle' just above the door. She zig-zagged between the rows of cars, making turns that Tron would be envious of, and shot out of the garage into the daylight. She slipped on a pair of Dolce & Gabbana sunglasses as she made yet another ninety-degree turn.

"How about we don't alert them where we are?" I said, while adding a second grip on the center armrest.

"Relax."

"Yeah right—is there something I can call you besides the Heretic?"

She looked over at me, smiling. "How about Lucy?"

I gave her the address to the safehouse. She took several other sharp turns, cutting people off before she turned onto the FDR and dropped the hammer. We went from uptown to downtown in about five minutes. Even when traffic started to slow down, she would just make a serpentine move and a path magically opened.

She finally let up on the gas as we rounded around the Seaport and I felt I could release the death grip I had on the handle.

"What's your story?" I asked.

"How do you mean?"

"Evil tyrant turned gamer? Do little Austin and Jake know they are playing side by side with an immortal?"

"Absolutely. It's the first thing I told them when I joined the squad."

"Why the change of heart?"

"Who said I had one?"

"Are you still manipulating and torturing humans?"

"Yes, but it is so much more challenging and rewarding without the supernatural powers. Which, by the way, I can use for good as well." She put a period on her sentence by removing her hand from the steering wheel and placing it on my thigh.

I picked it up by the wrist with two fingers and returned it to its proper place. "Two hands on the wheel of the million dollar car."

She pouted. "You're almost as boring as your predecessor."

"You were talking about your change of heart?"

She shrugged. "I tired of it."

"That's it?"

"You try doing variations of the same thing for a few millennia and see if it doesn't lose its luster."

"Was that before or after you were dethroned?"

She ignored me.

"Fine, can you help me out with my question at least?"

She scrunched her face like she had just sucked on a lemon. "You led my brothers, whom I have been successfully hiding from for ninety years, right to my door. Then you want me to answer a second question in the space of a few months. Did they tell you what happened to the last person who didn't respect my privacy?"

"They did."

"Are you brave or stupid?"

"The jury is still out. I had a vision."

"Stupid, got it."

I sighed and started again. "I had a dream—"

"So did MLK. Look what happened to him."

"I was in the future I think."

"I saw that movie. The book was better." Lucy shifted and punched the gas. I felt myself being pushed back against the seat, which was impressive seeing as how we were already going eighty.

"We lost the war. Apparently your family found our…weakness. A barely alive version of Hager told me to find you."

The screaming of the engine reduced to a growl and the pressure pinning me eased. She stared into the rear-view mirror. "We're being followed."

"I'll take care of it. Take the next exit and get back on going the other way."

"What are you going to do?"

"That depends if one of your siblings is in the car." I pushed the button for the window and unbuckled.

"What are you doing?"

"Don't worry, I'm kind of an expert at this now." I climbed out and onto the roof.

"You better not scratch the paint."

I caught sight of the vehicle following us and jumped, slipping into a short blur to compensate for the backward momentum. Leaning up against the cement side rails, I waited for our tail. They were a few cars back in a Ford SUV struggling to catch up to the land rocket Lucy was driving. Two more cars got off, yelling at me for being on the side of an off ramp. When the SUV took the exit, I stepped out into the middle. People who have been driving for years all have the same reaction to someone stepping out into traffic. The driver slammed on the brakes.

It was a good thing too. No matter what the movies say, whatever super strength I possess will not compensate for a few tons of car ramming into me. I may be able to protect myself, but the car will keep going and take me with it. They stopped short, about a foot from where I stood. Looking at me through the windshield were four guys: all normals trying to recover from the shock. Stepping up, I punched through the grill and released the hood. Shocked curses emanated from inside. I pulled out the easiest part that will disable the car, the battery. I ripped the cables right off the terminals, then yanked it clean out, tearing the mount that held it in place.

Closing the hood, I carried my trophy over to the driver's side window and slammed it down on the roof, caving it in and mangling all four doors so they couldn't be opened. I leaned down and stared at the driver, who I think might have wet himself. "I don't like being followed."

I walked back up the ramp and hopped over the cement median. Lucy pulled up in a different car. I climbed into the passenger seat and we took off.

"Where did you get this one?" I asked, admiring the Corvette.

"I made a trade."

"And they just agreed?"

"If someone hands you the key for a million dollar car, you don't argue."

"You didn't use your mojo on them?" I was afraid to know the answer.

"What if I did?"

"That would be wrong."

"How is convincing someone to take a deal that benefits them wrong? I basically handed them nine-hundred thousand dollars."

"It's the principle."

Lucy gave me a side eye. "You're losing this argument. *You* don't even believe that."

I scratched at the stubble on my cheek. I hadn't had time to shave in a few days. "Choice is important."

"Whatever. Anyway, I don't do that anymore."

"Why not?"

She stayed quiet.

I waved my hand in front of her with a mystical flair. "You want to tell him."

Lucy laughed so hard she lost her breath, then inhaled with a shrill squeak.

I pulled my head back, chin almost touching my chest. "What the hell was that?"

"Don't make fun of me."

"I'm not. That was a serious question."

"It's how I laugh."

"It sounded like a pig being tortured."

She backhanded my shoulder.

"So, tell me."

She looked over at me for what felt longer than prudent for the speed we were going, then back to the road. A smirk painted her face. "It has to do with the source."

"What source?"

"Our source of power."

"The Tainted's source?" I almost salivated at the idea that I might get first hand info about our enemy.

"All of ours."

I sighed. "Somehow, I doubt our powers come from the same place."

"Not now. But a few millennia ago, it wasn't so different. You bathed in sacred water from Israel, we bathed in blood."

I stared at her, keeping silent, trying to hide my shock.

Lucy glanced at me and made a face. "Yes, I know what your source is and you can relax, the others don't. We are not really into sharing intel."

"How did you find out?"

Lucy opened her mouth, then hesitated. "You probably don't want to know. The point is, we moved past needing a physical catalyst."

"I didn't realize the Tainted had a source. I thought your powers were part of you."

She barked out a laugh. "Everything needs a source. Humans convert food into energy. We convert emotions into power."

"Wait, pain and suffering isn't a drug for you?"

"That depends on your point of view."

"Okay, Obi-Wan, what does that mean?"

"Emotions fuel power. The greater the emotions, the more power. Power is addictive, so…"

"So what? You've got a new drug?"

"You could say that, and it does what it should."

"Touché. How does that work?"

"It's kind of like the differences in fuel for your car."

I thought about that. "So, if you use diesel you get better gas mileage, but your acceleration suffers. If you use electricity, your acceleration goes through the roof, but your range decreases and your time to re-energize is multiplied."

"See, you get it."

"What about the problem of using the wrong fuel for your engine? I can't just switch to diesel if I want more miles to the gallon."

Lucy's face blanched for a heartbeat then she was her old carefree self. "There is a transition period."

I thought back to the day we rescued Krissy. The process of purging the Tainted's influence was traumatic, to say the least. She had only been using that particular fuel for a few months. Lucy had lived on it for thousands of years. I shuddered, and we drove in silence for the rest of the trip.

Chapter Twenty

"If you want to be safe, you better lock all the windows and screens."

THE PRIVATE EYES - 1980

WE PULLED UP IN front of the safe house and Lucy put the car in neutral and set the brake.

"What are you doing?" I asked. "Parking garage is up there."

"I'm not going in."

"Why not?"

Lucy rolled her eyes. "You people are not exactly my normal entourage."

"We're not trying to start up a band. Though now that I think of it, Lucy and the Bishops is a damn good name."

"Ask me."

"What?"

"The question you were going to ask when you came to see me. Ask it."

"I thought you only answered one question every ten years."

"I'm not big on following rules, even my own."

I regarded her for a few seconds. "No, that's not it."

Her eyebrows tried to merge and sink down to her nose. "Fine, forget it."

"Seriously? The demigod is afraid to tell me the truth."

She sighed heavily. "It's that right there."

"The fact that I don't take your shit?"

"Actually, yes."

"Go on."

She stared out the windshield. "For thousands of years, everyone bowed and scraped around me. They were afraid of what I would do, or they wanted something from me. You are the first person to treat me like—well, a person."

I continued watching her. She was showing actual emotion. Not some fake manipulative version. Granted, she wasn't about to start bawling or anything, but I think it was more real than anyone else had ever seen her.

Lucy looked me in the eye. "So, ask."

"Where would Anton be holding Terrance?"

"Anton has an underground fight club. If he can't beat up on people, he at least wants to watch it. It's in the middle of the French Quarter on Barrone Street. Number one hundred thirty."

I smiled at her. "Thank you."

Lucy rolled her eyes. "You're welcome. Now get out."

"Why not come with us?"

She nodded at the safe house. "Look at this place. I have a four-star hotel waiting for me."

"Well, I owe you. If you need anything, just call."

"I thought you weren't interested."

It was my turn for an eye roll. "You know, you're not what I expected."

"Let me guess, something like one of the many roles Alan Rickman played."

"Yes, but that's not what I meant. I was told you burned the eyes out of a Bishop who pushed you too far."

She took on the far off look of someone reviewing a fond memory. Then she turned red and closed her eyes as though trying to rein herself in.

"That was a long time ago. Before I—converted."

"Hager believed you were still extremely dangerous. He worried about me being on your radar."

She smiled. "It takes years for humans to change their ways. You've got to give an Immortal a few decades at least. I'm sure I was still in the habit of leaving people with a certain perception back then."

I thought about that, then shrugged. "Sounds reasonable." I got out and closed the door. The window rolled down.

"Chris."

I ducked down, leaning one arm half in the car.

"Beware of Anton. He is a cruel, sadistic bastard and would like nothing better than to torture everyone you love while you watch."

"Thanks again."

"And tell Hager I will let him know when I set up in a new place." She peeled away, leaving twenty feet of rubber on the pavement.

The safe house was not as bad as Lucy made it out to be. It was an old abandoned building on the outside and the facade continued in for a few rooms. The real living quarters were accessed through a closet with a rotted out floor. Once the system identified me through my subcutaneous chip, a metal plate slid across the floor, covering the hole, and the back wall opened. Everyone was there, and we went through another flurry of heartfelt greetings.

"Where is the Heretic?" John asked.

"Lucy? She left." I nodded towards Hager. "She said she would let you know when she was settled in a new location."

"Why did you call her Lucy?" Hager asked.

"It's her name, isn't it?"

They all exchanged glances. Hager finally spoke. "No one knows. She refused to tell anyone."

"Why did she tell you?" Soon-Li asked.

I shrugged. "I asked."

They all stared, dumbfounded, at me. I walked into the kitchen with the team on my heels, opened the refrigerator and grabbed a water bottle. "She answered my question." Twisting off the cap, I took a big slug that drained a third of the bottle. Everyone started rattling off questions.

I addressed each person with their answer. "She offered. Where would Anton keep John's father? Yes, she answered me, fight club."

The last was to John.

He hung his head low and shook it, his dreadlocks brushing both sides of his face. "Of course."

"This fridge is bare. Is there any food here? I'm starving."

Tira crossed her arms. "Of course it's bare. It's a safe house. You're lucky I grabbed the water."

I looked over at her and she blushed. Something she would never have done when we first met. Putting me in my place seemed to give her unending pleasure. I smiled and shook the bottle. "Thanks."

John started packing up what little was brought. "We'll eat on the plane,"

"We need a plan," Hager countered.

"We can do that on the plane as well."

I swallowed another swig of water. "I've got to go with John on this,"

"Shocking," Soon-Li said.

"Yeah," Tira added. "Rushing into battle is so unlike him."

"Funny. Look at it strategically. This whole ruse was to flush out Lucy. They believe she gave us the secret to defeating Uji. They wanted her gone to reset the balance of power."

Hager put his hands behind his back. "Valid. Go on."

"They left John's father at the fight club just in case they needed him. They won't much longer and they don't yet know we are aware of his location. He is as close to unguarded as he is going to get."

"This is highly unusual." I'd almost forgotten Dave was there. He was sitting in the corner, almost in the shadows.

"You get used to it," I said flippantly.

"We shouldn't." He stood. "There is more happening here than one missing Bishop. I'm sorry, John, but it's true. There is a rebellion occurring within the High Council. They are not only manipulating activity, they are taking secretive action against protocols. These regulations were put in place specifically to ensure we don't experience the same issues our forefathers did."

I looked at Hager. "What's he talking about?"

He looked guilty, so I knew this was bad. He took a deep breath. "The Collective Covenants have had several occasions where our differing viewpoints caused, shall we say, friction."

"Friction?"

"Maybe heated disagreement would be a more apt description."

"So, infighting," I corrected.

"Well—yes." Hager seemed to rebel mentally against the word.

"So, while there are actual demons and demigods roaming the earth causing all types of havoc, the Bishops were squabbling over how best to battle them?"

"You might say it was more of a tiff."

"Seriously? When was the last one?"

"The Civil War," John said.

"Are you telling me half of us were condoning slavery?"

"There were some, but no," John said. "This was more a debate over getting involved."

David gestured toward John, highlighting his point. "And this occurred when our focus should have been on the instigators. It may have reduced the death toll or stopped the war entirely. Instead, we argued and fought each other when we should have been fighting the Tainted."

He looked at each of us, trying to drive his words home. "Rules were created to keep the peace. To give us guide rails on how to act based on the experience of what happens when you don't. We can't just toss out those rules when they aren't convenient."

I walked over and stood in front of him. "You're right, David. Rules should not be ignored simply because they are getting in the way."

He crossed his arms and nodded, satisfied.

"But," I continued, "nor should they be followed blindly based on the assumption that the people who created them knew better than us. Especially when those rules were created during a time when the world was a much different place. More importantly, we cannot allow rule following to impede doing what we know is right. That is rescuing Terrance."

David's face hardened. "This is going to lead us down a path into chaos."

"Maybe. But I'm going to make sure everyone can walk it with me, or choose their own. Including Terrance." I still held David's gaze. "John, get the plane ready."

Chapter Twenty-One

"You do not talk about fight club."

Fight Club - 1999

"SHE WAS KIDDING, RIGHT?" John asked, staring up.

The address was on Barrone Street, as she'd said, not even a block off of Canal. The building which housed the fight club was over four stories high, wedged in between a white high-rise with a restaurant (The Tackle Box) at its base, and a little tan building with a bookshop that was closed for business. Brown paper covered the windows. The location comprised two buildings, both red brick in construction. The one on the left was thinner and shorter, its bricks a rust color and heavily accented with tan.

The main building was filled in with slim arched windows framed by slender pillars. It was separated into three sections both vertically and horizontally, one of the three in each direction taking up half the overall space. An eight-pointed star window took up most of the upper middle section, while three double doors with archways domi-nated the lower. It looked as if it was sponsored by the number three. I could hear the count from Sesame Street laughing in my head. A white border cut across the building just above the doors. Carved into it were the words DE' PAR E VIRGINI SINE LABE CONCEPTAE.

"A church," I said.

"Not just a church. The Church of the Immaculate Conception," David added.

I looked over at him. "Is that even a thing?"

"Don't get me started." John walked towards the double red doors on the left. The other two sets were green.

David and I hurried to catch up.

"Are we really going to break into a church looking for a fight club?" David sounded more nervous than usual.

"I thought churches were always open," I said.

"You know what I mean."

We finally caught up to John, already at the door. I put a hand on his shoulder, letting him know I was behind him. Then I addressed David.

"We are just going to look around. Get a feel for the place." To John I said, "Has anyone in there been read in?"

John turned the handle and opened the door. I wasn't sure if it had been locked before. "Doubt it."

He slipped inside, and we followed. This was not the main entrance, but a side hallway. Even in here, I could see that this church was majestic in its design. We had pulled the blueprints and discovered there wasn't really a location where a fight club could be established unless they were brawling up on the dais. This side door appeared to be the best option, so we took it. We looked around but found nothing out of the ordinary.

Backtracking, we entered another of the side doors into the main area. I was awestruck by the beauty of it all. The ceiling extended to the roof. I could see rays of light shining down through the star window. The marble altar was ornately carved. The pews were a combination of wood and iron. It was less like a church and more like a palace. Intricately carved columns, archways and stained glass filled my vision at every turn.

"This is a bust," John wasn't seeing the majesty of this place, just the fact that it didn't hold his father.

A thought occurred to me. "Let's take another look from outside."

"How will that help?" John moaned.

"Humor me."

We filed out through the main doors, crossed the street, and turned back to face the church.

John seemed impatient. "So, what are we looking for?"

"Patience," I said. "Give me a second." I stood between the two. People passed behind us and traffic zipped by in front. I closed my eyes. I had done this once on top of a building in the middle of Miami, completely by accident. The question was, could I do it again? Reaching out, I found the shining source of my power and let it flow through me. I tried to remember what I was thinking back then. *Glimpse behind the curtain. See the reality through the facade. View the truth.*

I opened my eyes. The scene had changed. The church, which was beautiful before, now shone with a near blinding light. It wasn't the only thing that had morphed. People walking on the street had visible auras swirling around them, a complex conglomeration of light and dark. It was dizzying. I put a hand on both men's shoulders to steady myself.

"Everything okay?" John asked.

"Yeah. True sight has a tendency to put me off balance."

I could feel David turn in my direction. "I'm sorry, did you just say true sight?"

I didn't look at either of them, not wanting to become any more disoriented. "Yeah. I did it once before by accident while looking for the portal Kristina had fallen through. I thought it might help."

I could sense tension in John. "What does it look like?"

"People's auras shifted, which makes sense. Few people are purely good or evil. We all have our dark sides. The Church, however, is not where we will find your father."

"Great. Now what do we do?"

I looked to the left. "The rectory looks to be sitting on a seething mass of rotting earth."

The two regarded the other building.

"Let's check it out." John started forward and I held him.

"I'm going to need both of you to help me cross the street. I don't want to chance losing the site and not be able to get it back. Walking like this would be problematic."

I had to force myself not to let his nod in my peripheral vision draw my attention to him. We moved as a group while I kept my focus on the ground, which displayed the fewest images. My relationship with

David was tenuous and I didn't think it would survive me vomiting on his shoes.

As we got closer, I glanced up. The only thing that distinguished this building from a house or small apartment building was the thick white stonework around the entrance. It formed yet another arch framed by two simulated columns with capitals affixed with crosses. Above the arch was written: FIDES QVAERNES INTELLECTVM. Inside the arch encircling IHS with a cross extending from the middle of the H were more raised letters. AD MAIOREM DEI GLORIAM. That's what I knew to be there from what I saw before. What I was seeing now said, Faith of all Intellects, below, To the Greater Glory of God, surrounding a visage of Jesus.

It was as though someone photoshopped the translation over the original image, leaving both visible. It was even more dizzying and I leaned heavily on my two supporters. We reached the door and David moved to knock.

I shook my head and wished I hadn't. "Just go in."

He hesitated, then turned the handle. I guided them both in ahead of me. "You guys go first. I'll follow."

They did as I asked, and we stepped into a small greeting area. A desk faced the doorway from the right side. An older woman sat behind it and greeted us with a smile. No visions danced around her, for which I silently gave thanks. The space had the look of a living room that was doubling as office space. A conversation area with two comfortable looking couches at one end and a desk credenza and water cooler at the other.

"How may I help you, gentleman?" The woman's image shifted from a kindly senior citizen wearing a flowered dress with a cardigan to a shapely vixen with a tight dress that barely contained her curvaceous figure.

"Not like that." The words escaped before I could restrain them.

"Excuse me?" The vision of the stately grandmother returned.

"We were admiring the architecture and were wondering if we could have a look around," David said.

John and I both glanced over at him. Well, John did. I kind of looked at his shoes.

He ignored our stares and continued. "Are there areas open to the public that we could experience?"

The woman brightened up. "Why, yes. There is a gathering room in the basement. I'm afraid I can't give you a tour, though. I need to mind the front desk."

"I understand. Would it be okay if we explore? My friend's vision is failing and he always had an interest in churches."

A hand went to her mouth. "Oh, I'm so sorry. Yes, of course. Just down the hall first door on your right. Stay as long as you like."

I stared off in her general direction. "Bless you, my child."

They led me to the door, opened it, and made a show of helping me down the stairs. When we got down to the room and verified it was not currently occupied, I said, "That was quite a performance."

"I had to do something. John is trying to break down every barrier we encounter, and you could either be blind or drunk. I figured the latter wouldn't get us very far."

John looked at him askance. "With how much you like to follow rules, I wouldn't have thought you'd be so good at deception."

"Maintaining secrecy is one of our key edicts."

"Now that makes sense," John finished.

David sighed. "Can we move it along?"

"He's got a point. What do you see?"

I looked around slowly. The basement was a rec room, probably used for meetings, community service groups, and rented out for celebrations. There was a serving window where a bar could be set up, and stacks of folding chairs and tables. There were flashes of insight here and there, but nothing that would point to a source. Then I saw the cabinet.

It seemed innocuous. A cupboard that probably held odds and ends for parties. Non name-brand disposable plates and coffee cups. The party sized coffee pot, extension cords, boxes of those disposable salt and pepper shakers. No, it wasn't the cabinet, but what looked to be escaping from behind it.

The closest description I had was black mold soaked in blood. It pulsated and expanded almost imperceptibly. The True Sight didn't extend to my olfactory senses as far as I knew, but I could swear I could smell the putrid dankness wafting off of it.

I closed my eyes and released my hold on the supernaturally enhanced vision. My stomach stopped doing flips and my dizziness settled down to a slight vibration in the back of my skull.

"There." I removed my arm from around John's shoulder and pointed.

He took a step towards it, then turned back to David. "You got him?"

"Yeah," he said.

I gave him a thumbs up as well and made a shooing motion.

He got to it and started opening doors.

I waved my hand. "Behind it."

He looked back at me, confused. "There's nothing behind it. There aren't even scuff marks on the floor. This thing hasn't been moved in decades."

"Trust me."

Still looking skeptical, John wedged his fingertips behind the cabinet and pulled. It didn't budge. He put more strength behind it, still nothing.

"They must have screwed this to the wall. I could pry it off, but I think the sound of tearing wood may give away our true intentions."

He wasn't seeing what I had seen. I thought about the sickening image and remembered that the bloody mold had been emanating mostly on three sides. Reaching for my boon, I used it to delve the side that had the most contamination. I found the locking mechanism fairly quickly and triggered it. There was an audible click and the cabinet swung forward an inch.

John opened it further and it swung outward, silently revealing a staircase leading down. After a quick inspection, he said, "No wonder it didn't leave any scratches. It's not touching the floor."

I was feeling better and stopped using David as a crutch. At that moment, I heard the upstairs door open, followed by the voice of the attendant.

"How are you gentlemen doing?"

I motioned towards the secret stairs and pushed David ahead of me. We all filed in and I pulled the cabinet closed. There was a monitor on the wall showing the room we had just exited. The old woman appeared in the doorway and looked around. I extended my senses so I could hear what she was saying.

"Hm. They must have left while I was in the back. Shame. I would have liked to take that black beauty for a ride. Bet I could teach him a thing or two."

I looked at John, who must have been listening as well, since he was smiling.

"Does that mojo of yours have an off switch?" I whispered.

"Nope. Only an on switch."

Chapter Twenty-Two

"Where do these stairs go?"

GHOSTBUSTERS - 1984

"THIS PLACE IS COOL."

David and John regarded me in the dim light provided by small electrical sconces spaced out every twelve feet that projected light onto the ceiling.

"What? We just went through a secret door into a hidden passage."

They continued to stare.

"Fine, let's go."

The staircase started out straight down until we reached the first landing. To the right, a concrete spiral staircase wound its way down so that you could never see more than five steps ahead or behind.

John ran his hand across the cement wall. "How is this even possible?"

"What do you mean?" David asked.

"It is rare to find a basement in Louisiana, much less New Orleans. There is just too much groundwater to make construction feasible. That the rectory has a basement is rare, but this—" He patted the wall "—I would have thought impossible."

I regarded him. "Anymore impossible than building pyramids without the use of modern day machinery?"

He continued to look around. "I guess. But hauling enormous rocks is one thing, holding back groundwater?"

"Like Moses," David offered.

"But what's holding it back now? Concrete isn't waterproof."

"You ask too many questions," David said.

"Maybe you don't ask enough," John countered.

"Cut the chatter, you two. Who knows what we're walking into."

The staircase continued down what felt like an impossible distance. It reminded me of Kentucky's Mammoth Cave that we went to when I was a kid. We had descended into what my young imagination painted as the bowels of the earth. I half expected to step out into a cavernous room where I would be chased by half-animal, half-human cannibals. When we reached the bottom, it emptied into a corridor that extended out of sight in three directions like an upside-down 'T.'

David pointed right. "I'm sensing heartbeats that way."

I extended my own senses and heard them as well after separating those of my two compatriots. I nodded. "Right is right."

We started off in the direction he had indicated. The corridor curved to the left, which gave me the feeling that if I continued around, I would end up back where I started. I still had my senses beefed up and the smell hit me well before we reached the holding areas. It was the clawing odor of unwashed skin mixed with urine and feces. We came upon cells that reminded me of a medieval dungeon, and I wondered if this was the remnants of an old castle.

Ten of the twenty cells held prisoners. John peered into the last one then ripped the door from its hinges sending it clattering down the row of cells. Terrance lay in the corner. John rushed in and checked for a pulse.

"He's still alive." John's voice cracked and I caught him wiping at a tear. His words released a pressure in my chest. "He's unconscious and looks to have been beaten and starved half to death."

He sat his father up and pulled out a flask. He unscrewed the top and poured it over his head, while whispering a short payer. John's father convulsed and his breathing evened out. After a moment, he opened his eyes.

"John?"

"Yeah, Pop. I'm here."

"What took you so fucking long?"

"Sorry, sir. Can you walk?"

Terrance tested out his muscles hesitantly. "Anything left in that flask?"

John handed it over.

"Good boy." He drank the remaining holy water and shivered, his eyes closing. When he opened them again a moment later, he nodded. "Should be able to walk with help now."

"Good," I said. "David, let's get the rest of the prisoners out."

"NO!" Terrance grunted, while John helped him to his feet. "They're not human anymore."

"What do you mean not human?" I asked.

"They have been turned. Hard."

"What does that mean?"

John was grim faced. "It means they were pure of heart and have been turned with the blood of the pure of heart. The combination creates very violent, very strong Converted."

"Like Krissy?" She had batted Adam and I around like a shuttle-cock. I didn't want to get into it with even two like her, much less ten.

"No. But I don't think the three of us could handle them."

Terrance nodded. "I was in and out of consciousness, but what I figured is they keep them on the brink of starvation, so they are weak enough to be held in these cells. When a fight is scheduled, they release tainted blood into the basin." He motioned to the back of the cell where a metal receptacle was mounted on the wall. A pipe disappeared into the ceiling.

"How do you know that?"

"Because they tried it on me once. A buzzer sounds and the red light tells them it's feeding time. Gorging themselves on blood puts them into a frenzy. Gates funnel them to the battleground. I could hear them slamming into place and retracting after it was all over."

"How often do they do it?" David asked.

Terrance's cracked lips were pulled into a thin line. "Every night."

I grabbed him under the arm. "We need to go."

John lifted from the other side, and we got his father to his feet. We exited the cell, David leading, John and I half dragging Terrance after. A buzzer sounded and a red light shone under the cracks in the door nearest where we just vacated. Another buzzed and the following cell spewed light into the corridor. We all stood there staring at the floor, silently waiting, knowing we needed to move. But shock kept us in place. The rest of the cells, one after the other, lit up like dominos falling.

I looked at John. We both said, "Oh shit."

Chapter Twenty-Three

"Cry Havoc and let slip the dogs of war."

Julius Caesar - 1599

J OHN AND I GRABBED the back of Terrance's belt, pulled his arms tightly around our shoulders, then took off at a run. Going into a blur would have been helpful right then, but we couldn't do it while carrying anything of substantial weight. The old-fashioned two man carry was the best we could manage.

"Straight through the middle," I said. "I don't want to bump into an angry horde of converted just after feeding."

I caught John's nod in my peripheral vision. "Good call."

David blurred ahead to make sure our path was clear. The short corridor opened up into an open circular area about sixty feet wide with a thirty foot domed ceiling. A ring of glass sat at a second story height. The viewing area, I presumed. Large screens were mounted above the audience seating like one would see at a concert to give that closeup view of the spurting blood. There were four ways to enter and exit at the four points of the compass.

David stood on the opposite side of the battleground, anxiously waiting for us to catch up. We reached the middle as the gate slammed shut next to him with such force that I could feel the vibration through the concrete floor. All the screens came alive. Baldemar filled each of them.

"Christian, my good friend. It is so good to see you again."

"Hello, asshole."

"You are still not very complimentary."

"Sorry, was that not your name? Asshole, major asshole? Oh, maybe it's just your title."

Baldemar was still smiling. Not the insulted fake smile you get from people that find you offensive but are trying to hide it. He appeared to be enjoying the exchange. That pissed me off even more. He looked and acted like an aristocrat with his usual light colored silk scarf. Looming behind him, like a pet grizzly bear, was Anton. He leaned against a back wall, also wearing a shit-eating grin. His body somehow filled the background. He wore a curly black beard that was tied a hand's width under his lantern of a jaw. A big shiny belt buckle reflected the light from somewhere in whatever room they were in.

"See, you are so much fun to talk to. A pity I missed you in New York. But I did catch up with a new friend of yours."

Baldemar stepped back from the camera and motioned to someone. Two women dragged a bloodied figure into view. Her hair covered her face, obscuring her identity. Anton stepped up and wrenched her head backwards.

"Lucy," I said before I could stop myself.

She was conscious, but only barely. Blood flowed freely from several gashes across her face where bone was closer to the surface. Cheek bones, eye sockets. Her face was swollen with bruises already forming. That she was not healing spoke volumes about her state. Was she somehow cut off from her 'new source' as she put it?

"You two are on a first name basis. How nice. It's been a second since our last visit, but as you can see, we are getting reacquainted." Someone handed him a towel and he wiped his hands as though they were covered in excrement.

"I will make you a deal. Let her go now, and I won't feed your balls to you."

"Always so confident. But I'm afraid you won't be getting out of this one. Those bars are titanium. The surrounding walls are reinforced concrete with an astonishing amount of rebar."

"You really think that will stop me?"

"It doesn't have to stop you. It just has to slow you down." Baldemar nodded to someone off camera and the cascading sound of locks being triggered ran all the way around us. Anton's smile widened as he stepped closer to the screen.

We had found Terrance in the end cell on the right side. Apparently, there were an equal number of cells on the left as well. I heard doors crashing open mixed with the grunts and guttural noises of near-mindless, enraged creatures clawing over each other; each mad to be the first to draw blood.

I disengaged myself from Terrance and looked at John and David. "Get that door open. I will hold them off."

David's eyes went wide. "Are you crazy? You can't take on that many—"

"No time to discuss this as a committee."

I turned and committed myself to the fight. This was a battle and I couldn't waste energy or concentration on things like compassion, remorse, or guilt. I only had one thought in my mind: defend.

They poured in from both sides. Whatever had been done to these people, they no longer bore any resemblance to human beings. Whatever torture these creatures had submitted to, whatever heinous acts they had performed, had transformed their bodies into a hideous perversion of the human form. They were beyond skinny, their gray skin pulled taught against bone and stringy muscles. What hair they had left was in spindly grimy clumps. The nails on their fingers and toes were clawed and blackened. I could hear them clicking and scraping across the floor and walls as they scrambled to reach me.

I slipped down into a steady stance, pressing the ball of my back foot into the concrete as though I was stamping out a cigarette. I was sturdy as a tree rooted to the ground, but as fluid as a river. Dipping into the well of power bestowed upon me, I felt it fill me like molten metal, until I radiated power.

As they entered the arena and caught sight of their prey, they blurred.

They moved like lightning, their aims divided between the four of us. Some wanted me. Take out the top dog and show dominance. Others sensed prey that was more vulnerable and focused on taking down the wounded or distracted. I could feel each of their intentions and they enraged me with a righteous fervor. I let the fury envelop me, turning the liquid metal, white hot.

The horde was moving between the space of human heartbeats, but I was the flutter of a hummingbird's wings. The first attacker aimed at me, launching itself like a cougar pouncing. I let loose a strike that batted it mid-leap. It collided with another, and they both crashed into the wall with enough force to crack the cement.

The next was focused on Terrance but I grabbed it out of the air, spinning it into the flow of attackers on the other side. I slipped from one strike to the next. The end of one move became the start of another. When I trained with Soon-Li, she connected moves with forces of the world. She would tell me to choose a style that countered your opponent. Now I embodied not one element, but all of them. I was fire burning a devastating path. I was water flowing around their strikes, guiding them away from their points of focus. I was as immovable as the earth and they crashed upon me, a ship onto the rocks. I danced like lightning avoiding their attacks, then struck like thunder.

One tried to get past me, but I straight-armed it so hard in the throat it somersaulted backwards twice before smacking into the ground with a sickening crack. Continuing the move around, my fist pounded into the side of another's head, sending it careening into its fellows. With my other hand, I grabbed the downed creature at my feet and launched it into another crowd of claws and teeth.

I saw five moves ahead, instinctively knowing what attack was coming and what to defend it with. I slipped from iron to whip-like speed as though I had been doing it for hundreds of years.

Blood spewed in all directions, making the floor slippery for my opponents, at least. I could not be moved, could not be daunted. Still, they scrambled at me or about me, desperate to reach a victim that was just out of reach.

As I twisted low into a leg sweep, taking a creature on one side down, I grabbed the ankle of another on the opposite side. The momentum brought me around and I used the one in my grasp as a flail, its head colliding with the head of a third. Both exploded into a spray of blood. I stomped my foot down on the neck of the one whose leg I had just swept, bringing forth a satisfying crunch.

Then everything went quiet. The only sound was my pounding heart, the gasps of my breathing, and the constant dripping of blood. I was coated as if I had bathed in it. I turned to see if John and David had gotten the gate open. Two of the bars had been bent open enough to fit through. Terrance was on the other side. All three were just staring at me.

It was John's father that finally spoke, "Angels and ministers of God, defend us."

I glanced up at the monitors, now splattered with blood, even at their height. "I'm coming for you next."

Baldemar looked perturbed for the first time since I met him. His eyes narrowed. "Give it your best shot. But you will need to dig yourself out of your grave first. Goodbye, mister Bateuler."

He reached for a switch, and behind him, Anton waved his hand, yelling, "No!"

A barrage of explosions echoed from above and the ceiling started raining down. I reacted without thought, forming a barrier of air trapping the tumbling debris. The pressure was massive and I felt like an ant being stepped on.

"GET OUT!" I growled through clenched teeth.

"Not without you," John said.

"I can't hold it. Just go. That's an order."

David stepped through the bars and pulled Terrance to his feet.

John stood resolute. "I'm not leaving."

"Get your father out. I'll be right behind you."

"You better." He stepped through, took up his father's other arm and they scrambled back up the stairs.

The weight was unlike anything I had ever experienced. I was being slowly crushed. I felt like the pressure was pushing my eyes from my skull. It roared in my ears and pounded at my chest. *Keep going!* I silently urged them. When I thought they'd had enough time and I didn't think I could hold back the landslide, I let go and blurred as the world crashed down around me.

Chapter Twenty-Four

"Come to the coast, we'll get together, have a few laughs."

Die Hard - 1988

W AS I DEAD? I coughed. Nope, not yet. But where the hell was I? Everything was black. Were my eyes open? I blinked a few times. They were raw and crusted with something, like waking up with a cold. I reached into my pocket and whaled my elbow against something. Cursing as pain shot up my arm, I dug in and retrieved my small flashlight.

Gray dust coated the air in what looked like a fog from the John Carpenter movie. Despite that, I could see what was restricting my movements. I was trapped under a crap ton of rubble. My plan as the roof literally came down on me had been to get to the most reinforced place, the cells. The dust was settling and I could make out the squared off corners of the cell where we had just freed Terrance. I guess I'd made it. Well, almost. The falling rocks had caught up with me and had trapped me up to my waist in dust and stone. My torso stuck out at an odd angle, like I had been caught mid-dive. I saved myself from being crushed so I could die slowly buried alive. *Buried alive.*

I arched my back towards the ceiling and screamed, "KHAN!" The echoes bounced back, creating a dramatic effect, making me smile. At least I haven't lost my sense of humor.

I checked my well of power. Not empty, but it was as close as I had come since November. I had learned it was less like a well and more like a pair of lungs. The more frequently it was used, the more it could hold. Though its capacity was not unlimited. I had used a lot. I wasn't even sure how I held up the collapsing structure. Most Bishops had a modicum of telekinetic ability. Enough to pick a lock or flip a switch. But I hadn't heard of a display of such magnitude. Whatever it was nearly drained me. That and the fight.

The battle came back to me more clearly now that the bloodlust that had lifted from me. Who was that? It didn't feel like me. I had shied away from killing indiscriminately my whole life, including during my Army days. I rarely even kill bugs. It just always felt wrong. I always considered it a strange part of my personality, especially when you contrasted it with my love of eating meat.

But that battle. I ran through it in my mind again and cringed at every blow. The savagery of it went against everything I had been preaching since I obtained these powers. These were people, plain ordinary people, who had been coerced into taking the wrong path. They weren't born evil; they were tempted. It wasn't death they deserved, but a chance at redemption. My stomach turned and it took all of my willpower not to vomit.

I recalled one of Father Murphy's favorite sayings. There was nothing I could do now. The past is something to learn from. *Let it guide you into the future, not hold you back.* It had been months since I last saw the old priest. He had watched me grow up, knowing about the dormant powers I possessed. He'd tried multiple times to steer me back to the Church and my birthright. Between my father's stubbornness and my own, it had taken a chance encounter at a small church in upstate New York to make the connection.

I squeezed my eyes shut. Ruminate later, survive now. I shifted my weight tentatively, waiting for a burst of pain. None came. Either I had gotten lucky or I had healed. I used a lick of power to enhance my strength and pulled myself free. I examined my legs and found several gouges soaked with blood. The skin under the fabric, however, was unscathed. Definitely healing involved. I stumbled around the rock strewn floor as I inspected the cell.

It had been about six by nine feet with a ten-foot ceiling and it was half filled with rubble, which sloped from the top of the door to the opposite wall. There was a vent in the ceiling, which I assumed was to provide fresh air. Can't let the warriors in an underground epic fight club suffocate. That would be poor business sense. The opening was not large enough for me to pass through. But with some power-assisted demolition, I thought I could get through the concrete, however thick. I might burn through the rest of my reserves and the chances of the air shaft being clear all the way through to the surface were very slim. On the other hand, I had a lighter. I could reenact the scene from Die Hard as I crawled through the shaft. I put that option on the back burner.

I considered opening a portal, but that had a few issues. The least of which being I only knew how to get to one place. The only way to identify where a rift would lead was to memorize the harmonic resonance of the area I wanted to portal to. I had memorized only one, a rooftop in the middle of Miami. Granted, being there would be much better than here. I had been meaning to study other places. I just hadn't gotten around to it. The real problems were much more concerning. Did I have enough power left to open, not one but two portals? The first would provide entrance to the Divine plane where it was said that no human could survive. The second rift would go from there, back into our world. Also, I'd only ever opened portals in well-ventilated areas. I had no idea if doing so would suck out all the air I had left.

Leaning against the wall, I closed my eyes and extended my senses. I tried to ignore the scurrying scratching sounds of life that lived primarily underground. Instead, I searched out something that would connect me to the outside world. Then I heard it. The distinctive sound of water in a cavernous area. It was flowing, though barely. The image in my mind tickled a memory. Charity. It was one of the runoff systems she had told me about on our walk. But was it close enough? I focused harder; tried to gauge the distance. It was two or three feet of concrete, followed by dirt, more concrete, then bricks. I might get through all of that with some enhanced excavation. But could I make an opening large enough before I ran out of juice or drowned in the flooding cavern?

It was too risky to make the attempt alone. I needed help. I pulled out my cell phone, only to find that it hadn't survived the ordeal. The chances of getting service down here were slim to none, anyway. What about a more magical version? I could astral project myself and was fairly confident I could reach the surface. But when I got there, I could not communicate with anyone. Either John or David would need to be actively looking for an astral projection and even then, all I could do was pantomime. My problem needed an arrow not already in my quiver.

This was one of my issues. I was a person who believed in technology, in science, and in logic. There was little of that in what I did. I could accept the things that I achieved as fact. I had faith in myself and in what my friends taught me to bridge that gap. But to do something new, I would need to base a hypothesis on scientific fact. Another idea occurred to me. What about theory? Brainwaves were well documented. There are many theories that state miracles, derived from prayer, are nothing more than the harmonized focus of large numbers of people on a single idea.

There are also arguments that psychics, telepaths, and empaths are people who can receive and translate outside brainwaves. So I extrapolated. People could receive brainwaves, and I could enhance my physical traits. It was logical that I should be able to enhance my brain waves so that someone else might receive them.

I sought the field and the lake: the place in my mind where all new ideas started. The water line had receded as though a drought had hit the area. It looked more like a pond. The grass, normally a vivid green, was the color of straw. The trees were wilted, branches hanging low to the ground.

I ignored the depression that the sight evoked in me and focused on the crushing barriers of dirt and rock that separated me from John. I cleared a small space against the wall, sat and pushed my consciousness upward. My mind passed through layer after layer, touching living things all the way up. I breached the surface and began touching minds. There were a lot of them. A jolt of excitement went through me that I could get this far, but I still needed to find John and figure out a way to communicate. I believed I could pick him out—someone I had stood side by side with in battle; someone who was linked to me in a way that science could not explain. I assumed I could identify John by that spark that distinguished him from every other person in the world.

I started delving into the minds around, searching for something familiar. I wasn't getting particulars. There weren't any images, or memories, or even passionate emotions. Just a feeling, like tasting food blindfolded. I picked over mind after mind, looking for that familiar flavor. I worried about how much power I was using, but pushed it out of my mind as just another distraction. Then I hit one. Recognition tugged at me but it was vague. I guessed that it was David or Terrance.

Should I try communicating with them? I decided that was a bad idea. If I tried with Terrance, who was tapped out, I could waste time and energy. My best chance was a mind I was more connected to. I moved on and found a stranger. Shifting back to where I thought they were, I encountered yet another. Panic grabbed me by the throat. I fought it down, drawing a deep breath, and took a careful mental step back. A stranger, but the one I was just touching. *Okay, think. Which direction?* After a second tentative step I was again touching someone familiar. *Good, now focus.* Another step.

This was as familiar as my mother's macaroni and cheese. John. I breathed a sigh of relief. *So, you found him, now what?*

"John?"

No response, either because he didn't hear me, wouldn't acknowledge me as something other than a random thought, or couldn't communicate back. I was going with option two since it was the most self serving.

"John, it's Chris. Can you hear me? Okay, not hear, but are you receiving me?"

I thought I felt a question ripple across the consciousness. Time to up the gain. "John! Sound off like you've got a pair."

I heard a faint buzzing like it was a terrible connection.

"John, you need to use your power. Focus on projecting your brainwaves."

"*Chris?*" There it was. "*Are you dead?*"

"Not yet. I'm trapped in the same cell we pulled your father out of. I was able to get into it before the billiard parlor walls came a-tumbling down."

"*What?*"

"Forget it. I'm trapped."

"*Yeah, I got that. Are you okay?*"

"Yeah. Whatever injuries I sustained are already healed. But I'm running out of power and air quickly. I'm not sure how much this communication is costing, but I don't want to risk losing you to find out."

"*About that. How the hell are you doing this?*"

"This isn't a standard power?"

"*Ah, no. Let's put that aside for now. What's the plan?*"

"How do you know I have a plan?"

"*You usually do, they're just normally stupid.*"

"Yeah, this one's no different."

"*Okay, I've got you,*" John said in my head.

I dropped the rock I had been pounding against the wall to help him and David locate where the sewer crossed closest to my location. I had to keep in contact for fear of losing him. Unfortunately, I couldn't estimate distance with the mind meld, my name for this new power. Since I was unable use two powers at the same time, my arm was killing me. Stupid rule.

"*Can you hear this?*"

"Barely."

The next one was louder but still muffled.

"That's better. Yeah, I heard that."

"*Good. Disconnect for now. Save your energy. We've got to get some tools to get through this. I will pound on the wall when I need to communicate.*"

"Will you be able to find the spot again?"

"*Uh, yeah. That second hit that you heard put a gigantic crack in it.*"

"Great, what do I do in the meantime?"

"*Meditate?*"

"Wonderful."

I broke the connection with no small amount of trepidation. I rarely have a problem with being alone. In fact, I need regular solitude. But there was a vast difference between choosing to be away from people and being placed in a dark, underground, solitary confinement. There was a distinct possibility that might be my last conversation ever. I could run out of air any time if that air vent was blocked in the explosion. A second collapse could crush me. Water from the sewer could flow in and drown me. No one would be there to witness my passing. I would die alone; cut off from everyone I knew and loved. They would only realize what happened as they finally breached the room to find my lifeless body staring up at them.

I growled at the tangent my brain took me on. "Maybe meditating *isn't* such a bad idea."

Looking around, I tried finding something to do. I thought about moving some of the debris to make it easier for me to reach the hole when they broke through. That would use up the limited oxygen faster. Not a good plan.

What else? Nothing? Seriously nothing? I was completely reliant on John. The frustration built until I started shaking and I wanted nothing more than to punch something with the last bit of power I had left. Taking several deep breaths, I calmed myself.

I swept away the debris on part of the floor with my foot and sat with my back against the wall. I sought the meadow and the lake again. This time, it resembled more of a deep puddle. I didn't reach for the power. The depressing post apocalyptic landscape had me reconsidering my decision. Then I remembered this was not an actual place. It was an image that I created: my happy place, if you will. Apparently, it was also a reflection of my mood. Mood however, like breathing, was both involuntary and voluntary. If ignored it would react to my surroundings. Focusing on it, I would have the ability to affect change.

Instead of allowing the feeling of impending doom to dominate me, I concentrated on the positive. My friends, both old and new; some of whom were working right now to get me out of my current predicament. I forced myself to release my death grip on the reins of my situation. I had to trust that someone else could do what needed to be done. I was not alone. My new family of Bishops had my six. They could carry the load.

My connection to them had brought me closer to my mother than ever before. Because of them, I'd met Marie. Just picturing her face made me smile. I hated being away from her and couldn't wait to see her again. I glanced around and the meadow was renewed. The grass was a bright green, plants were standing tall and leaning towards the light. Even the tree branches appeared fuller. The lake was still shallow but looked less bleak. A more optimistic perspective shone through me, promising nourishing rain.

I nodded at the results and my astral self sat down in the field. I let my mind drift, the opposite of meditating. This wasn't to clear my thoughts, but to analyze them. The thoughts that bubbled up were, of course, emotional and full of longing. Those, I brushed aside.

Use the time wisely.

Lucy appeared, so I focused on my conversations with her. I looked for little things that were present in my subconscious but hidden from my conscious mind. I started with our most recent connection and worked backwards. Replaying the video in my head, I tried to build a complete picture. I concentrated mostly on her face, which was beaten and bloody, hair falling down around it. Anything else?

She was being held by two men. Mercenaries, if the uniforms were any indication. Her clothes were the same as when I saw her last, so she must have been captured shortly after she left me. Then I noticed her hands. One was still. The other was dancing about like it had a mind of its own. Not dancing, signing.

She was sending me a message, and I missed it. I replayed the exchange over and over in my head, but couldn't extract any detail from it.

Distant thunder rolled and I pushed it out of my thoughts, annoyed. Was there anything else I was missing? I scanned my memory for any other details. But the picture was blurry. I knew there was more, but I couldn't see it. A louder boom echoed through my mind and it tickled a thought. I stopped what I was doing and listened for it again. Another thunder clap. This time, I recognized it for what it was. I pulled myself out of my meditative state.

The pounding through the wall became more insistent. I extended my thoughts out and found John where he had been before.

"Okay, easy before you bring down more of the ceiling on me. Again."

"*Shit, man, you scared the hell out of me.*"

"I'm feeling a little lethargic, so some fresh air would probably be a good thing. But otherwise, still kicking." I put my palm on the ground to help me sit up. It splashed. I was sitting in a puddle. "However, we have a new problem. That crack you made looks to have created a leak in here."

"*I'm not surprised. There is about a foot-and-a-half of water here and you're below the water line. How bad is it?*"

"Not an issue now, but I'm thinking it will get a lot worse once you start excavating."

"*Well, we have several twenty pound sledge hammers being wielded by a couple of super humans. We should get through it in no time.*"

"No explosives?"

"*Yeah, we've got them though I'm not sure it's such a good idea under the circumstances.*"

"This should be fun."

"*Are you ready?*"

"No, but since when does that matter?"

"*Okay, here we go.*"

The sound of the sledgehammers against the brick sewer wall and floor was unmistakable. John and David were apparently alternating their strikes. The rhythm reminded me of documentaries I had seen about laying tracks for the railroad. Two men working in tandem, striking a metal spike.

The flow of water increased almost immediately. The puddle was expanding, though slowly. Concrete is porous. It allowed water through, but it took time. Water would seep in through cement slowly if it was surrounded by saturated soil. A pool was a completely different scenario.

I stayed silent, knowing that John would have to redirect power from what he was doing to talk back. The hammering would stop momentarily now and then, presumably, to remove the larger chunks. After a few minutes, a much shorter time than I had predicted, it stopped altogether.

"Okay, we're through. Switching to shovels."

"Thanks." I honestly didn't know if I was thanking him for keeping me informed or for the actual rescue effort. I guess both. The digging wasn't loud enough to hear without enhancing my senses. But I couldn't do that while maintaining a connection with John. The sewer water seeped in faster now that there was, what I assumed, a gaping hole in the water duct. That wasn't the worst part. The sound of the gurgling water, as it found its way into the room, was ominous with a promise of death.

It took another few minutes before John finally said, *"I think we've got it."*

"Great, I'm more than ready to go."

"You were right."

"Words I will never tire of hearing."

"We are going to need to blow this. Get as far away as you can and protect yourself. After this, we shouldn't need your mind meld."

That John called it that, even in these circumstances, made me smile. "Give it one minute and let it rip."

I scampered up to the opposite corner, reinforced my skin, covered my ears and opened my mouth. With such a small room, I wasn't sure what the concussive force would do to my innards and I didn't know how far the protection went. I started counting down as soon as I disengaged myself from John's mind. It was only a moment or two past the sixty mark when the blast hit me.

The initial impact drained the rest of my power just before it flung me into the wall. My head slammed into the cement, sending the room spinning. I fell backwards and rolled down the rock debris into the rapidly rising pool of water. The gurgle had turned into a roar as water gushed into the room like a horizontal waterfall. I was dizzy, in pain, and I'm not ashamed to admit, scared.

"Chris! Let's go, soldier!" John's words were muffled, but they spurred me on just the same. I pushed myself to my feet, and staggered over to the hole. It was too high. The hole was big enough for me to pass through, but it was near the ceiling. The bottom of it was a foot and a half over my extended hand.

In my current state, I couldn't see a way to reach it. Then a knotted rope dropped through.

I leaned against the wall and sighed. "John, you are the man." Even with the thick knots, it took all my strength to haul myself up.

As I reached to get a handhold, the velocity of the water threw my arm back. I tried again, this time bracing against the force. My fingers found purchase on the other side of the wall, the dirt and concrete digging into my skin. Still gripping the rope, I brought my feet up to the next knot. I held my breath and pushed with all the energy left in my legs.

The water pressure in my face was incredible. I could feel it pushing into my mouth, nose, and under my eyelids. With my current state, and all the work I was doing to get out, my lungs strained with the need for air. I grabbed higher on the rope when a large rock or brick broke loose from above. It struck me right above my right ear. The last thing I felt before I lost consciousness was someone grabbing my wrist.

Chapter Twenty-Five

"Doctor. Doctor. Glad I'm not sick."

SPIES LIKE US - 1985

I OPENED MY EYES and stared at the white ceiling tiles, trying to figure out where I was. The soft rhythmic whir drew my attention to the I.V. pump on my left. To my right, Charity slept in the chair next to the bed. Between her and me, on the wall near the headboard, was a touch screen with all my information. The lack of windows and the high-tech medical room told me I wasn't in any hospital. So I had to be at the New Orleans Covenant house. I sat up and gave my vitals a quick check. All looked within normal limits. I reached over and turned off pump, closed the clamp on the line, then ripped it from my arm. I always wanted to do that, though it hurt more than I thought it would. Putting pressure on the injection site with my thumb, I pulled back the covers with my other hand. I was completely naked.

A pile of new clothes was stacked in a small cubby on the opposite end of the room. I eyed Charity, who breathed evenly. I slid off the bed, padded over and started dressing. My body didn't seem any worse for wear. I presumed they had given me a holy water sponge bath to help with my healing. I buttoned my pants and was grabbing the shirt when she spoke.

"John asked last night why I was watching over you. Now I know the reason. That show was worth the wait."

I slipped the t-shirt over my head and pulled it down. "Funny. I have a girlfriend."

"So you've mentioned."

"Where is everyone?"

"Not sure, but I can take you to the usual place."

"You're not going to try to talk me into staying in bed?"

"I thought you said you had a girlfriend." Charity got up and walked out.

I followed, shaking my head. We stopped by the kitchen so I could grab some food and coffee. I picked up a banana and a beignet. We were in New Orleans. How could I not? By the time we got to the meeting room, the banana was gone and the coffee was halfway there as well. I was still hungry as I started on the pastry, but the shaking had subsided a bit.

The room was filled with a combination of Bishops from New York, Miami, and New Orleans, all standing shoulder to shoulder. I stepped in with Charity at my elbow like she was waiting for me to swoon. I swallowed what I was chewing and followed it with a swig of coffee. When my mouth was clear I said, "What's up, docs?"

I expected some kind of greeting based on my return from the dead. 'Great to see you, glad you're feeling better, I was so worried.' What I got was silence. The entire room went quiet and all eyes turned to me.

"What did I do now?"

Hager stood. "It's not what you did, it's what we did. Disobeying a direct mandate from the High Council. They have ordered us to appear before them and explain our actions. We knew this was coming."

"Why? Because we went to see Lucy?"

"He is on a first name basis with the Heretic?" Ima said. "Why am I not surprised?"

"Yes." Hager's answer was for me, not Ima. I think.

"But we were only denied because Miriam had already visited without the council's approval." I was being stubborn, and I knew it.

"Do you have any proof of that other than the word of one of the Tainted." Ima stared down her nose, looking very much like a principal scolding a wayward child.

"Lucy is not a Tainted anymore."

Soon-Li's thin eyebrows came together. "Chris, what if we were under similar circumstances in a regular court and your proof was based on Charles Manson's testimony?"

"He's dead."

She squinted at me, telling me just how stupid she thought I was being. "Whatever leaf you believe she has turned over does not eradicate her crimes of the past. It calls her entire testimony into question, and that is if she showed up in person to give it. Right now, all you have is hearsay from an admitted international terrorist."

I considered her words and could find no way to debate them. "Fine, but this is on me. I'm the one who met with her."

"Admirable, but as the Bishop in charge I am ultimately responsible. Not to mention it was I who provided the address."

"I can provide my testimony," Amanda said.

"Which will speak to the circumstances around the infraction, not argue guilt or innocence of the act itself." It was Tira who spoke this time.

I gave her a look. "Did you pass the bar while I was gone?"

"Since I don't plan on practicing, taking a test that would allow me to do so would be a waste of time." She tried to hide a smile. "But I could."

"Does the High Council work like a modern court system?"

"It is similar but probably closer to a court martial than a public trial from any country."

"Great, we just need to convince Miriam to admit that she ordered the code red and we are good to go."

A collective sigh ran through the room.

"What?"

When Hager stopped shaking his head, he asked Tira. "Is there any defense we can use?"

"Not that I can think of."

I crossed my arms. "What if we ignore the order?"

"Why, do you have something better to do?" Ima asked.

"As a matter of fact, yes. We need to assemble a rescue."

"Of whom?" David asked.

"Lucy."

The room went into an immediate uproar. Ima and Hager stood and got everyone settled. Then she faced me, leaning forward on her balled up fists. "Have you lost your mind?"

"No, I would say I'm the only one thinking clearly."

Ima stood up straight and started counting off on her fingers. "Let's review, shall we? You visited the Heretic against strict orders. You broke into a church rectory without proper backup or equipment and caused a sink hole the size of a city block. Now you want to ignore our highest laws to go off and rescue one of the Tainted?"

I crossed my arms. "Good synopsis."

"Can you answer one question?"

I nodded.

"Why?"

"Because it's what my mother would want me to do."

"I have a better question." Adam interjected. "Where? You needed the Heretic to find Terrance. Who will guide you this time?"

"Same person."

"I think he hit his head harder than we thought," John offered.

"Sitting in the collapsed cell gave me time to meditate on everything that happened yesterday." I glanced at Charity. "It was yesterday, right?" She smiled, nodding, and I continued. "I presume John and David gave you a full report?"

"They did," Hager said.

"When Baldemar was on the screen, Lucy was in the background signing with one hand. I can't remember exactly what she was saying, but I'm pretty sure she was giving me a clue to where she was being held. Is there a way to pull more details out of a memory? Like hypnosis or something?"

"No need. I recorded it."

I turned and regarded David. "Excuse me?"

He held up his phone. "Regulation 46A, all communications with the Tainted or their minions will be recorded."

"David, you go right on quoting regulations! Please send that to me. Hager, what would happen if we ignore this request, even for a little while?"

Hager steepled his hands on the table. "Then we would be considered rogue Bishops and the High Council would order a decree for our immediate capture."

"We have a police force?"

"There is a group of Martial Bishops who are tasked with such responsibility along with their normal duties."

"How long would it take them to mobilize?"

John put a hand on my shoulder. "Not long."

I regarded him, confused until his statement sank in. "You?"

Amanda raised her hand. "And me."

"Why you joined those brown shirts I will never know." Terrance said.

"Can we not do this now?" The exasperation in John's voice was clear.

His father grunted but otherwise stayed quiet.

"And to answer your next question," Hager continued, "the same would happen to any Marshall that failed to perform their duties."

John crossed his arms. "That's not an issue for me. I've got your six."

Amanda motioned with her head. "Me too."

She was a person I'd just met. But she had put her status and her freedom at risk for me and was willing to do it again.

"Thank you both. I don't mind putting myself in trouble, but I'd rather not have you sacrificing yourselves just yet. I get the feeling *that* time will come. So ignoring the problem is not an option. What happens if we are found guilty?"

"That depends," Tira explained. "It could be as light as a warning, suspension of privileges or go all the way up to expulsion from the Covenant."

"They would chance the loss of two Bishops? I thought our numbers were dwindling as it was."

"We have had issues in the past," Hager said quietly.

I frowned. "Issues?"

"Dark Bishops," John said.

"That's a thing? Why have I not read about it in any of the tomes?"

"It's not something we like to publicize," Ima said.

I snorted. "You people are amazing. A group of supernatural beings who are supposed to represent the very best of society. Thousands of years of history derived from the most advanced civilizations. But you fall into the same pitfalls as every other person."

Hager sighed. "We are all still only human. Subject to the same faults and flaws."

"That's a bullshit excuse," I said with a level of venom I couldn't keep out of my voice. The ripple of shocked faces circled the room. "It's what you say when you are tired of trying. I'm still breathing, so I'm not done yet. When and where is the hearing, or trial, or whatever it is?"

"It is customary for the High Council to come to the capital Covenant of the country."

"So, Pennsylvania," I said. "Fine, we get to visit David's house. When?"

There was a moment of silence before Hager answered, "Tomorrow."

I nodded. "First things first. John, charter our flight back tomorrow morning with that private airline. I'm not flying coach to my court martial."

John pulled out his phone. I stepped away and sat down, my gaze circling the room before settling on Tira. "You know what we need now?"

She nodded. "A good defense."

"Nope. There is nothing to defend. They said don't, we did it anyway. I'm not about to dance through loopholes. What we need is an offense."

Chapter Twenty-Six

"You can't handle the truth!."

A FEW GOOD MEN - 1992

I STOOD ON TOP of Municipal Pier Number thirty-eight, according to the large rusting metal sign below the fanlight with equally rusty mullions. It was a large, old building with peeling white paint. The upper portion, where artists had to lean over the edge of the roof to get the right angle, was covered with graffiti. At least that was what it was intended to portray. It was a facade, as were the rusty metal bay doors, partially repainted blue doors at either end. Even the notifications about a development opportunity and location for Penn Warehousing and Distribution weren't legit. The only real things about the three hundred sixty square foot building front were the two small signs warning that any parked cars would be immediately towed.

The prep work for this trial had not gone well. David had introduced us to Fallon Ardkill, the Philadelphia Covenant Head. He was tall and well built, but with a head and hands that appeared too big for him. He was also a stuffed shirt if I'd ever seen one. We had a few in the army: people who pursued power and rank. Those who had to remind everyone they were an officer. Some had knowledge and wisdom to go with their positions, but rarely to the degree they thought they did. I've found that the best leaders never sought leadership. It was thrust upon them, or they were asked to take on the role—like Hager.

One thing this Covenant did have was an extensive library. New

York was the second established in the then new colonies. Pennsylvania was the first. It held volumes that were copied over from the great library in Portsmouth in preparation for their journey. We had pored over one after the next; created and dismissed strategy after strategy. My gut still told me there was a path through this, but as of now, I couldn't see it.

So here I stood on the roof, one foot was propped up on the parapet as I stared across the Delaware River towards Camden and sipped coffee. David had told me about this spot. There was no furniture to make it comfortable, which is why it was almost always empty. Camden had been my first mission. It was where I first met Jelena when she'd decided not to kill me. Well, I persuaded her with my superior acting.

The Camden incident had taken place in November. Not even a year had passed. Now this trial would determine if I could continue in my role as a Bishop or if I would be cast out from yet another family, taking Hager with me. How bad do you have to screw up to be kicked out in under a year? I took another sip of coffee, then walked to the other side of the building, which faced Christopher Columbus Blvd. I looked southwest to the top of Gloria Dei Old Swedes' Episcopal Church, which poked up above its ring of trees. It was the location of the court we would visit shortly. It seemed fitting. This whole thing started in an Episcopal Church in upstate New York. Now it may end in one in Pennsylvania.

I took another swallow.

"Are you brooding again?"

I glanced over my right shoulder to find Father Murphy standing next to me, hands clasped in back of him. I put my cup down on the wall and moved to hug my old friend. "What are you doing here?"

"I'm here to lend you my support. Plus, if I waited for you to pop over for a visit, my beard would be down to my knees."

I pulled away. "Like you would ever let that happen. Now your mustache, that's another thing entirely."

He stroked the thick 'stash that would have made Hercule Poirot jealous. "It is, isn't it? So why are you brooding?"

"Still not brooding. Just thinking."

"About?"

"How fast this has all been going." I expected some kind of response, but he stood there, continuing to fiddle with his mustache. "It hasn't even been an entire year and I may already be drummed out." Still no reaction. The silence that I had sought up here became uncomfortable. "I was just feeling like I fit in."

"Ah ha!"

I jumped a little.

"My boy, you felt like you were fitting in because you finally let people in. You opened yourself up to family again. Powers, no powers, it doesn't ultimately matter. Do you think Marie fell for you because of what you could do, or who you are?"

I thought about it and tried to see my life without Bishop's mantle. Pick up Miser Brothers Heating and Cooling? Though if I moved to Miami with Marie, I guess there would be little heating involved. Was she ready for that type of commitment? I hadn't spoken to her since the Han Solo response to my profession of love. I admit, I would miss the whole superhero gig, but it was not altogether unappealing.

I shook my head. "Yeah, but I still have so much to do here."

Father Murphy looked around. "In Pennsylvania?"

"You know what I mean."

"He put a hand on my shoulder. Not even the Mets would bench their star player in the middle of a winning streak."

I squinted at him. "Darrel Strawberry."

"Yeah, but he was caught up in a major scandal—oh, I see your point. Okay, but let's look on the bright side."

"Which is?"

"Like the Mets, you're not out of it yet."

"Great, that makes me feel so much better."

"Come on. Let's go down. I brought you a present."

"What kind of present? Will it solve all my problems?"

"It's a couple of books. They may not fix everything. But I have a feeling they may solve some of the more pressing ones."

It was a brief ride to Gloria Dei. Hager and I hopped on South Christopher Columbus Blvd, hung a U-turn at the first opportunity, then accessed the grounds from Christian Avenue. I've said it before and I'll say it again: you can't make this shit up.

The Church itself was not large. Simple in design, similar to the one where I inherited my powers. The obvious difference was that it was surrounded by a graveyard. The headstones listed out names of soldiers who fought under General George Washington. My own service gave me a feeling of kinship to these men, long dead. I wanted to spend some time with them and extract their stories. Listen as they talked of their shoeless trek over the frozen ground. Did they believe in their fight as much as we publicize it? Was each young man as dedicated to ensuring the freedoms we all take for granted, or misinterpret, today?

I walked up to the door, the rows of headstones still in my thoughts. "I'm sorry. We will try to do better."

"What's that?" Hager asked.

I raised my eyebrows. "Nothing."

We stepped inside.

The church was brighter than any I had encountered. Though, admittedly, my experience was not vast. The pews were painted cream and capped with a darker wood, running along the back and on each end. The off white color extended to the wainscoting, window trim and the two balconies which ran lengthwise down both sides. Large plain windows brightened the space. The only stained glass was a small window on the wall above the altar. Its mullions were in the shape of a cross.

As we stepped into the main area and the doors closed behind us, all the people filling the pews stood as one. I thought for a second there was a mass going, but realized it was a sign of unity, a symbol of support. I could feel it emanating from them. I wondered who they all were until I gave them closer inspection. They were everyone I had come to know over the past few months. Every Bishop I had been in contact with was there. From the New York Covenant were Soon-Li, John, Tira, and Richard—Tira's brother-in-law and NYPD police lieutenant, Father Murphy, even Jackie, my friend before all this started, was there. The small New Orleans team included Terrance, Blessing, Charity, and Tiffany, who refused to be left behind this time. The Miami contingent included Ima, Adam, Jelena, Janice—Jelena's mom—Krissy, and… My heart stopped for a beat when I saw Marie. I had to resist the urge to run over and embrace her. She smiled at me and blew me a kiss. Whatever doubts I had walked in with fled with the overwhelming turnout.

There were many other faces I didn't recognize who, I assumed, were there to support Hager. Out of the corner of my eye, I saw him nod his thanks.

The council was sitting in a line up on the left of the altar. We made our way into the two high-backed wooden chairs that had been set up for us on the right. As we sat, so did all our supporters.

Althea stood. "I call this hearing of the High Council to order. As we have a celebrity in our midst, I would ask him to honor us by leading the opening prayer."

I leaned closer to Hager. "Celebrity?"

He smiled in answer. Then, to my shock, Father Murphy stood, walked up, faced the crucifix, and bowed. He turned to face the congregation and with a small motion of his hand, everyone was on their feet again.

"In the name of the Father, the Son, and the Holy Spirit." We all followed his lead, making the sign of the cross. Well, the Catholics did. "Heavenly Father, we thank you for your guidance in our lives. You help us to see when we have strayed from our path and, with your eternal patience, help guide us back. We ask for that wisdom again today as we search for the truth. Show us the true hearts of the men that stand before you today, so we may lead them into righteousness, or be guided by their wisdom." There were a few quiet grumbles at that and I snuck a peek at the High Council. There was a mix of deep frowns and open smiles. "We ask this Lord through your name. He who is all religion, She who is all love, They who are one."

"Amen," the congregation responded as one. Everyone sat and my old friend, who apparently was famous among the Bishops, returned to his seat after a quick glance of support.

Ali stood again with a smirk on her face. "Thank you, Father. Your wisdom is always appreciated." She faced us and became all business. "Amram Hager, Christian Bateuler, please stand."

I huffed a little as we did. What is it with the constant up and down in church?

"You have been charged with acting in direct opposition to a High Council mandate. How do you plead?"

Hager opened his mouth to respond as we had discussed ad nauseam over the past day. Apparently, my subconscious had other ideas.

"We have not come to plead in your court."

Hager closed his eyes and sighed deeply.

Ali was taken aback, but Miriam immediately jumped in, her taut bun seeming to pull her head skyward. "Excuse me? You are here because you were ordered here, and you will—"

"Wrong." There was an intake of breath that affected every person there. I stepped forward. "I am here out of courtesy, something you have failed to show us from the moment we met."

"You are out of order." Miriam looked like she was ready to chew iron and spit nails.

I miraculously resisted quoting Al Pacino, though I think I drew blood biting my tongue.

"There are rules which must be followed," she continued.

"That is the problem. You are so focused on the rules you are missing the point."

"And what point is that?"

"What is the decree of the High Council?"

"We are not on trial here."

Hager stepped up next to me. "Maybe you should be."

"How dare you?" Euzebia piped up her slight double chin jiggled with her excitement.

"Answer my question," I pushed.

"We are not here to answer your questions. You are here to answer ours."

Althea spoke up. The neckline of today's dress was no higher than last time despite us being in a church. "To support all Bishops in defending humankind against the Tainted. To guide the Covenants in their righteous endeavors, and to act as the catalyst for communication and partnership."

I nodded. "Thank you. Nowhere in that decree does it give you authoritative or judiciary rights over the Bishops or the Covenants. The rules and traditions that the High Council has initiated in an attempt to guide have, over the decades, become a means of domination. The positions you hold were once given to the oldest, so they could continue to serve as their powers were handed down to their grandchildren. Now they are sought after as titles of power and control."

I glanced back at Althea. "Again, I thank you for indulging me. But I'm afraid you have left out a key part."

She gave me a questioning look. "There isn't any more."

"But there is."

I nodded at Hager, who pulled a book from inside his large jacket pocket. He held it up for everyone to see. "This is an excerpt from a copy of the original book of the High Council. There are five known copies of this book held in each of the great libraries. This one was in the Philadelphia Capital Building."

I caught the eye of Speranza. She nodded, nearly imperceptibly.

Hager flipped to the first page. "We the Covenant of Bishops do hear-by establish a High Council to ensure that as we move forward into the next Millennium we act with a single purpose. As such, the High Council is mandated to support all Bishops in defending humankind against the Tainted. To guide the Covenants in their righteous endeavors, and to act as the catalyst for communication and partnership until such time as technology makes the need redundant, or the focus of the Council becomes contrary to the aforementioned mandates."

Hager closed the book and removed his glasses, staring pointedly at each of the High Council members.

"I submit to you that we have reached such a crossroads."

Miriam looked down her nose at me. "How dare you? This council has become more than just a communication hub."

"That is the problem," I countered.

She continued as though I had not interrupted. "We are here to ensure Bishops stay on the right path. Countless times our kind have succumbed to temptation. Only our guidance and influence has limited the devastation—"

I held up my index and middle fingers. "Two."

Ali's face became a mask of shock. "What do you mean, two?"

I regarded Hager, who pulled a second book from his pocket. He held it out first to the High Council, then to the congregation. "This is the official log of all Dark Bishop activities." He set his glasses on his face and opened the book. He started from the back and flipped nearly all the way back to the front. I silently applauded his dramatic flair. "There have been thirty-seven logged investigations over the hundred and twenty-three years since the High Council was established. Thirty-five were deemed unfounded. The other two were identified and confronted by the members of the *local* Covenant." Hager locked eyes with Miriam. "It appears we are more than capable of policing ourselves."

Shock and rage were barely restrained in Miriam's face. "That is an official document which cannot leave the sanctity of the motherland." The spittle flying from her lips was clearly visible in the light streaming through the stained glass windows. "Where did you get it from?"

"I gave it to them," Speranza said, her ancient head held higher than I had seen since the moment I met her.

Miriam rounded on her. "What right have you? Your role is to guide silently. To break the tie."

"*That* is all of our jobs." The woman had enough energy to power a city.

"It wasn't I who made the rules," Miriam retorted.

"No, but you have perverted our mandate to muscle control. Break the tie? What tie? You have controlled every vote since you recruited these two. And do you think I don't know about the private army you have been organizing? Dark Bishops are not around every corner as you would have us all believe. And the few that do exist are quickly dealt with by their peers as we do now."

"Are you calling me a Dark Bishop?"

"No, Miriam. You are just misguided. But the High Council's time has come to an end. We must disband."

Miriam's face was beet red. Her fists were clenched and trembled at her sides. "Who will guide us, then? This war is coming to a head. You can feel it as much as I do. Who will lead us against the armies of darkness? You?"

"No. I took on the mantle of High Council Mediator at the request of my old mentor. While I am a very capable guide, I am not quali-fied to lead." She turned toward Hager. "We need someone who has proven themselves repeatedly on the battlefield." She walked toward us with purpose. "One who has demonstrated outstanding leadership even without the position of authority." She stopped in front of him, staring into his eyes. "One who unerringly does what is right, despite the consequences."

I held my breath. This is what we needed. Hager would cut through the bullshit and just get things done. He had a moral compass that always pointed true north. But would he accept the role? He gave her a subtle nod, and I practically jumped with excitement.

"One who does not even wish to lead and even now has no idea what is being asked of him."

Did she not have her glasses on? He just nodded.

"The only one of us who has ever killed one of the Tainted."

Wait...Speranza turned her attention to me.

"Oh, shit." It slipped out before I could stop it.

She lowered herself to her knees. "Christian Bateleur. You are the light in the storm, the voice on the mountain, the guardian of the valley. My sword and my life are yours."

I stared at her, not understanding. Trying to find the words to tell her she was making a mistake. It was Hager that should lead. I didn't know what to do. I looked to him for guidance. He nodded again and I felt a wave of relief. Hager would explain it to her. He lowered himself to his knees next to Speranza. I presumed to whisper to her so as not to cause her further embarrassment.

Then he raised his eyes to me. "You *are* the light in the storm, the voice on the mountain, the guardian of the valley. My sword and my life are yours."

Miriam was silent for the first time since I met her. She stormed out. Euzebia was right on her heels. Shakini followed as did Cili, tugging at one of her myriad of ear rings. Half of the congregation left with them, including all the members of the Philadelphia Covenant. David still stood in the pew rubbernecking from his leader to me and back. I could practically feel the conflict radiating from him. When he met my eyes again, I smiled and nodded to him, mouthing the words, *"It's okay."*

He nodded once at me and followed his Covenant out.

Jelena stood and stepped up behind the two kneeling before me. *Good, she will talk some sense into them.* She kneeled behind Hager. "You are the light in the storm, the voice on the mountain, the guardian of the valley. My rifle and my life are yours."

I felt my mouth open, but no words came out. I thought if anyone would remind these people of my lack of experience, it would have been her.

Soon-Li, John, and Tira lined up behind Jelena, kneeled and spoke the words, the only difference being John, who replaced sword with knife. Then Ima, Adam, Krissy and Amanda followed suit, lining up next to Speranza. They had arranged themselves, consciously or not, into a circle with me at the apex, leaving a space for two more at the base.

Father Murphy took Marie's hand. A question etched into her expression. Thanks to the acoustics of the church, their words reached me with no need to engage my boon.

"I'm not a Bishop."

"Neither am I. But I will stand by his side and give my life for him. Somehow, I get the feeling you will do the same."

She smiled, standing up straighter and they came forward. I shook my head. A small movement, but one that she caught. The look she gave was very clear. Stop being stupid. They both dropped to their knees and repeated the devotional.

Without a word, they all joined hands as if they had practiced this hundreds of times. Hager reached up and grabbed my left hand, and Speranza grasped my right. As one, they all repeated the lines again. Power flowed from my hands through the connected group. I could see it pass into each of them as their backs arched and they lifted their gaze up to the rafters. I watched it enter Marie; saw the rapture in her eyes. The love. Then I recognized the same in all of them. The love they felt for me was a reflection of the feelings I had for each of them.

The clouds outside parted and a beam of bright light shone through the stained glass window, illuminating the group. I thought for a second that I should say something, but quickly realized despite their oath, this was not about me.

The rest of the congregation knelt and recited the words as well. The feeling of power flowing through the circle increased, then slowly receded. As the power ebbed, so did the beam of light. I pulled the two hands I still held and brought the small group to their feet. Everyone in the pews rose with them.

They were all staring at me, and the time came for a response. I looked into each of their faces. The ones standing beside me as well as those watching from the pews. "Thank you. All of you. For your support, and your trust."

"Okay, boss man," Jelena said with a smirk. "What do we do now?"

Hager nodded. "Indeed. What is the first order of business?"

"We are going to rescue one of the Tainted."

Chapter Twenty-Seven

"We are at DEFCON 1"

Wargames - 1983

I T WAS OFFICIAL. THE Bishops were torn in half. In eight months I had broken apart an organization that predated the United States. Hager was on the phone with Covenant after Covenant like a campaign manager, drumming up support. We were moving in a fleet of rental cars making our way back to New York. I was in the middle car based on the insistence of both Hager and Ima. I felt like a fool playing at being a VIP. John was driving. Hager sat in the passenger seat up front, reminiscent of when I first started. The one major difference was Marie sat next to me.

I was trying to focus on the video David had sent me before he chose the other side, but was having a hard time. I kept having to rewind and replay it.

"Splendid," Hager said into the phone. "We shall be in touch once we have a game plan." He ended the call. "We have Portsmouth."

"Great," I said with an utter lack of enthusiasm, and rewound the video again.

"It *is* great. Many Covenants take their cues from Portsmouth."

"What does it matter?"

Hager turned in his seat to meet my eyes. "It matters because we cannot fight alone. You cannot fight alone. We have chosen you as our leader. The more Bishops that answer the call, the better chance we have of ending this war."

I made a scoffing sound and put the phone away.

"Don't do that," Hager said, his tone acidic.

"What?"

"Dismiss your destiny so flippantly. Again."

"What destiny? You told me when we first met that there wasn't any prophecy heralding a savior."

John glanced over at him and returned his eyes to the road.

I met John's gaze in the rearview mirror, then Hager's. "What?"

Hager took a deep breath. "I lied."

I stared at him, unable to speak. Several options came to mind, some venomous, some accusatory, others just curious. I couldn't get any of them to stick long enough in my head to make their way to my mouth. I was just staring at the car radio, which was playing with the sound off. The display showed the artist was Bob Dylan, the track, *Knockin' on Heaven's Door*. The song started playing in my mind.

Hager continued. "I am constantly astounded at the level at which you are able to block out reality to suit your internal narrative. Everything you have done from the time you connected with your power has put you squarely on this path. Every decision you have made cemented you as the one that could change the tide of a war that has raged since nearly the dawn of humankind. Reality bends itself to your will. People flock to your silent call. Your enemies cower at your very presence. You are the sword of God, his wrath, and his passion. You could no more escape it than your mother could escape her fate. You have been chosen, Christian."

"Chris." I croaked out of habit.

"No, damn it all! *Christian.*"

I finally looked at him. His eyes were brimming with tears as he looked at me with a feverish glow. "Christian Bateleur. Son of Angela Bateleur. Named after your great grandfather. The man who gave his life to keep his family safe, knowing his lineage would one day end the war. It's time to stop hiding and take on the responsibility handed to you. Pick up the sword."

Hager turned back and stared silently out at the road, scrubbing at his beard.

Marie reached over and slipped her hand into mine, lacing the fingers. It felt good, grounding me, and the turbulent world steadied somewhat. We all spent much of the rest of the car ride in silence, except for Hager's campaigning. He was getting constant reports from other Covenants. He had established a substantial network over his many years. Becoming the volun-told leader of the combined power of all the Covenants may have been a new concept for me, but it appeared Hager had been working up to it for a while. Maybe even decades.

I spent the time doing what I did best, thinking and planning. I thought about asking for a notebook, but I didn't want a record of what I was bouncing around my head. There were two excellent reasons for this: If my thoughts were documented they may fall into the wrong hands. If anyone else read them there was a good chance I would be committed. Luckily, while not someone who coveted leadership as an Ex-Army Ranger, I wasn't a stranger to it either.

A war is won by battles, but those battles had to be strategic. Stepping stones to get to the objective. Step one was always to identify the destination. If one doesn't know where they're going, how do they know what direction to go in? Up till now, the Bishops' aim was to limit the damage at the hands of the Tainted and slow the spread of the infection plaguing the world for which they had no cure. We had a new objective now, a cure. And I wanted to shove it right down Baldemar's throat.

I smiled.

Marie gave a little tug at my hand. "What?"

I put my other hand on top of hers. "Nothing. Just setting my compass."

By the time we pulled up in front of Lucy's building, I had a game plan. I had thought about relaying my requirements to Hager, already firmly placed in my head as second in command. My *number one*, if you will. However, this whole thing was new for everyone. They had taken a leap of faith and put their future in my hands. Hager was right. I needed to show that I wouldn't drop them. Hell, I had already pulled off my first miracle; finding three parking spots in a row in uptown Manhattan.

As we all piled out of our cars, the team encircled me. Several pedestrians eyed us, trying to figure out who we were. Were we making a movie, delivering food to shut-ins, on a scavenger hunt? Others pointedly ignored us like just another pile of dog crap to be avoided.

I looked around at the faces that stared at me, waiting. Some I had known for several months but already considered family. Some I barely knew. I became painfully aware that I was going to send some of them to their deaths at a future point. The weight increased as I realized that they knew it as well. I had been fighting for control for a while, but recently more than ever. Now I had it. Hell, I had too much. These people were descendants of those who guided the world through history from the sidelines. Yesterday, they had been sure of their own path. Now they stood in anticipation of my first decree. They gladly handed me the reins, steadfast in the belief that I could guide them to victory. Talk about being careful what you wish for.

I took a slow breath. "First, before we get deep into it, I want to say thank you." I regarded each for several heartbeats as I continued. "Thank you for coming to Amram's and my aid. Thank you for standing by my side in whatever trials we have had together. Most of all, thank you for putting your faith in me. Based on who we are, that is not done lightly or without great prudence."

Around me were smiles and nodding. Marie blew me a kiss, and John tapped his chest with a fist.

"Now to business. We are at war. Do any of you disagree with that?" I studied their faces for opposition. Not just obvious but subtle call outs they were not aligned with the vision. I found none and nodded. "Good. Because that is the basis for how we will work from now on. War, I understand. I don't like it, but I understand it. The word has gotten muddy over the past few decades being used at the drop of a hat. People say they are going to war when what they really mean is they are standing up to something. They are at war with their competitors, at war against pollution, or corruption, even their neighbor.

"That is not war. War is sacrifice. It is giving yourself to the task of not just defeating your opponent, but eradicating their entire existence. It is being willing to lay down your life for a cause you believe in with every fiber of your being. War is the acknowledgement that you plan to wade through blood and commit acts that, during any other time, would be considered heinously immoral. All with the singular cause of preserving your way of life." I looked around again. "Are you ready to do that *with* me?" They would not be doing this for me, but by my side. Within each of them, I saw resolution, focus, and determination.

"Tira."

She placed her fist over her heart, palm facing in. The image was familiar and caused me to pause. She raised her eyebrows at my hesitation and I continued.

"Wars create casualties. We need a hospital that will not ask all the usual questions. I would like you to oversee its inception. I'm sure we have enough doctors and nurses that we have helped over the years that would support the cause."

She clasped her hands behind her and shifted her weight to one foot.

"You want to know the reason but are afraid to ask." I said.

"Not afraid," she said with a smile. "But, yes. For people who can self-heal, a hospital seems redundant."

"Fair enough. For anyone else who may be hesitant, don't be. I will explain my reasoning when feasible. But I also ask for your patience and trust when circumstances aren't optimal for a debate. To answer your question, the hospital is not for us. It's for those who will fight alongside us. Which brings me to the next order of business. Who among you has the most connections with military or ex-military forces that can be recruited?"

It took a few seconds, but Terrance spoke up, "I guess I do. I will hold off my questions until we are not on the street."

"I appreciate it."

He rubbed the back of his hand across the stubble on his chin. "How many do you need?"

"All of them. Raise me an army."

"You will need a place to house them." Ima spoke up. "If it is okay with you, I will organize barracks. Any location in mind?"

"If we have enough, I would like them stationed all over the world. I don't want to worry about transporting them."

"I will take care of the food and finances," Adam said. Then to each of the Covenant heads, "I will need access to your funds."

"I have the High Covenant financial details," said Althea. "They are—" She cocked her head as she searched for the right word "—substantial. I can help with the finances." She flushed a little as she spoke to Adam.

He nodded.

Jelena spoke up next, "The army will need weapons. I know a guy."

I turned to Speranza. "Would you coordinate all the activities?"

"Finally do something again?" She poked me in the stomach. "You bet your ass."

"Let's try to do this the right way. I don't want to give either the Tainted or the other Bishops a way to shut us down because of missing permits."

She moved to see to it, but I stopped her. Most were busy suggesting ways they could help one team or another. John, Hager, and Marie were standing close by, but I was less concerned with revealing my doubts to them. "One more thing."

She cocked an eyebrow.

"I would like your thoughts about rescuing the Heretic."

She smiled and patted my shoulder. "What is it your savior was fond of saying? Let she who is without sin cast the first stone. If we were all to be judged by our worst acts, I dare say there would be few left to do the stoning. From what I have been told, and seen for myself, you have a strong moral compass. I think you should trust it." She waved a hand at the gathered team. "*We* all do."

She shifted her attention to Hager. "Is it okay if we use the New York Covenant as our base of operations?"

Hager nodded and smiled. "It'll be nice to see it bustling with activity again."

"That it will."

"Should we be concerned that the Tainted know the location?" I asked.

She looked around dramatically. "With this many Bishops in one place? Let 'em come." Speranza stepped into the escalating conversation and immediately took control.

Everyone climbed into the other cars and took off again, except for Father Murphy. "Mind if I tag along?"

Marie strode up and grabbed him by the arm. "You knew Christian when he was a boy, right?"

"That I did."

The two walked towards the building. "Great, start when he was three and go from there."

Hager moved closer and asked, "How many embarrassing stories does Angus know?"

"Too many."

"Oh my."

"We are looking for a safe," I said when we were back in the apartment.

"I will search the living room," Hager volunteered.

"I'll take the dining room," offered Father Murphy.

"Kitchen," John claimed.

"I'll take the bedroom," I said.

Marie gave me a side eye. "*I'll* take the bedroom."

"Okay, then I guess the office."

Surprisingly, it took a while to find. After about twenty minutes, John called out. "Got it. But I think we have a problem."

We all joined him and I admired the setup. "In the kitchen. That's a new one for me," I said. It was behind a good sized pantry. The whole unit slid partway into the wall against which it butted up. Wall and ceiling molding was still in place, but looked strange with the cabinet's adjusted alignment. The safe was mounted flush and was fully biometric.

Hager asked, "Are you sure she was signing 'safe'?"

"Not safe," I replied. "She signed 'money'."

"May I?" Father Murphy held out his hand.

I queued up the video and handed it over. I was peering over his shoulder as he watched, so I didn't see the cuff to the back of my head coming.

"Where did you learn to sign?"

"I saw a brochure once."

"You should have looked at it a little longer. She's not signing 'money', it's Monet."

"That's not a 'y?' Huh. Then what does a 'y' look like?" John offered a suggestion. "Oh, that's just rude. Marie, are you going to let him talk to me like that?"

"I just spent twenty minutes rummaging through things I cannot unsee. So, yeah."

We returned to the dining room and cautiously removed the priceless painting from the wall, making sure there were no alarms. Marie and I cleared a space on the table so Hager and John could place it face down. The back was covered, as was customary. We carefully removed the backing and found nothing. After a few minutes of careful prodding and poking, Hager removed a piece of paper that was wedged in between the frame and the back of the painting. It unfolded to the size of a business card. On it was an address. Above it was the name Anton Mueller.

Chapter Twenty-Eight

"Well, we really didn't expect the first part of the plan to work."

THREE AMIGOS - 1986

THE NEW YORK HEADQUARTERS was bustling. A few people milled around the common room, drinking coffee while excitedly discussing plans. The talking stopped as they watched the five of us enter. I didn't recognize them.

"Where is everyone?" I asked.

The two glanced at each other and one said, "The war room."

My eyes narrowed. I'm the one who named the main conference room when I first joined the Bishops. It had stuck, much to Hager's chagrin. I nodded and walked past them to the spiral stairs through the library. The stairs by the front door were actually closer, but my affinity for books drove me to at least pass them by, even if I couldn't sit and lose myself in their pages. The two men followed. As I climbed past the first floor, I noticed several more strangers with tomes open, debating what they found there. As they noticed us, they stopped dead, then followed as well. I presumed those I picked up along the way were contacting others because by the time I got to the war room, I had a fairly large entourage. I stepped through the door and all activity ceased.

It was crowded with all our supporters from the trial and a great many strangers. One person started clapping. It escalated quickly, and I looked around to see who the fanfare was for. Then I realized they were applauding for me.

"Okay, thank you. I appreciate the sentiment, but we have a lot to do." There was a single seat vacant at the large table. Speranza gestured with her eyes. I rolled mine, stepped over, and sat down. Everyone else took the cue and sat, if they were lucky enough to have a place to do so.

"Any progress?" I asked.

"Tactical," Speranza said.

Terrance nodded at Jelena. She swiped on the tablet in front of her and the large screen came to life. There was a breakdown of multiple paramilitary units, four highlighted in green, two in red, which I assumed meant available or not interested. "Jelena and I put together a list of personal military units for hire, and started making phone calls. We are a little over halfway through the list and have successfully hired four."

I nodded. Each record had a detailed breakdown. "Good. How many total personnel can we count on right now?"

"That depends on what you mean by right now," Jelena answered.

"Wheels up within twenty-four hours."

"Two hundred and sixty-three."

"How many within striking distance of Louisiana?"

She perused the tablet and poked at it. One unit flickered and expanded to fill the screen. The name of the organization was the Creole Mavericks. "Seventy six. It will take a few hours to spin them up. Should I give them the word?"

"Put them on standby."

"Do we have a target?"

Hager handed over the piece of paper with the address. "We will need an analysis of the location for a tactical strike."

Jelena motioned to one of the crowd standing on the side, and a tall guy with cropped blonde hair stepped up and saluted. She gave him the paper and said, "Twenty minutes."

He examined it and gave her a questioning look. Then he apparently decided it was safer not to argue. He saluted again and sprinted off, practically pushing people out of the way.

I met Jelena's eyes. "Friend?"

She smiled. "We've worked together before."

"I can tell."

"Armory?" Speranza spoke up again.

Jelena flipped the display in her hand, and the large monitor shifted. "Two hundred AR-15s, two hundred M4A1s, three hundred Mossberg 500 series shotguns, two thousand rounds for each to start, and six hundred grenades."

"What about non-lethal alternatives?" I asked.

Jelena caught Terrance's eyes. "Told you." Looking back to me, she continued. "Three hundred tasers, two thousand rounds each of rubber bullets and beanbag rounds, along with tear gas, flash bangs and the like."

"Will we have what we need for the rescue?"

Jelena nodded. "The team will come at least partially equipped. I'll verify after the briefing."

Is that what this was? I never saw myself running one, but I couldn't deny what was occurring. I felt like I was supposed to say something, then it dawned on me. "Good job."

Jelena smiled at the compliment, which really unnerved me.

"Life sciences." Speranza's voice pulled me back as my mind became buried in an avalanche of thoughts.

"Leasing properties and obtaining equipment is not as quick of an endeavor," Tira said.

"Usually," Althea commented.

Tira inclined her head and continued. "However, we were able to convert a few struggling clinics. We'll continue to run under their current shingles while folding them under one of our umbrella corporations. With a new influx of money and equipment, we should be up and running shortly."

I opened my mouth to ask a question but was cut off.

"Yes, I have one set up near the operation. I will make sure we have enough supplies on hand to deal with any issues. I have also hired field medics to accompany us."

"Good idea," was all I could think to say.

"Do we get hazard pay?" I hadn't even realized Charity, who I hadn't noticed was in the room.

"What do you care? You're not going," John said.

"The hell I'm not," she retorted.

"You don't have any military training."

"I'm not going as a soldier. I'm going as a medic."

"Since when are you a medic?"

"You've been gone a long time, big brother. I've been an EMT with the local volunteer fire department for a few years now."

John asked his father, "aren't you going to talk some sense into her?"

"I can talk to a gator all day, but she'll still eat the duck."

John looked at me. I held my hands up. "I'm not touching that with a ten meter cattle prod."

He shook his head, and Charity's smile spoke volumes.

"Technology." Speranza tried to get us back on track.

Soon-Li stood. "I have personnel trackers coming in for all the troops. And we are planning to launch that satellite you wanted."

"Wait, really?"

"It was the only reliable and secure way to monitor a few thousand troops across the globe."

"A few thousand?"

Soon-Li smirked. "We figured you were just getting started."

I took in all the faces. They were not nervous or hesitant. They were excited and it was infectious. "Yeah, I guess I am."

My office in the New York Covenant was sparse, to say the least. Hager had one set up for me before I'd left the year before. It felt like a lifetime ago. I had a desk with nothing on it but a lamp and a plant. Behind me was an empty credenza flanked by two empty bookcases. Two chairs sat facing the desk and a small round table with three chairs stood off to one side. It reminded me of a Whoville house after the Grinch had rolled through.

However, there was no dust anywhere and it smelled of furniture polish. Someone must have anticipated the need. I couldn't imagine one of the Bishops dusting. Though they have had to play many roles in the past, we had too much going on to be worried about such a thing.

As if in answer, someone knocked. I made a face and called out, "Come."

A young man with short buzzed hair stepped in. He closed the door behind him as though the gesture was ceremonial. Then he faced me and saluted.

"There's no need for that," I said.

"Very good, sir. I am Jeremy Stark, and I have been assigned to you, sir."

"You can drop all of that sir crap as well."

"Understood, sir."

I sighed. "What do you mean, assigned?"

"In other circumstances, I would be your Yeoman."

I considered that a moment. "Do you like Star Trek?"

"No, sir. I was referring to the Navy, sir."

I grunted. "Were you in the Navy?"

"Yes, sir. Six years."

I nodded. "So, Jeremy, is there something I can do for you?"

"Sir?"

"You knocked. I presumed there was a point behind it besides this thrilling conversation."

"Yes sir, I brought dinner."

"I will eat with everyone else."

"Permission to speak freely, sir."

"Jeremy, this is not the Navy. You can speak your mind whenever you want."

"Eating with the men is a bad idea."

"How so? It shows them I don't set myself apart from them. I am no different."

"That's just it."

"Get to the point, Jeremy."

"You are different. You are a leader. There needs to be a sense of awe about you."

"Good leaders don't need that."

"Very good, sir. There is another reason you shouldn't eat with the troops."

I sighed, thinking that maybe I should adopt a more militaristic atmosphere for my new army. "And what is that?"

"Eating is a time for them to relax. To let their guard down and joke around with each other. Maybe even to complain about their commanding officer. If you are there, they can't be themselves."

I thought about that for a moment. Nodding finally, I motioned towards the lonely table with three chairs. "How about over there?"

Jeremy smiled. "Very good, sir." He removed a white cloth from his jacket and dusted both chairs, then the table. Stepping out of the office, he returned a second later, wheeling a small cart. Silently going to work, he put down a tablecloth and set it for two, smiling the whole time.

"Will you be joining me?"

"No. Miss Valentina will."

I was about to ask why he went through that entire argument when he could have just said that. Then I realized. "This was a test."

His smile got wider. "Multiple tests, actually. All of which you passed with flying colors."

"Are you not really my Yeoman?"

"No, I am. I just like to know what kind of person I'm working for."

Marie breezed in, saw Jeremy, and stopped just inside the door.

He didn't rush, knowing we were both waiting for him to finish. He examined the glasses and silverware for spots and arranged the place settings meticulously. Then he opened the wine bottle he had chosen without asking my opinion. Jeremy poured two glasses no more than an eighth full at a proportionate level that might normally have required a laser level to attain.

Placing the bottle back on the table, he nodded to himself. Then he addressed me. "Will there be anything else, sir?"

"Yes, don't call me sir."

Jeremy gave a slight nod. "Very good, sir." He left smiling.

Marie watched him leave, clearly amused, then stepped up and kissed me.

"You had to wait for him to leave to do that?"

"You are the boss now. Need to maintain an air of majesty."

I gave a derisive snort. "I think there is enough false eminence to go around." Marie punched me in the stomach, eliciting a grunt. Grabbing my stomach, I managed to say, "You've been hanging around Jelena too much."

"I think she's on to something. It feels like the proper response to you being stupid."

"How am I being stupid?"

"Have you ever heard the phrase, fake it till you make it?"

"That's what I'm doing."

"No, you're not, because you don't have to fake it. You are a legitimate superhero with powers unlike anyone has seen in centuries, even among the Bishops. You are a natural born leader with a near genius IQ, an ex-Army Ranger and a moral compass that makes any normal person look like Genghis Khan. And you have an incredible girl friend that loves you. Tony Stark would be envious. So stop wallowing in self doubt and just do what you know is right."

I stared at her for several moments, and apparently she read something in my expression.

Her eyebrows knitted together and she said, "What?"

I smiled. "You said you loved me."

Her eyes went wide for a second. Then she sat down and took a sip of wine.

"You're not going to admit it, are you?"

"How about you sit down and eat, or do I need to punch you again?"

"Once was enough."

She eyed me, and I saw she caught the double meaning.

"Whadaya got?" I strode into the war room again thirty minutes after Jelena had sent her man scampering.

"A less subtle Fort Knox," she answered, pointing at the screen. It showed an infrared satellite image of the area. There was one huge main house. Towards the back was a large garage and a building off to the left. "This place is in the middle of nowhere and is heavily guarded. They have about a hundred and fifty troops on location. Half are housed here—" She pointed to the side building "—While the rest are patrolling the grounds."

John walked in, took one look at the map and said, "Oh shit."

Jelena and I stared at him.

"I thought that address sounded familiar."

"Care to elaborate?" I asked.

"My father was kept there the last time he was taken."

"What is he related to Liam Neeson?"

"You are fucking hilarious. Did anyone ever tell you that?" Terrance walked in with most of the rest of the devoted.

"Several, usually with the same tone of voice," Jelena replied.

"This place, huh?" Terrance crossed his arms. "Did you tell them about the underground bunker?"

"Not yet."

I stared at both men. "Say that again?"

Terrance moved closer to the screen, pointing midway between the main house and the garage. "There is a converted bunker right here. It's accessible from both. They used it for human trafficking about ten years ago. It's where she kept me and several others until John stepped in." There was a hint of pride in the gruff man's voice.

"She?" I asked.

Terrance stared out into nothing. John said, "Another time."

I did my best to push my curiosity to the back of my mind and focus on the present. "So, there is a possibility that more guards are in there, heat signatures hidden by the ground."

Terrance moved back. "I would say it's a good bet."

"Do you think it's where they are keeping Lucy?"

"More likely it's a trap knowing your history," Ima pointed out.

Jelena nodded. "That's what I would do. Fill the place with explosives, let you 'sneak' in and boom. If the explosion doesn't kill you, being trapped under all of that rubble will, eventually."

It was a little too soon after the last attempt. I swallowed hard. Jelena realized after a second. She grimaced and looked sheepishly at me. It was as close to an apology from her as I'd experienced.

Marie chewed on the inside of her cheek. "I don't know. For that to be the case, they would have to expect that you would escape the explosion. They would have to surmise that the Heretic would communicate her location to you and that you would head straight for the bunker. Seems a little far-fetched."

Adam crossed his arms. "More than immortal, evil creatures that can corrupt the minds of humans?"

Marie considered that. "Funny how quickly the fantastic becomes commonplace."

I took a breath and pushed on. "So, covert extraction is out. We are going to have to clear the place room by room before we go near the bunker. And even then, we need to be cautious. They could have moved to a completely different location and are just watching through cameras like they were in the fight room."

Jelena swiveled in her chair. "There are cameras all over the place, but it's impossible to tell where people are monitoring them from. Experience has shown the tainted consider their hired help expendable."

Apparently, she hadn't gotten over Baldemar literally dropping a bomb on her team at the end of an op.

Hager sighed. "So, they will know we are coming long before we get in range to do anything."

Ima tapped her lip with a finger. "Maybe not. What if we drop in from above?"

Jelena shook her head. "There are too many troops to not see parachutes."

I glanced at Adam, and a smile split my face.

He caught my reaction and appeared confused, which quickly shifted to horror. "No."

"I have an idea," I said.

Adam had his head in his hand. "This is a stupid plan."

John cracked a smile. "Here we go."

Chapter Twenty-Nine

"Give me that letter!"

HARRY POTTER AND THE SORCERER'S STONE - 2001

S INCE MARIE WAS HERE, my new room was a double. I still remembered Hager's reaction when I had requested one soon after I arrived. *Sure, right after you get married and have children.* Was this a subliminal message?

Marie was already there with me. She was unpacking the small bag she'd brought with her from Miami.

"How does it feel to be home?" I asked.

She made a face. I didn't realize how much I had missed her myriad of expressions until that moment. "I was born in Brooklyn."

"Yeah, but I meant New York."

"I live in Miami."

"Forget it," I smiled. "Where does everyone think you are?"

"I took some personal leave for a family emergency."

"Speaking of family, don't your parents still live here?"

"Yup."

"Do they know you're here?"

"Nope."

"Why not? Maybe we can visit."

"I brought you a present."

I acknowledged the deliberate subject change. "Okay, is it something for me that you will wear?"

"How do you get anything done with that one-track mind of yours?" She handed over a wooden box of a size that made me think of cigars.

"Is this for celebrating the win?"

"Just open it already."

I lifted the lid. Inside was a stack of envelopes. Some were opened, others still sealed. I recognized the flowing script immediately, the yellowing of the old paper, the hint of my mother's perfume as it clung to the letters.

Around twenty years ago, my mother had walked into battle knowing she would probably die. Before she did, she had left a stack of letters with Hager with the instruction to give them to me when I asked. The initial one was in a box similar to this, which had been waiting in her locker for me. She presumed I would find it after my first communion, which should have been shortly after she passed. This, shall we say, did not go as planned and I finally received them last year just before we went out to foil Baldemar's plans.

There was one for every year up to my eighteenth birthday, along with a few extra for special occasions, like each sacrament I was to receive. I hadn't read all of them because if I did, there would be no more letters to anticipate. My mother's voice would finally be silenced, her wisdom complete. I wasn't sure what I was waiting for, but presumed I would know it when it arrived. I shuffled through them quietly until I found the one I was searching for. It was the only letter not addressed to me.

"Are you going to read one? I can run down to the kitchen if you want to be alone."

This was something I normally did in solitude. Often I would tear up. I took a deep breath, picked up two sealed letters and held one out to Marie. "I think we both will."

She looked at the envelope then up at me. She licked her lips as though her mouth had suddenly gone dry. "Are you sure?"

I nodded and swallowed hard in order to allow myself to speak. "It's addressed to you, after all."

Her eyes sparkled with unshed tears. She reached out and carefully took the envelope. Across it, written with my mother's flowing script, were two words. *For Her.*

Marie sat on the bed and I took the desk. We both opened our
letters.

Dear Christian,

*Each of these letters is harder than the last. I think about
all the milestones I will not be there for and my heart breaks
a little more. It is not my intention to burden you with this,
but you are sixteen now and I want you to know that I
didn't make this decision lightly. I have always known what
my destiny was, since I was a little girl. I couldn't see the
details, just the highlights. Kind of like the trailers we love
to watch for the new movies coming out. It was one of my
gifts. Now, though, as the hour approaches, I am no longer
as sure as I once was.*

*This was my decision. The story may get altered in the
coming years, or be completely buried. I feel a shift in the way
the High Council is managing itself. They are implementing
more and more self perpetuating regulations. Since Speranza
ascended to the head position, as little more than a tie breaker,
her control is slipping. Maybe I am just being paranoid, but
be wary. Remember, rules are there to make things clearer.
They are guides that help us stay on the path. They can also be
manipulated and few stand up to the scrutiny of circumstance.*

*I don't mean to turn this into a lesson. But as I get closer
to my final days, I worry I haven't prepared you enough for
what is coming. Luckily, Mr. Hager and Father Murphy will
be there for you, two of the best guides anyone could hope for.
With their help, you will be more than ready for what is to
come. I'm sorry for not being there for you. I'm sorry I could
not guide you and watch over you myself. But in order for
humanity to have its best chance, I need to make this sacrifice.*

*Surround yourself with those you feel are worthy of your
trust. Steel yourself with your faith and do what you know in
your heart is right. But be cautious not to confuse righteousness with hubris. History is filled with people who believed the*

*monstrous things they did were for a greater purpose. Make
sure you are not one of them.*
  Love always
  Mom

I wiped at a few tears that had blurred my vision. I glanced over at
Marie, expecting to see the same. Or rather hoping. I was comfortable
with my own emotions, though didn't know if there was a strong
emotional pull for someone who was not her son. What I saw was
not what I was expecting. Marie had gone pale. The shock on her
face was unmistakable. I wanted to ask what was causing so much
distress, but I didn't want to interrupt her. I watched her eyes, but
they didn't appear to be scanning the text. Her head moved, but not
in a way consistent with reading. It looked more like she was shaking
her head no.

"Marie?"

She regarded me, looking even more grave.

"What is it?"

She opened her mouth but said nothing. Then she shook her head
more vigorously. Her hand dropped to her lap, which drew my eyes
to the letter.

"What does it say? Can I see it?"

She snatched the letter to her chest, her expression turning horrified.

"What is going on?"

She practically jumped up and headed for the exit. I followed.

"Marie."

She stopped at the door and put a hand out, halting me. She finally
looked me in the eye. "I need to think. I'm going to find somewhere
else to sleep tonight."

"But—"

"Chris, please."

I nodded and she disappeared out the door, closing it behind her.
I stared at it, as though answers might be found in the wood grain.
I turned as a splash of white on the bed caught my eye. The empty
envelope, still addressed *For Her.*

Chapter Thirty

"Run, Forest! Run!"

FOREST GUMP - 1994

I RAN ANOTHER LOOP around the regulation sized track in the hidden complex several stories below the house. Each lap I moved faster, adding more power each time. My speed didn't even approach the level of a blur, but I was able to maintain it for a sustained period. It was a technique that Tira had taught me before I left. It was a combination of normal human running with a small flow of supernatural energy feeding the muscles. She could sustain speeds that would probably earn her a ticket on most throughways, while I would have had trouble catching a slow cheetah.

Sweat flowed freely, soaking my shirt and dripping from my hair into my eyes, causing them to sting. I wiped at it and dug in, picking up speed. As I came around where the doors led to the showers, I noticed Hager sitting by the small fountain of holy water off to the side. I slowed to a stop, putting my hands on my knees, gulping air like a drowning victim.

I could have allowed more power flow into me to hasten the recovery process, but I wanted to feel the strain. Let it distract me from whatever had just happened. I picked up the towel and water bottle I had dropped near the track and threaded my way around the few pews, that made up the small reflection area, and plopped down next to Hager.

"Good workout?"

"I guess."

"I'm not a fan of that response. It has become the obnoxious form of no or a copout when you feel obligated to say yes."

"Yes, the workout was fine, but it didn't help. Happy?"

"Actually, yes."

"Did you come down here just to bust my chops, or did you have other information?"

"Why do you assume I came down for you?"

"If you really intended to pray, you would have done so in the temple."

"Oh good. Your head is not fully implanted in your nether regions. I was hoping for an intelligent conversation."

"Shoot."

"What is troubling you?"

I mopped sweat from my face and neck. "What makes you think something is?"

"The time to leave is quickly approaching. Can we dispense with the denials?"

I peered over at him.

"I am here for you, my boy. How can I help?"

I thought about the advice in my mother's letter and sighed, returning my gaze to the towel. "Fine. I gave Marie the letter."

"Which letter?"

I stared at him. "*The* letter. From my mother."

Hager had been in possession of the letters for twenty years. While he didn't know the contents, I was sure he had memorized the envelopes. It took him another second before his eyes went wide. "I see."

"Yeah."

"I presume she did not respond well to its implication."

"That part was fine. After reading it, she looked as though she had seen a ghost and bolted."

Hager was silent for a few seconds. "Any indication of why?"

"No."

"Do you know what the letter said?"

"I never read it. It wasn't addressed to me."

Hager nodded.

I wrung my hands. "I need to know. What freaked her out like that?"

"Have I ever asked you what was in your letters?"

"No, but—this is different."

"Is it?"

Frustrated, I took a swig of water.

Hager pushed on. "Do you trust Marie?"

"Of course."

"Do you love her?"

I met his eyes. "I do."

"Then let the rest go for now. She will talk to you in her own time."

"What if she doesn't? What if whatever was in the letter made her change her mind?"

"Would your mother jeopardize such an important relationship?"

"I guess not."

Hager grimaced.

I couldn't help but smile. "No."

"And do you think that after everything she has been through with you, that it could shake her enough to walk away?"

I thought about that for a few moments. "No."

Hager placed a hand on my shoulder. "Control that which you have power to influence. Have faith that the rest will sort itself out."

I nodded. "Thanks."

"Now stop your brooding. You need a shower before we implement this stupid plan of yours."

Chapter Thirty-One

"I have a plan: attack!."

THE AVENGERS - 2012

"YOU REALIZE HOW MASSIVELY crazy this is?" Adam yelled over the engine. The deafening sound from the open belly of a prop cargo plane was like riding the back of a thirty-foot bumble bee. We wore our coms. However, the engine noise mixed with the wind drowned out much of our conversation.

We sat on thick plastic seats bolted to the fuselage of the C23A Sherpa we'd chartered. Each had a seat belt (for all they would do in a crash, but we were wearing them, anyway.) The inside looked like a miniature version of a commercial plane with all the other seats ripped out. The noise level had even been tolerable, until our spotter opened the small door on the side. Now she held onto the two inch pipe that surrounded it, her head sticking out into the night as we approached our target.

I smiled at him. "No more than my other plans."

"We are going to jump out of a plane without a parachute."

"What are you talking about?" I reached across and turned him so I could see his back. "Your chute is right there."

He eyed me. "Yeah, but we won't be using them."

We both were back in our wingsuits, our breathing units connected to the onboard system.

"You can choose not to jump. I will take care of this."

"Hell, no. You jump, I jump." Adam pantomimed along with the words. I gave him a thumbs up.

He was right. What we were attempting had never been tried before. Well, Gary Connery jumped out of a helicopter twenty-four hundred feet in the air and landed on a massive strip filled with cardboard boxes. We were at twenty-five thousand feet, which was just under the service ceiling for this plane. There wouldn't be any boxes and our target was substantially smaller. But hey, we had superpowers. Back in Miami, we'd evaded police entanglement by performing a controlled drop off of a tenth-floor balcony, which I hadn't even heard of prior to the attempt. I was somewhat successful. That is to say, I succeeded in not dying. The concept was to increase drag during a fall so as to create a supernatural parachute of sorts. My description differed somewhat from Adam's because his directly defied the laws of gravity. Since I don't have a big red 'S' on my chest, I found a better way for my fact based brain to accept it.

Despite Adam jump-shaming me, I came to find out that this was not a typical talent. He had feigned ignorance since he was trained by his mother, who also had the gift to a much lesser degree. No one else besides he and I were confident enough to attempt an incursion of this magnitude. As it was, Adam was only semi-confident. I had been practicing the controlled descent for the past few months and gotten it down to a science, more or less.

Our spotter pulled her head in and triggered the ramp which slid up to expose the whole rear of the plane to open air.

"One minute," she yelled, holding up a finger.

We both unbuckled our seatbelts and moved towards the back door. Running through our final checks, we zipped up the sleeves of our wingsuits. The problem with this plan was that we couldn't bring any gear. A wingsuit was about aerodynamics and we would need as much advantage as possible. We both had concerns but had to shed them and don a cowl of confidence. Doubt could corrupt the delicate balance of our faith. My mind was also stuck on my last conversation with Marie. I triple checked my jumper's watch trying to refocus on the task at hand. Our spotter raised an open hand indicating fifteen seconds until we were over the jump point. The next seconds seemed to take forever. My brain tried desperately to insert any distraction from what I was going to do. Faces started appearing in my thoughts; Marie, my mother, Hager, Jackie, Father Murphy, then the litany of faces that had hooked their destiny with mine. All of them had put their faith in me, believed in me. They were putting their lives in my hands. I desperately wiped each image away as it appeared, clearing my thoughts. Then a single face appeared and I latched onto it. Lucy. My objective. It focused me like an arrow seeking its target.

The spotter closed her fist and we jumped.

It is difficult to explain the feeling of skydiving to someone who has never done it. I could say it's like flying, but I'm pretty sure no one else has that frame of reference. That feeling one gets from a long drop on a roller coaster or jumping from any kind of height only lasts for a few seconds. Once the body equalizes, we were just rocketing through open air. Nothing tethering us, nothing forcing us to be this or that, not even gravity. The absolute freedom is beyond exhilarating. After the euphoria passed, I refocused.

My watch showed twenty-four thousand, six-hundred and sixty feet. I searched the sky and found Adam. "You reading me?"

"Five by five."

I reached up to switch on the heads up display of my goggles. It took a second to orientate, then a digital map of the terrain below us appeared.

"Looks like we drifted a few degrees north of our target," Adam said.

"Confirmed." We shifted our weight and realigned ourselves to the digital glide path. "Back on target."

"ETA to max flare: ten minutes, seven seconds."

"Roger."

The flying squirrel suits made maneuvering far easier, but if we were not careful, we could veer well off course with minimal movement. I did my best to stay in mid swan dive position.

I keyed my long distance radio via the switch on my glove. "Havoc, this is Phoenix One."

"Go, Phoenix One."

"We have passed Wolfman."

"Roger that."

"I can't believe Hager agreed to those mission goals." Adam yelled over the short range coms. It wasn't necessary, but you try talking in a normal voice in the middle of a hurricane.

"I didn't give him enough time to come up with another set. If you are going to do something, you might as well have fun. Especially if it may get you killed." My attempt at modulating my volume was equally unsuccessful.

Adam checked his watch. "Nine minutes, thirty seconds."

The time was digitally counting down on my heads up display, but it was so easy to lose track of time he liked to keep the habit. At this height, the lights across Louisiana resembled a firefly town hall. Large clusters shining brighter than any single one could, while individual lights off on their own spoke of cozy secluded spots where maybe lovers sat by a fire, or a family watching TV. Solitary, but not lonely. We were aimed for a small, unusually bright set. Anton's compound. The green glide path had us aimed right for it.

"Thirty seconds."

See what I mean about losing track of time? We were not directly over our target yet, but we were coming in fast— about eighty miles an hour. As we hurtled towards the central building, it rapidly grew in size. The moon was on the opposite horizon. While the compound was lit up on the ground, the rooftop was in virtual darkness to save the night vision of the sentries on duty.

Adam started calling out the last seconds, "Ten."

I reached out and dipped into my well of power. I felt its warm glow, like the sun on my skin.

"Nine."

Enhancing my senses, I could see each of the guards at ground level as well as the two on the roof and marked them in my mind.

"Eight."

The wind across my face became like needles in my enhanced state. I backed off, having mentally mapped the compound already.

"Seven."

Our glide path was perfect. We skimmed about three hundred feet over the trees. Then a gust of wind blew in from the east, throwing us off track.

"Shit! Six."

Alarm bells went off in our coms. The digital glidepath before my eyes changed to red and two words started flashing above it. *OFF COURSE. OFF COURSE.*

"Five." Adam's voice carried the stress we were both feeling. I twisted by body back toward the target and saw him doing the same. We were like two fighter jets in formation.

"Four."

We turned back towards the building in a maddeningly slow arc. I wanted to force the turn more, but doing so would stall what little lift I had. If that happened, I would end up painting the side of the wall with my face.

"Three." Adam spoke through clenched teeth.

"Two." The panic in his voice made me glance over. He was still too far off course. There was no way he was going to make it.

Chapter Thirty-Two

"You are a toy!"

Toy Story - 1995

INSTINCT KICKED IN. POWER radiated down my arms to my back. I felt the air gliding across it, an icy river flowing around me. I increased its surface area and turned to my wingman.

"One." The finality in Adam's voice was heartbreaking. His head darted about, desperate to find me or something to save us. But I was already above him. I grabbed him by the collar and redirected us towards the rooftop, my wings of faith acting like a hang-glider.

Now back on target I shouted, "Flair."

Adam and I both arched our backs to catch the most air. We slowed dramatically. With my halo wings, I rode the wind up a few feet. Then I aimed Adam at one of the guards and let him go.

I was too busy to see the results as I tilted down into a dive and went streaking for his partner. I hit him high in the chest as he was reacting to the sound of Adam's attack. He didn't even have time to be surprised. A few seconds later, they were both zip-tied. I keyed the long range mic to my coms.

"Havoc, this is Phoenix One. We have passed Slider."

"Good copy, Phoenix."

I finished removing my wingsuit and helmet. We wore black underneath, which would help us blend into the shadows but also screamed intruder. We didn't intend to leave anyone conscious in our wake, so wasn't concerned.

Adam was already done. He strode over to me.

"What the hell was that?"

I knew what he was asking, but played dumb while I finished extracting myself.

He grabbed my arm. "You were flying."

"That wasn't flying. It was falling with style."

"Will you cut that shit out? You maneuvered over me and lifted us both. It's impossible."

I crumpled up my suit and threw it to one corner of the rooftop, then turned on him.

"Adam, we do the impossible every day. How is it you keep adhering to the limits other people have invented? You are tethered but cannot see the ropes that constrain you."

I wasn't sure where the little speech came from and I felt myself flush. "Sorry for sounding preachy." I stepped over to the hatch leading down into the house and opened it. "Shall we?"

Adam took another second to come back to himself, then pulled down the full face mask attached to his beanie. He stepped up and did a handstand on the ridge, his hands in the position of a chin up. Then he slowly lowered himself down so only his head protruded into the room below.

"Showoff," I whispered.

"Clear."

He lowered himself the rest of the way, slowly and deliberately.

Smiling to myself, I pulled down my face mask and followed him into the house without the extra dramatic flair. I used the ladder to descend into a narrow hallway next to equally tight stairs continuing down. The plans that Soon-Li had found online showed a central hallway with rooms on either side. The grandeur of this type of building existed on the outside. Inside it was a maze of rooms; small only by comparison to the huge exterior with its twenty-eight Roman columns supporting the wrap-around porch. The exception was the attic, where we now stood.

At the time it was built, this was the servants' quarters. Individual rooms were not deemed necessary. Therefore, half of the hallway was dedicated to a separate dining area. The two large, open areas were where they all slept and went about their daily lives during the few hours when they weren't catering to the robber barons they worked for.

I heard movement and talking from the adjoining areas. Motioning for Adam to take the right side, I went left and poked my head through the doorway. Beds lined multiple walls while the dormer windows created little alcoves made for sitting, changing, or storage. Two guards sat at a small central table.

"I have two on my side, playing cards," I whispered into the coms.

"Same here, but mine are sleeping."

"Of course. Take care of yours first."

"Already done, just waiting on you."

"Okay, I see how it is."

I took a deep breath and blurred into the room. Sliding across the table feet first, I kicked the guard on the far side in the face while I grabbed the other's head as I sailed past and slammed it into the table.

"Clear." I keyed my long range radio. "Havoc, this is Phoenix One. We have passed Ice." I zip-tied and gagged them.

"Roger, Phoenix One, confirming Ice."

Adam appeared in the doorway and was about to say something until he noticed the arsenal in one alcove.

"Why keep the ammo up here?" Adam asked.

"I think this is just for the roof. It's the most defensible area with the longest line of sight. Five or six people with the right equipment could hold back a small army."

I could see the realization of what we could have walked into reflected in his eyes. "I guess your plan wasn't so stupid."

"Subject to change without notice. John's intel said there was a hidden entrance to the bunker through the basement. Let's go."

"About that. I found something else not on the plans."

I followed him to the adjoining area, which was set up almost identically. The only difference was that, in the place the west side held ammo, the east sported a very narrow circular stairway.

Adam pointed. "Servants' stairs. Probably leads to the kitchen. Can't have the help using the main stairway."

I smiled. "Shall we use them for a nobler purpose?"

"I think it's only fitting."

We equipped ourselves with some sidearms just in case, but left the assault rifles where they were. If we were going to do this quietly, we needed our hands free.

With me leading the way, we crept down the stairs. They moaned at our every step. I kept my senses extended, but didn't catch any acknowledgement of our presence. My shoulders nearly scraped both sides of the narrow passage at the same time. I couldn't see how someone was supposed to carry a tray of food through here as well.

One level down was a door that looked fancier than I would have expected. Until I realized it was for the benefit of those on the other side. I could hear movement in rooms to the left and right.

"I don't suppose we can use your slip technique to check each room," I whispered, barely audible.

"I can make us fade into the background in public places. No matter what I do, a home intruder will be noticed."

"I'm not a fan of the epithet, but I get the point."

"What would you call us?"

I took him in, dressed in black from head to toe.

"I said I wasn't a fan, not that it wasn't accurate. You go right, I take left."

He nodded. I listened for another second to make sure no one had wandered into the hall, then crept out. My estimates placed us in about the middle of the second floor and I was not far off. There were six bedrooms on this floor. The master, where I expected Anton to be, was where I was headed.

The first door I encountered was an unoccupied bathroom of all marble with a claw-foot bath. There was also a couch, which confused me. Who the hell wanted to lounge out in the bathroom? Then again, I'd had some hangovers where a couch to lie on in between bouts bent over may not have been a bad thing. Shaking my head, I moved along.

The next room was occupied in the most extreme way possible. One man and two women engaged in sensual acts. Well, they would have been sensual if all participants were fully willing. The women gave off an air of resigned ambivalence, much as I might give to mopping the floor or taking out the garbage. One woman was facing me, alarm on her face at my entrance. I placed a finger to my lips. She didn't react, which I believed was more out of fear and confusion. It was as though she was trying to decide if her situation had improved or worsened.

I grabbed the man by the throat from his kneeling position on the bed and hauled him across the room, pinning him on the wall near the ceiling. He let out a squeak, restricted by my increasing the pressure on his trachea. He was skinny and gangly with splotches of hair in strange places except on top of his head. This was thin and combed over in an attempt to cover the bald areas, but currently fell over his bulbous nose. Pulling my knife, I placed the blade against the part I thought would capture his attention the quickest. Another squeak tried to escape. I didn't need enhanced strength to hold him in place, so I engaged my heightened senses to see if anyone had heard the scuffle. I hadn't raised any alarms, but my more acute vision saw the bruises and cuts on the two women who were now huddling together.

I spoke through my gritted teeth.

"A woman was brought in here recently. She would have been heavily guarded. You couldn't have missed her. I'm not in the mood to be lied to, so answer carefully. Your favorite toy depends on your honesty." I increased the pressure on the knife and I saw a tear slide down his cheek. As I allowed some air back into his throat, he gasped, trying to catch his breath.

"The bunker," he croaked.

"Are you lying to me?" More pressure on his genitals.

His eyes went wide and he tried to shake his head. "No."

"Is it a trap?"

He hesitated. It clearly wasn't a question he was expecting.

My knife drew blood and I thought his eyes would bug out.

"Yes," he squeaked out.

I let him down. "Put on some pants. We're going to have a little talk." Adam stepped into the room. "All good here?"

I nodded. "Other than having to sanitize my knife, yeah. I may have found an excellent source of information."

"What makes you think he'll be useful?"

"He doesn't have the build or temperament for a hardened soldier. Plus his accommodations and fringe benefits puts him in strategy. Can you call it in and take care of the ladies while Sméagol and I have a talk?"

I caught Adam nodding in my periphery. "Havoc, this is Phoenix Two. We have passed Jester and Merlin." He gathered up the women who were murmuring their thanks while trying to find clothes. He looked back as they were exiting. "Just don't ask him what he's got in his pockets."

Chapter Thirty-Three

"It's a Trap!"

STAR WARS EPISODE VI-
RETURN OF THE JEDI -1983

T HE REST OF THE house was eerily empty. There were guards for sure, but not enough for a house of this size. Gollum had informed us that the main contingent was out on another mission which, of course, was the trap. It also took very little coaxing to get him to reveal the secret entrance to the underground bunker through one of the three wine cellars.

"Are we really doing this?" Adam asked.

"Do you see an alternative?"

"Someone has pointed out a hornet's nest, and you are just going to stick your hand in there, anyway."

"There's someone trapped in that nest getting stung over and over. Plus, that's what they make bee suits for."

"Great, do you have a couple of those?"

"Relax," I assured him. "We secured the remaining guards in separate rooms. We know what their plan is and we've taken steps to foil them."

"Foil? Do they all have waxed mustaches they twirl while anticipating our demise?"

"They might, rabbit, they might."

Adam perused the enormous wine rack. "What bottle did he say to pull?"

"The only one with a twist cap."

"Of course. Can't be wasting good wine as a doorknob. I still think we should have taken him with us."

"No way. He may have been chicken-shit and had a creep factor of ninety-seven but he was too smart. The last thing I wanted was another variable walking around. Didn't you like the position I left him in?"

"Yes. Hannibal Lecter would be very proud."

He pulled on the requisite bottle, and the wine rack pivoted on hinges away from the wall. The tunnel beyond was made from poured concrete. LED lighting lined the upper walls. I could feel the dampness beyond. The humidity was controlled in the cellar, and possibly the bunker beyond, but the passage between was not.

"Aw crap," I said.

Adam looked around. "What?"

"I was hoping there would be a torch."

"There is something seriously wrong with you."

"Are you just realizing that?"

"Can we go?" Adam pushed past me, taking the lead.

"Apparently."

We walked about forty-feet on a slight downward slope. The dank air and descending path reminded me of my recent experience of being buried alive. I wasn't claustrophobic, but the walls appeared closer than when we'd entered. The door at the other end had no need for secrecy. It had instead a biometric lock attached to a hatch that would be more at home in a submarine.

Adam placed a hand on it. "This was not what John described. Can you get through that?"

I scrunched up my face in a derisive expression.

"Of course."

I approached it with trepidation. This was indeed much tougher. Luckily, I had the opportunity to visit a modern sub during my time in the army. The key to this entrance may have been digital, but the lock itself was still mechanical. I put my hands on the door and pushed my senses into it. An image formed in my mind of the array of locking mechanisms within. Like those on a submarine, this one had eight points of contact with the frame via three inch diameter steel rods. They could be extended or retracted manually with a central wheel on the inside once the locks on each rod were disengaged—simultaneously.

I found each pin holding the rods in place, fixed them in my mind, and pushed. An audible click emitted from the door. Now came the hard part. While still holding the pins open, I had to find the wheel and spin it. It was like patting your head and rubbing your stomach at the same time. When I figured out the motion needed to twist the wheel, the pins would slip back into place.

I nearly had it when Adam's question broke my concentration. "Anything I can do to help?"

"Yes, stop talking."

He crossed his arms and frowned. "Should I cut down our informant?"

I refocused on the task and, after two more failed attempts, I finally got it. Taking a deep breath, I pulled the door open. I smiled at Adam.

His arms were still crossed. "Took you long enough."

"Everyone's been hanging out with Jelena too much."

He huffed in response.

I took point this time, entering a kitchen area. It was spacious for a bunker, about what could be expected in a decent size house. The appliances were all high end, sitting at the border between industrial and 'I can't cook, and have too much money.' Granted, this had to support all the residents, which from what John had described, could number from twelve to fifteen. A small, square table sat in a corner and a counter with stools ran across the wall opposite the work area. Two doors on opposite sides of the room led further into the lair. Dramatic, yes, but that was the word that came to mind.

"You take right, I'll go left."

Adam nodded and stalked through his after checking the area. Once again, I pushed out my senses and found only a singular heartbeat from the connecting room. I opened mine and rushed through. All the cells were as John described; rooms converted into holding pens by replacing the doors with more secure versions that locked on the outside. All except one that gave the impression it was made to hold King Kong. Through the small, barred window I could see the three inch thick steel of the door. Looking through it, I found Lucy chained to the ceiling, hanging a good foot off the floor. Her legs were secured to the floor with chains more suited to hold up a bridge than to keep one small teen girl restrained.

"Adam, I found her."

"Coming."

I didn't need to manipulate this lock to get it open. The mechanism was similar to the one we passed to get in to the bunker. The central wheel was locked with a simple, though hefty, pad lock. I grabbed it and twisted, snapping the thick arc and tossed it aside. Spinning the wheel, I hauled open the hatch and ran in to check on her. She was fully naked, covered only with welts and bruises from what appeared to be constant beatings. I checked for a pulse out of habit, even though I was still sensing her heartbeat. The rhythm I felt under my index and middle fingers didn't match what I sensed. Hers was thready and barely there. Then I realized the stronger heartbeat was not in front of me. I turned and found Anton Muller crouching in a corner, since his massive bulk couldn't fit in the room if he stood at his full height.

I keyed the mic on my coms unit. "Maverick."

Chapter Thirty-Four

"Pneumatic tire is flat."

THE GREY HOUNDED HARE - 1949

"I KNEW YOU COULDN'T resist a rescue."

"Funny, I didn't think you were capable of thought. I figured you for an enormous lap dog."

I was barely able to prepare myself for the backhand that sent me sailing back out the door. I crashed into the opposite row of cells just as Adam rounding the corner.

I regained my composure enough to mouth, "Hide."

I didn't want to take the chance of speaking in case Lurch on steroids could overhear. There was just enough time to add, "Get Lucy out."

Anton wedged his bulk out of the cell. He had to turn sideways to get through the door.

In my ear I heard, "Lead him out to your left. I will go around the way you came in."

Adam was whispering as well, and I hoped Anton was too focused on me to be listening for anyone else. I had a better idea. I blurred in the small space right at the giant. Then at the last second, I hardened my body into a speeding mass of steel. When I was very young, one of the older kids dared me to run down the rectory stairs and crash through the wall. He had assured me it was flimsy and that the priest wanted it taken down. It was a brick wall. However, I had better luck with it than I did with Anton.

He chuckled in his gravelly way, picked me up and launched me in the opposite direction that I was trying to get him to go. My skin was still reinforced, so no actual damage was done. But between colliding with an immovable object and being thrown into my second wall in as many minutes, I could hear church bells where there weren't any.

Adam whispered in my com, "Your other left."

Anton followed up with, "That tickled. Do it again."

"Great, everyone's a comedian."

I did attack again in the same way. But this time I aimed low, sweeping one tree trunk of a leg. He didn't fall, but staggered to keep his balance. I spun up and threw everything I had into a back kick, which doubled him over. To finish him off, I hammered him with a jumping right cross. I heard the satisfying crunch of breaking bones. Until the pain hit me and I realized it was my hand that shattered, not his jaw.

Anton looked up at me from his hunched over position and smiled maniacally.

"Aw shit." I headed for the exit.

"That's it. Run, little rabbit. Let's make this last."

"Good. He's following you," Adam said.

I wasn't convinced about how great it was, but kept going anyway. Passing through the door from which Adam had previously emerged, I took a left through another, which led to a cement stairway. I started climbing, my shattered hand cradled protectively against my chest as it healed. I could only run at normal speed while my body repaired itself, so I could hear Anton's long thumping strides close behind.

"Where are you, little rabbit?"

Him constantly calling me rabbit made me picturing him as Elmer Fudd. I wondered if a good game of rabbit season, duck season, would be effective. Then again, a shotgun to the face might be how he brushed his hair in the morning.

After I'd climbed a few levels, the stairs flowed out into another tunnel. I picked up speed as I shook out my newly healed hand. I was almost to the other end when Anton's voice echoed from behind.

"There you are. No more running. Let's play some more."

"Fuck you, asshole," I called back in my best Schwarzenegger impression. Not my finest repartee, but it had the intended results.

He growled and picked up speed. Remembering John's description of the place, a plan was developing. I crashed through the door into the large garage at the end, jumping the four additional steps to the level with all the cars. Right next to me was a little two-seater sports car. I hurried over, engaging my holy strength, and prepared to lift more than I had ever attempted.

Grabbing the frame under the passenger side, I tilted the car onto two wheels. Thinking that wasn't too bad, I squatted down and grabbed the other side, which I was just able to reach. Knowing Anton was right on my heels, I only had one chance at this. Taking a deep breath, I pulled for all I was worth while attempting to stand. The convertable dipped forward from the weight of the engine and I nearly lost my grip. It took excruciatingly long to get into place and I waited for his next attack while I was unprotected.

I had timed it right, though. As he burst through the doorway, I said a brief apology to the auto gods and launched the vehicle using all of my strength. It hit him full in the chest, taking him down, his hands slapping against the hood from the impact. Since I was positioned above him, I was pretty sure he was pinned under it.

I keyed the mic to my coms. "Adam, how is Lucy?"

"Semiconscious. I am half-dragging her out since she won't let me carry her."

"You're going to have to go out through the house. I blocked this entrance with a car."

"Where's Anton?"

"Under the car. I threw it at him."

"You threw a car?"

"Yeah, it's not as easy as it looks in the movies. This whole thing about picking up a car from the front is just BS."

"You—threw—a—car?"

"Well, lobbed is probably a more accurate term."

"Is he dead?"

"No. I'm just hoping he is pinned long enough to delve into his mind for his Kryptonite."

"Are you sure you can do it on purpose? Wasn't the last time kind of a fluke?"

"We have little choice, don't we?"

"I guess we do. Okay, I will meet you at the back of the house."

The unmistakable sound of gunfire broke the air.

"Did you hear that?" Adam asked.

"Yeah. We have company. Switching to monitor the main channel."

As soon as I clicked over, the coms unit squawked with other voices. "Sniper! On the roof."

"Man down."

"Multiple hostiles ground level."

"We are under fire from the southwest building. I repeat, we are under fire."

"Tactical, this is command."

"Go command."

"Take Alpha to lay suppressive fire while Charlie moves up. Bravo team, move towards the barracks."

"Roger, command."

The trap had sprung shut. The small army Anton had waiting nearby advanced on the compound. "Adam, looks like you are walking back into a shit storm. Stay frosty." The radio was monitoring all channels, but Adam and I were still only transmitting on our secured channel to avoid cross communications.

"Roger that. Hey, at least you took Anton off the board."

The car shifted.

"You had to say that."

Chapter Thirty-Five

"Sometimes, you just gotta say what the fuck, make your move."

RISKY BUSINESS - 1983

"SHIT." I BATTLED INTERNALLY with staying and fighting, or turning tail and running until I came up with another stupid plan.

The garage was built kind of like a big a Jiffy Lube where mechanics could access the bottom of the cars through a lower level. The trench that provided access to that area ran along the back of the garage, where a thick, metal railing prevented drivers from pulling too far forward. Stairs descended from the main floor to the lower and also led to the tunnel I'd just exited. The sports car leaned at a downward angle over the now bent railing where it was pinning Anton in place. I had hoped that the initial movement was the weight of the car settling, but no such luck. It shifted again, this time against gravity.

Maybe he was trying to get loose, but was really stuck? The car slid up another two feet.

I raised my face to the heavens. "I'm the good guy, remember? How about you cut me a little slack here? I hit him with a fucking car."

"I have to give it to you," Anton said. "That was a pretty good hit. Maybe you have a bit of fight in you after all."

I stepped to the side to get a view of him. His clothes were disheveled and torn in places, but there didn't appear to be a mark on him otherwise. He saw me and smiled.

"Let me show you how it's done." Anton leaned forward and grabbed either side of the hood, which his massive arm span made easy. The fenders on both sides crushed in as he set his grip. Then the bastard lifted it from the front.

"Son of a bitch." I just could not catch a break.

He swiveled his hips, making the car arc widely.

"Shit!" I blurred out through the nearest window in a shower of glass as the car tore through the building after me. Looking back, I dodged to one side. The vehicle landed on the lawn next to me, tearing up vast swaths of grass and soil.

"Freeze!" A squad dressed in black fatigues had their weapons trained on me. They seemed unphased by a flying convertable and a man appearing out of nowhere. I held out my hands, trying to make myself appear as non-aggressive as possible. My only weapon was my pilfered side arm, currently holstered.

The squad leader checked the tactical info strapped to his forearm. "Hold your fire if you want to get paid. That's our boss." Everyone lowered their rifles as one. "Mr. Bateleur. I'm Sergeant Vulpe. How can we help?"

Anton broke through another part of the wall, drawing all our attention. The team took aim and I held up my hand again. "Hold up. Don't shoot him. You will just put yourselves on his radar."

"Sir, we have some heavy artillery we can use on him."

"Anything stronger than hitting him with a car?"

Sergeant Vulpe stood there with his mouth open for a second. "You hit him with a car?"

I pointed. "That one, to be specific. Somehow, I think whatever you're carrying won't do anything but piss him off." I walked up to the wreck and ripped off the steel bumper. "Just keep anyone else from interfering. I'll take care of Anton."

I said it with much more confidence than I was feeling. The bumper was just for effect. I didn't believe it was going to do any better than the car. But it made me feel a little better holding it.

I swaggered up to the giant, and he stomped toward me. His smile oozed confidence and amusement, like an adult being threatened by a five-year-old. As we moved in close, he reached out for me and I ducked under his grasp, swinging my big steel bludgeon at his nearest leg. Anton stumbled and I spun around, connecting with the back of his head. As he pitched forward, I twisted again, this time hitting him clean in the face. He was still up, so I wound up for another try. He caught it, tore it from my hands, and swung for the fences.

I was able to get my defenses up before his grand slam, but the ferocity of the hit pierced my hardened skin. Pain bloomed across my side as I went airborne. Luckily, he'd hit me so hard, I landed a good thirty feet away. That's a sentence I never thought I'd say. It gave my body a few moments to heal before he was on me again. I stood up to face him and he met me with a punch to the stomach that I felt all the way up to my hair. I stayed there hunched over, struggling to get my lungs to remember how to breathe. Anton grabbed me by the back of the pants and for a split second, I was afraid he was going to give me an atomic wedgie. Then his other beefy hand encircled my throat and he spun, launching me into the air.

The shock of floating out in the night sky kicked my lungs back into gear. The feeling of falling reminded me of the near crash I had. Out of need and instinct, my angel wings unfurled and caught the air. Without realizing how, I turned in midair and streaked towards him in a full Superman pose. Having made the mistake before, I reinforced the skin from my fist all the way down my back, building layer after layer of protection to where the weight of it tipped me sideways.

Anton's shocked expression right before I connected with his jaw was priceless. The crack that resounded off the walls and trees was akin to slamming two rocks together. The big Tainted stumbled as I landed with one knee, fist on the ground. Yeah, I was posing. Anton fell on his ass and it was my turn to grin confidently at him. His expression was pure shock as he rubbed his jaw. Then he did something that sent a shiver up my spine. He smiled. I had hurt him, and he was happy about it.

Anton climbed to his feet. "Finally, someone who can hit back."

"So, where's Baldemar?" I needed time to come up with a plan, since I was running out of ideas. I was hoping he was in a talkative mood enough for me to regain control of the situation.

"I don't need him to beat you."

"Was that his idea, or yours?"

"Mine." Anton maneuvered himself to his feet.

"Let me guess, he suggested you needed his help to take me down, which you found insulting?"

I could see the wheels turning. "So?"

"It's obvious he was hedging his bets. If you defeated me, I would be gone and he'd still have his place as the head honcho. If I defeated you, he wouldn't be caught in the crossfire and would know for sure that I wasn't getting my information from the Heretic. Plus, I think he wanted to see if Uji's death was a fluke. If I could do it again."

Anton considered my words for more time than I gave him credit for. Finally, he waved me on. "Bah! It makes no difference. I will kill you now, then take my rightful place as the new Korol. Come, let us go again."

I ground my teeth and fixed the image in my mind of my skin as titanium and my fists as anvils. I took several running steps and started swinging. Gone was any semblance of style or finesse. This was a slugging match. I tagged him with everything I had and he hit me right back. We weren't exactly going punch for punch, but neither were we wasting a lot of energy trying to block either. I drove my fist into his gut and a foot into the back of his kneecap. Then I knocked him down with a spinning roundhouse kick. He got up and backhanded me, followed by a right cross.

We kept at it, taking turns pummeling each other and pausing only long enough to see if the other would stay down. The fighting had died down around us and a crowd formed. I could feel my power dwindling. My typical supernatural fighting used my boon like a hybrid used gas. This craziness I had engaged in was burning through it like a nineteen-sixties twelve-cylinder big block. I had lost all semblance of control. I just knew if I failed, the devastation he would let loose on my team would be unprecedented. But I was almost out, and it didn't appear Anton was going to tire before me.

I had one chance. Putting everything I had left into one final blow, I wound up like Popeye and let it loose. The big man did something he hadn't before. He ducked. His fist came up into my gut, blowing through the last of my defenses. My ribs shattered and some of my internal organs ruptured. Anton grabbed me by the feet and lifted me up high enough that my dangling hands didn't touch the ground. Pain rippled throughout my whole body, nearly causing me to pass out.

"Victory!" he yelled to the growing crowd and held me aloft as proof.

My team stood around wearing shocked expressions, upside down from my viewpoint. I recognized one man out of them. It was David. His expression showed only determination and confidence, despite the clear failure at hand.

"Yet another challenger beaten. Is there no one that can stand up to the mighty power of Anton Mueller?" He shook me, and my view swung so that I was facing his belt line. I felt myself slipping away and could only think that this was not the view I wanted to die seeing. Then I recognized something.

It was Anton's belt buckle. Why was it familiar? It was a rhino in front of a six-pointed star. Where had I seen that before? Then it came to me. It was in the picture from decades ago, but there it was pinned to his shoulder like a rank insignia. I searched my memory further and found it again on a painting of him that dated hundreds of years. There it held a cloak closed.

As he ranted, I reached out and pulled it free, unsnapping it from the belt. He was too pleased with himself to notice. The effort caused so much pain, blackness crept into my periphery. With how much just getting the buckle had taken out of me, did I have the strength to drive it home? I wanted nothing more at that point than to take this blowhard down but I had a choice. Do it myself and probably fail or ask for help.

Taking a deep breath, I twisted from my hanging position, found David again and, with the last of my strength, flicked it at his feet.

He looked down at it, then at me.

I pointed at my eye.

David smiled, reached down, and picked it up. "Hey Anton!"

The giant wasn't paying attention. "Even among gods, I reign supreme."

"Hey!"

"Anton the Mighty!"

"HEY!"

"ANTON THE INVINCIBLE!"

David closed his eyes and took a deep breath. When he opened them, his eyes crackled with intent. He opened his mouth and bellowed, "SHUT THE FUCK UP!"

Anton finally turned to face whomever dared to challenge him.

David smiled and added in a quieter tone, "Please."

Then, with a front flip and flick of his wrist, he sent the buckle spinning so fast I thought it was going to break the sound barrier. It impaled itself into Anton's eye socket. The shock of it caused him to drop me and my body exploded with pain.

David was at my side in an instant, pulling me out of range and propping me up. We both watched as black ooze flowed from first his eyes, then his nose and mouth. It didn't pool on the floor, but writhed as though being dropped into turbulent waters. The mass finally coalesced into the billowy shape of a rhinoceros, which took off at a run. It then circled back and ran through Anton's still form, shattering it like a statue made of glass. It kept going, heading straight towards David and me, letting out a scream that echoed off the buildings. It dissipated inches in front of us.

Quiet settled over the grounds. The battle was over. Then a raucous cry of celebration pierced the air as though everyone had caught their breath at the same time.

"You did it, Chris!"

I grabbed his hand in mine. "You did it. And it's Christian."

He nodded and wiped away a tear.

"Now," I said. "While there is time, I think I may need a hospital."

I passed out.

Chapter Thirty-Six

"Tis but a scratch."

MONTY PYTHON AND THE HOLY GRAIL - 1975

I DIDN'T WAKE UP in the hospital again. I was still on the battle-field. Lucy stood over me on one side and Marie on the other. I smiled, then confusion set in. I turned my inspection inside and took a gauge of my internal organs. There was no pain. I took a deep breath. My lungs weren't rattling and I didn't feel like someone was sticking a knife in me. I looked from one to the other.

"I don't understand."

"Lucy healed you," Marie said.

"How is that possible? How are you even standing?" I asked. "Adam was practically dragging you around."

"I told you I changed the source of power. I no longer feed off of misery and pain. Before you all showed up, that was all I was surrounded by. Once you arrived, I could start recovering."

"And you can heal people now? Can all the Tainted heal?"

"I am not one of the Tainted. And no, they can't. My new source has several interesting new powers."

"Where do you get your power?" Marie asked.

Lucy ignored the question and laid a hand on my chest. "You will be fine. I have others to attend to." She got up and walked away.

I watched her go as Marie studied me, apparently unconvinced that I was completely healed. "I thought we talked about this weeks ago on the mountain. No more putting your life at risk."

I propped myself up on my elbows. "This was different."

"How so?"

"I wasn't in control. I wasn't doing it for myself."

"It was just the right thing to do?" she suggested.

I nodded.

"Well, maybe you can try to find a way to do good that doesn't have you trading punch for punch with a demigod."

"I will keep that in mind for next time."

Marie glanced away. "I wanted to apologize for last night."

I tapped her on the shoulder until she looked at me. "You did nothing wrong. It was my fault. It was obviously not the right time for that. I usually read those before a critical moment, and I wanted to include you."

She started shaking her head midway through. "No. It was perfect, and I loved that you shared that with me. I just wasn't expecting what was in the letter."

"What was in it that freaked you out so much? Can I read it?"

"NO!" She shook her head again. "Sorry, not yet. But I will let you read it one day."

"That's very cryptic."

Marie's smile returned and became mischievous. "There's nothing wrong with a little mystery in a relationship." She leaned down and kissed me.

When she pulled away, I lifted myself up into a sitting position as Hager, Tira, and Soon-Li walked up but stayed far enough to give us privacy.

"They've been hovering since Lucy offered to help. They weren't completely sure that she wouldn't try to finish the job that Anton started."

"Did you stop them from interfering?"

"No, you did."

I regarded her, baffled.

"Hager said it was what you would have wanted. A chance for her to prove her loyalty."

I grabbed the back of her neck and pulled her into a hug. She hugged back, squeezing as hard as I did. When we finally let each other breathe, I said, "Thanks."

"For what? You hugged me."

I touched her cheek. "Just for being there. For being you."

"That's all I know how to be."

"That's the cool part."

"You better let them come over before they bust."

"Help me up. I will go to them."

She did, although I didn't really need the aid. I felt a hundred percent. There may have even been a little juice in the holy tank again. I wasn't sure how that was possible, but it would be something I would consider later. We walked over, me dramatically leaning on Marie because she insisted on it.

"Thank you. All of you," I said when I reached them.

"Thank us?" Tira asked. "We had the easy part."

"Indeed," Hager added. "There were more Bishops in one place than in hundreds of years."

"Good thing too," Soon-Li said. "Anton had an army of his own. There had to be thirty converted, plus a demon and all the normals."

Tira nodded. "If you hadn't brought us together, this attempt would have gone a completely different way."

I crossed my arms. "I wish I could have seen that. It sounds like an epic battle."

Soon-Li grabbed my arm. "Let me tell you about it."

I extracted myself from her grip. "While I would love to hear the story, I need a sitrep."

Soon-Li huffed.

"With you down, David has taken incident command," Hager said.

"Stepping right up. I see."

As if on cue, David came running over. "Thank God. I was certain that creature would have done something unspeakable."

"I'm fine, thank you."

"I wanted to say—"

"Later. Sitrep."

David stood straighter. "Local authorities are on site. Terrance is dealing with them, as he has a past relationship. Ali is coordinating, triaging the wounded."

"Any losses?" I asked

He nodded. "Seven unblessed—that is seven of the military team, and—" David's mouth opened and closed a few times.

A sense of dread gripped at my heart and I looked around and realized John was not there. "Who?"

Everyone's expressions revealed how shaken they all were.

"Dammit, answer me! Who?"

It was Hager that spoke. "It's Charity."

A flush of relief flooded through me, then a wave of guilt that nearly knocked me to my knees. I tried to control my voice, but it still trembled. "How?"

David was able to speak again. "It was the sniper. She was dead before any of us heard the shot."

My breathing became rapid, and my sight began developing a reddish haze. I looked across the manicured yard turned battlefield and growled out the words, "Where is he?"

I felt a hand on my shoulder and I turned with venom on the tip of my tongue.

Hager met my gaze, concern etched on his face. "Breathe, my boy. The sniper is dead."

"Then he got off easy." The guilt I had felt was compounded by the truly barbaric thoughts that were running through my head—The ways I would have punished him.

As if he could read my mind, Hager said: "Feelings are not bad in themselves. But acting on them often is."

I took a few deep breaths, which helped somewhat. The red haze dissipated and my breathing became more controlled. The anger, however, was still there.

"Where?" I asked.

Hager brought me over to where Charity lay cradled in John's arms.

He stared up at me, tears streaming down his cheeks. "Heal her."

His request shocked me, and I struggled for words. "John, she's dead. There is nothing I can do."

He laid what was left of her head down gently on the ground.

Stepping up to me, completely covered in her blood, he said. "Lazarus was dead for four days before Jesus resurrected him."

I glanced from John to his sister and back. "Lazarus was sick, not—" I gestured at Charity's ruined head. "With the state of medicine at that time, he may not have even been dead. But most importantly, I am not Jesus."

John looked down at her again, his bottom lip trembling. When he turned back, there was something behind his eyes I couldn't pinpoint. "I believe you are the Messiah, the son of God, who is to come into the world. You are the resurrection and the life. The one that believes in you will live, even though they die."

The mere thought of what he was requesting was completely insane. I felt not just John's eyes on me but all the Bishops. They had all gathered around. The words "I can't" were on my lips.

What I said instead was, "I'll try."

I kneeled at Charity's side and took her still warm hand in mine. The coppery smell of her blood attacked my senses, and I forced myself to block it out. I didn't know where to start, so I started where I always do: the meadow and the lake. The water level was low, not nearly enough for anything of the magnitude that I was attempting. I wiped my hand across the horizon and the view changed back to the battlefield. But I viewed it from a different angle, as if I stood next to my physical form. I was astral projecting.

"It's about time you got here. You just love to keep a girl waiting."

I turned to find Charity standing behind me. I glanced over at her body to make sure it was still there, then back.

"Yup, I'm dead."

I didn't know what to say. So the only thing that came out was, "How?"

She shrugged. Or rather, her projection did. Her spirit?

"Damned if I know. I couldn't tell you that any more than I can explain a Bishop's powers or how I knew you would find me here."

"Don't worry, I will figure this out." I bent over her form. I was still not sure what I was supposed to do, but that never stopped me before. I felt Charity's touch on my shoulder.

I looked back and she shook her head.

"What are you talking about? I can do this." I wasn't sure I believed my own words, but I wasn't about to let her down again.

"I don't want you to."

I stood and faced her. "How can you say that?"

"Christian, look at my head. There is almost nothing left. You might heal the brain tissue, but the memories that were contained there are gone. My mother's cooking, my father's awful sense of humor, playing basketball with John. Who I was as a person. That's all gone."

"But you remember all of that now."

She nodded. *"And I know that if you connect my spirit with a rebooted brain, it will all get reset."*

"Maybe it won't."

"It will."

"How do you know?"

"I just know."

"I can't accept that. I wasn't sure if this was even possible, but if you're here then—"

"Christian. I loved my life, loved my family and who I was. I don't want to go back as someone else. I don't want to lose them—or me."

I wanted to fight her on this. To tell her she was wrong. To explain that there was still a chance. But I realized my concern was not for her. I would miss her, even though I had just met her. I would grieve for John's loss. I was afraid he would blame me—Hate me. I didn't want to face Blessing with the news of her daughter's death. My concern was for myself.

I nodded and a tear ran down my face. "So, if you are not waiting to be made whole, what are you doing here?"

"I want you to take a message to John and my parents. Tell them I hope they understand my decision. That I love them and miss them, but will see them again. I have two diaries that I keep. Give the pink one on my nightstand to my mother. The red one is in a secret compartment under it. Don't open it, don't read it, just burn it. I am trusting you with this."

"What's in it?"

"Let's just say that it is not the thing you want your family flipping through."

I nodded. "Anything else?"

"Yes. When you return to the physical plane, the first thing you say to John is: 'Charity says you can have The Patrick now.'"

I nodded again. "Charity, I'm sorry."

"Me too. I would have liked to see if I could have stolen you away from Marie."

I half laughed, half sobbed. "Not a chance."

"You may not say that if you saw what was in the red diary. But don't."

I held my hand up like taking a vow. "I promise."

"Take care of my family."

"I'll do my best."

"You'd better. I can still haunt you."

Her image dissipated with her last words. A dread came over me unlike any I had ever felt. I didn't want to do this. I would rather trade places with Charity than deliver this message. Steeling my resolve, I stepped back into my body. I felt John on my left. I dropped Charity's hand, embraced him tightly, pulling him to me; offering him support as I relied on him. Then I whispered his sister's message.

I felt his expression crack and he started to shake. His grip on me tightened to where I could barely breathe, but I didn't care. His body jerked with the sobs that followed. I don't know how long we stayed there. I felt like I had failed all of them. I held on to John, afraid that if I let go, I might lose my friend forever.

Chapter Thirty-Seven

"Rebellions are built on hope."

ROGUE ONE: A STAR WARS STORY - 2016

"ALMIGHTY GOD, WE REJOICE in your promise of love, joy and peace. In your mercy turn the darkness of death into the dawn of new life, and the sorrow of parting into the joy of heaven; through our Savior Jesus Christ, who died, rose again and lives for evermore."

The priest's words still rang in my ears hours later. I sat on a wooden bench staring out at the water from John's family home. I was alone, listening to the soft lapping of the bay against the stone retaining wall. My brain was on a loop. The image of Charity's ruined head, John's pleading for me to help her, my conversation with Charity's spirit. I wasn't there when John told Blessing, but my mind created the scenario, anyway. Her crumpling into a chair, wracked with grief. Her last words to me: See that you don't disappoint me.

But I had. She hadn't spoken to me, but I could feel her eyes on me throughout the service. Terrance and Blessing were both well-known so Charity's funeral had all the pomp due their station. The slow progression to the cemetery was longer than a city block. The brass band played "Just a Closer Walk with Thee" and other similar dirges. Both of her parents were somber though stoic. I presumed they were keeping up appearances again.

On the walk back to the house they played more upbeat music including songs like "When the Saints Go Marching In." Everyone seemed to be in a more cheery mood. People even joined the procession waving handkerchiefs and dancing. The whole thing was foreign to me and I felt uncomfortable.

Now half the community were inside paying respects, expressing condolences, and talking about their memories of Charity. That's why I was here. I had few memories I could share and I wasn't sure if I could handle listening to the life that had been cut short. Plus, I wasn't convinced anyone wanted to hear from the person who got her killed.

My thoughts did another loop and tears breached my lids and rolled down my cheeks. I lacked the strength to wipe them away, and I felt the itch they caused was the least I deserved.

"May I?"

I turned wiping my face to find John holding a bottle of scotch and two glasses. I didn't trust my voice so slid over and motioned for him to sit. He did and placed the glasses between us.

"Would you join me in a toast?"

Drinking was the last thing I wanted to do but how could I say no. I nodded.

He pulled the cork and inhaled the oaky aroma. Pouring two fingers into each glass he recapped the bottle and put it in the grass next to the bench. He picked up both glasses and handed me mine.

I took it, my hands trembling slightly.

"My sister lived life on her own terms. I may have been gifted with superhuman powers but she was always the strongest. She was my little sister but I looked up to her more than anyone in my life." John lifted his glass. "I love you and will miss you Char."

Emotions that had been pushed down for days came exploding out. I couldn't hold them in and started sobbing uncontrollably. I covered my face with one hand as the scotch sloshed around in the glass in my other.

John put a hand on my back. I felt stupid and embarrassed. I tried to stop but couldn't. The more I did the worse it got. Finally, after a few minutes I settled down and was able to take a deep breath.

My friend pushed the bottom of my glass towards my lips. I complied and took a sip. The liquid burned as it went down.

"Better?"

"Yeah, sorry."

"Why are you sorry?"

"Because it was your sister and I'm the basket case."

"Nope. Try again."

I wanted to ask what he meant, but I knew. I took a bigger sip.

"I'm sorry I got Charity killed."

He nodded. "Yeah."

The pit in my stomach doubled in size. I assumed he blamed me but getting confirmation was devastating.

He drained his glass. "Yeah, I figured you might be blaming yourself."

I looked over at him my eyebrows knitting together. "Of course. It was my fault."

John handed me his glass to hold, refilled both and took it back again.

"Christian, did you listen to my toast? Charity did what she wanted and no one in Heaven or on Earth could have stopped her. Least of all you."

"But it was because of me that she was there. It was my idea to attack the house. She died in my plan to save one of the Tainted for God's sake."

"John shook his head. She died doing what she always does, helping people. And my dude, you may be nearly all powerful, but you had no control over her. Was it tragic? Definitely. Does it suck? Epically. But we don't blame you for the same reason we don't blame God."

My blank expression showed how lost I was.

"Many people talked about God's plan. They use it in a way to explain things they have no control over. Especially death. Want to hear my theory?"

I nodded.

"There is no plan. You are given an unknown amount of time on this earth. It is made clear by the death and destruction we witness every day. God wants to see what we will do with it."

"That's it?"

"Has to be."

"Why?"

"Otherwise he is taking back the greatest gift he has given humanity. Free will."

I sat back taking another sip and thought about that.

"So you came out here to cheer me up?"

"Naw. I came out to apologize."

"For what?"

"What I asked of you that day. It wasn't fair. There was nothing you could have done. I knew that. I was just hanging on to a last glimmer of hope. I'm sorry I put you in that position."

I considered his words. "I'm glad you did."

It was his turn to look at me with a puzzled expression.

"I got to see her and pass on her message. I'm sure it helped me, despite my previous outburst. Hopefully, it helped you guys as well."

John nodded and took another swallow.

It reminded me of something. "I didn't think you drank scotch."

"Only on special occasions."

He picked up the bottle. It was a colorful label with no visible brand. "Single Malt" was prominently displayed with a smaller script "Louisiana" above the first four letters.

"Atelier Vie was Char's favorite. I thought it was appropriate."

I held out my glass and he refilled it and his once more.

"Since I screwed up your toast, how about we try it again? To Charity. You will be missed."

John clinked glasses. "Amen."

"The note didn't say anything else?" I asked as I opened the door to Lucy's apartment. It had been several weeks since the battle with Anton.

"Only what I told you several times," Hager said. "She left a clue to the next step in our evolution here."

"What the hell does that mean?"

"I haven't the foggiest."

"And no clue where she went or when she would be back?" Tira asked. Hager only shook his head.

"We already searched this place while trying to find a safe we didn't need, remember?" John grunted. We had resolved the main issues staring out over the water and drinking scotch. He wasn't himself though.

"Yeah, yeah, I will brush up on my sign language for the next time someone sends me a coded message while being kidnapped." The attempt at our normal banter fell flat.

Adam though huffed a laugh. "For how much it's happened since you joined, it's not all that farfetched."

"Not cool. And Krissy was taken before I joined."

"If you are all finished with your immature antics, maybe we can get back to it?" Hager chided.

Tira opened a closet. "Back to what? I'm still not sure what we are looking for."

"Maybe it has something to do with her new source," I suggested.

"About that," Marie said. "You told me they were drug addicts and misery was their drug of choice."

I shrugged and pointed at Hager. Everyone stopped what they were doing to listen to his explanation.

"That was the prevailing theory."

"Were there other theories?" She continued her interrogation.

"A few."

"One that linked it to where they got their power?" I offered.

He crossed his arms. "I believe so."

"Any reason they were discounted?" Marie asked. She and I were tag teaming him.

His eyes narrowed. "I presume they didn't hold with the thoughts and ideas of the time."

Stepping over, I smiled and put a hand on his arm. "I'm not judging. I know I have been quick to criticize. I am only trying to understand, so I don't make the same mistakes in the future."

Some tension went from his posture. "I would have to say that they were afraid of the consequences of that discovery."

I thought about that for a second, attempting to divine the logic. It didn't take me long to connect the dots. "Unlimited power."

Tira stepped up. "It has always been our Achilles heel. The hope was that they had one as well. Some source we could eliminate that would make them vulnerable."

John added. "To admit they were getting power from the very misery they were causing meant they had a virtual unending source."

"I think I found something," Marie called suddenly. Her voice was coming from the bedroom. We all filed in.

She stood in front of an armoire, and I stepped around to see. "I'm not following. It's just a closet."

"It's empty," she said.

I looked at her and then back to the armoire. "Are you not seeing the clothes hanging there?"

John stepped over. "Naw, that's empty."

I stared at them both like they had two heads. "Okay, are you guys punking me?"

Marie reached in and pushed the garments aside. They squished down to about six inches.

John gave my shoulder a playful punch. "You need to up your fashion game."

I gave him a side eye. "I'm fashionable."

Marie laughed.

John said, "Keep telling yourself that."

I was now feeling self conscious about my jeans and t-shirt declaring that 'Goonies never say die.' Putting a hand on the rear of the closet, I used my boon to search for a secret door. In the back of my head, a twenty-sided die hit the table as I found the mechanism. It was a simple latch with no physical method for triggering it. If you didn't have the ability, you weren'y getting in.

The door slid sideways; probably into the wall itself, leaving no mark of its passing. It was a personal elevator that would hold one or maybe two people. I went inside.

"What are you doing?" Marie asked. "You don't know where that goes."

I smiled and held out my hand. "Only one way to find out."

She made a face, then stepped up into the confined space with me. "Are you sure about this?"

"What can happen?"

"Do you want me to list the movies where this exact scenario ended up in tragedy?"

"No, that's my job."

I pushed the only button.

As the door closed, Hager said, "Do be careful."

Not able to resist, I replied, "Hey, it's me."

I expected a tumultuous ride full of creaking and banging as if this thing was built in the turn of the nineteenth century. However, it elicited no sound as it began its descent.

Taking advantage of the close proximity, I moved to give Marie a hug.

She put her hand out violently.

"Hey, I was just trying—"

"And I'm trying not to lose my shit in this moving coffin."

"Oh, sorry. You could have stayed up there."

Marie made another face. I decided my speaking was not helping the situation. After about thirty seconds, the elevator stopped, but the doors didn't open.

"Christian?" The rising panic in her voice was clear.

"Got it." I reached out and performed the same process I had on the upper floor. Knowing what I was searching for this time, it was much quicker—though probably not for Marie.

As the panel opened, she flung the garments to the side and elbowed me getting out. There must have been a weight sensor on it because it closed after I stepped out.

"Sorry about that. I didn't realize how much that was going to affect you."

"I don't even like you sleeping that close to me because it makes me feel closed in."

"Sorry, I didn't make the connection."

I looked around, trying to think of something to say, and immediately knew where we were. Turning back to the wardrobe, I distributed the garments along the rod. They were vestments.

"This is a sacristy," I said.

"A what?"

"It's where the priests and altar servers prepare for mass."

"How do you know?"

"I was an altar boy."

"*You?*"

"Is that so hard to believe?"She put her hands on her hips. "Yes. Alter boys are supposed to be attentive and observant. You didn't even know I had crippling claustrophobia."

"I knew about the claustrophobia, just not the crippling part."

Marie chewed on the inside of her cheek. "Why the hell would Lucy have an elevator to here?"

"Quick way to get to mass?" I offered.

"Not likely. More like she was raiding the wine storage."

"If you tasted her scotch, you would not be saying that."

She stopped what she was doing and faced me. "What were you doing tasting her scotch?"

"She offered."

"So, you just go around tasting other women's scotch?"

"No, but this was superb scotch."

"Oh, so only if it's really good?"

"Okay, you win."

Marie folded her arms. "I win what?"

"I will only taste your scotch."

She nodded. "Now let's get out of here."

Luckily, there was no mass going on, but a priest did eye us warily as we made for the door.

"Good morning, Father," I said.

We stepped out into the street on a side block. We both glanced up and down for something that would give us a clue as to Lucy's note.

"Well, that was useless," Marie said.

I looked back at the front of the small church and it hit me like a punch to the gut. "Maybe not."

"What?" Marie looked at me, then at where I was staring. "Oh, shit."

The name of the church was "The Perpetual Power of Hope".

The End

Get Exclusive Content From
W. J. Grupe Jr.

If you have enjoyed this book, I would really appreciate if you would leave a rating and a review.

If you haven't already, check out the first two books in The Tainted War series, Awakening & Unworthy.

Sign up for my newsletter to stay up to date with everything going on .

Visit me on Facebook, Instagram, Twitter, and Linkedin.

Get the John McCaw novella and learn how he came to join the New York City Covenant of Bishops.

Available exclusively on my website:

www.WJGrupeJr.com.

Acknowledgements

As always I need to start out by thanking my family. You are still my biggest supporters and I couldn't do this without you. But specifically:
Marie- Always my apha reader and biggest cheerleader.
Kristina & Will - My semi-unpaid staff. Money cannot buy the support you guys provide, but that doesn't mean I shouldn't try.

Special thanks to:
Lawrence Mangine for his help with the military elements,

my beta readers Jim, Marguerite, Jen, Lawrence, and Sarah for their insights,

my editors Mark Stay and Liv Mammone that kept me focused on my voice instead of others;

and the gang at The Best Seller Experiment - Thanks to the Best Seller Academy I was able to complete this book in one year instead of three.

www.ingramcontent.com/pod-product-compliance
Lightning Source LLC
Chambersburg PA
CBHW050415260626
47156CB00003B/1015